PRAISE FOR
TIME/LIFE

'Breathtaking, heartbreaking and also full of love and hope, what a journey this book takes us on – with love, time travel and a toxic tech magnate.'

SANDI TOKSVIG
Author and broadcaster

'Multiplexly brilliant, intricately fascinating, harrowingly emotional fiction, sprung from this century's first and possibly final quarter.'

WILLIAM GIBSON
Author of *Neuromancer*

'Mayer's genre-bending riff on H.G. Wells is as clever as it is poignant. A dark and sharply contemporary pleasure.'

LUKE JENNINGS
Author of the *Villanelle* series (the basis for *Killing Eve*)

'Mayer's reimagining of H.G. Wells' *Time Machine* is a profoundly moving exploration of loss and love. *TIME/LIFE* delivers a wild blend of unreality with chilling elements that are all too real.'

BEE ROWLATT
Author of *In Search of Mary* and *One Woman Crime Wave*

'Catherine Mayer's unique and prescient *TIME/LIFE* playfully repurposes H.G. Wells's *The Time Machine* for the post-truth generation, creating and recreating worlds like a computer game. Yet it is also a devastating meditation on grief and the ephemeral quality of time. It might make you cry but it will also make you laugh.'

ELIZABETH FREMANTLE
Author of *Queen's Gambit* (made into the movie *Firebrand*)

'Timely and utterly compelling, breaks your heart then makes you laugh.'

MONIKA RADOJEVIC
Merky prize-winning poet and author

TIME/LIFE

A MEMOIR BY DORY SILVER

(A NOVEL BY CATHERINE MAYER)

SPECIAL PRE-PUBLICATION

EDITION

RENARD PRESS

RENARD PRESS LTD

124 City Road
London EC1V 2NX
United Kingdom
info@renardpress.com
020 8050 2928

www.renardpress.com

TIME/LIFE first published by Renard Press Ltd in 2025

Text © Catherine Mayer, 2025

Cover design by Will Dady
Proofreading by Elleni Yapanis

Printed on FSC-accredited papers in the UK by 4edge Limited

Limited edition hardback ISBN: 978-1-80447-155-5
Paperback ISBN: 978-1-80447-141-8

SPECIAL PRE-PUBLICATION EDITION

CLIMATE POSITIVE Renard Press is proud to be a climate positive publisher, removing more carbon from the air than we emit and planting a small forest. For more information see renardpress.com/eco.

EU Authorised Representative: Easy Access System Europe – Mustamäe tee 50, 10621 Tallinn, Estonia, gpsr.requests@easproject.com.

CONTENTS

TIME / LIFE

'There is no difference between Time and any of the three dimensions of Space except that our consciousness moves along it.'

H.G. Wells, *The Time Machine*

'The future's done, the past might never happen, but the present – that's what matters. And it is wherever the time machine takes you.'

Elo Ó hAllmhuráin, *Today Programme*

I

00:00

A **woman stands at her bedroom window, listens intently.** *Just three days to summer, yet a frost, hard and unexpected, has whorled the glass.* Ne'er cast a clout till May be out, *she mutters. The cold turns her words to smoke. She would kill for a cigarette.*

Outside, plastic scrapes across a rutted windscreen. Perhaps she should haul herself downstairs. This might anyway be the moment, or past it. She is using her kitchen timer to log the minutes between contractions, but the signals from her body prove as indecipherable as patterns in ice.

Breathe. Again, smoke spirals from her mouth. The thing distending her belly must be a lump of coal. Chilly light shows up every defect in the room – fingerprints on the vanity mirror, a misalignment of wallpaper that severs the stems of its roses. Spatters mark the timer, residue from long-forgotten meals. She picks at the largest fleck, then winds the dial forward as far as it will go. Expecting, people call her condition. Though she has glowered rather than glowed through these last long months, she takes no comfort in their expiration. As night follows day, so expectations cede to harsh reality and she knows, in her bones, what happens next. She will flunk the primary duties of motherhood, to love and to care. If it weren't too late for prayers, if she believed in God, any god, she'd pray. Please, *she'd say,* let me be whole again, unburdened. Let me wind past the early years, entrust to time the raising of this child until it shies from my kisses rather than begging for them, withdraws its hand instead of trying to slide sticky fingers into my fist.

But no god oh god, this deep, dark ache. Breathe, breathe. She surrendered her life at the moment of conception, refuses to sacrifice another. Surely such pain isn't natural. She has no frame of reference, no idea how she should feel. Words have failed her. Not one of them prepared her for this: the anguish of expelling a soul into the frozen world.

Across Europe, soil and air have turned to crystal. In Bordeaux, they walk the rows in silence. A mild spell tricked the vines into early flower and now estate managers see death wherever they look. They cannot know that the vitality of the surviving plants will yield one of the great vintages.

Decades later it lingers on the palette of a microbiologist called Leonard Hayflick as he toasts an award for scientific achievement. He has identified a pathogen that causes respiratory illnesses and developed a cell strain used in the manufacture of vaccinations against lethal viruses, yet it is a different strand of his work that secures the honour. Hayflick has determined that most cells cannot keep dividing, but like life itself must come to a full stop. His discovery, published, by chance, on the day of the Great Frost, is christened the Hayflick Limit.

You may prefer to ignore it. Many people do, and their denial is reinforced by a huge industry that feeds on fear. The woman at her window, her hourglass figure temporarily inverted by another cellular process, already invests in the promise that mortality can be avoided – at a price. Those jars on the vanity table contain what she calls lotions and potions. Though she tries to give up cigarettes, then gives up giving up – they keep me in shape, she says, by which she means thin – she will devote hours of her life to extending the hours of her life, cycling through aerobics, yoga, Pilates and Peloton, training for her first marathon in her fifties, completing her last at eighty. And on she runs, even after this victory, as if to pause might prove fatal. When, finally, she is forced to do so, consigned to bed for the second and last time, she complains that science has let her down. I swallowed everything the experts told me, she protests. The advice, the supplements.

Briefly I am grateful for a new topic of conversation. By now, Mum and I have spent a lifetime (mine) circling the personal, focusing on novels we might read, the comfort of TV series that never end, even if characters come and go. Morgen usually accompanies me, chatting easily through the pregnant silences. My love's absence today is a black mark against me, yet I have no intention of explaining, much less apologising. For one thing, Mum would turn the information into a goad, implying that I'd neglected Morgen, too preoccupied with my work to notice anything amiss. For another and more importantly, Morgen has helped me to understand that Mum won't change. These days

I respond to the words Mum utters, not to the rage and disappointment she transmits in the spaces between them.

Worlds can be detected in the complaint she has just voiced, parallel universes in which she is resplendent, and I, her only child, have never existed. I pretend not to see them. Science is not, *I reply,* a single discipline. *(Pompous, I know; Mum has that effect on me.) The cheerleaders for the idea of immortality are neither biologists nor medical practitioners but computer scientists who model life from the safe distance of their screens.* Like writers, *she sniffs.*

I persist. Their recipes for resisting death, whether melding flesh and blood with technology or resetting the body's internal clock, its telomeres, are perfectly logical – and just as perfectly divorced from reality. Hayflick co-authored an open letter that I quote to Mum from memory: The prospect of humans living for ever is as unlikely today as it always has been.

As I speak, my gaze falls on the alien poking its head through the skin below her collarbone. Cells that carry on dividing are the ones that should worry us. This tumour, closer to her heart than any other living thing, will kill her, but not for a while. Right now, though weak, she is unmistakably herself and infuriated by defeatism, Hayflick's and mine. She hauls herself up against her pillows, presses the buzzer and stares at me, triumphant, when a nurse answers her summons. See, *her look says,* I still call the shots. *And she does. She will force me to witness her final moments, choosing to die before emergency measures bar visitors from hospitals and as Morgen's own life hangs in the balance.*

Staff fix a picture of a swan above Mum's bed as the time approaches, signalling that she is not to be disturbed for medical checks. This, they believe, is the last opportunity for us to commune and connect. They're wrong. Mum continues to assert herself, making noisy interventions whenever my guard is down. ('It's amazing that Morgen puts up with you,' she says. 'Red was never your colour,' she says. 'Nobody loves a smartarse,' she says.) She elbows her way into my dreams, too. How persistent are the dead. It is the quick who abandon us.

Another surprise: Mum's intrusions are indistinguishable from grief, whether for her or the loss to come, or maybe for both these things and more: that portion of my life receding to a pinprick in the rear-view mirror. What bliss it was to be young, feet planted in the present and the future shimmering into the distance like tarmac. Too late I realise that the past builds, minute by minute, into a responsibility. Who will tend to this history, identify its cast of characters, remember them on my behalf? When I go, these things go with me, and that feels like failure.

Already I live with ghosts, a haunting of gaps and missed opportunities. Here she comes again, stomach swollen with discontent. Watch as she crosses to the window. We cannot see the street outside but hear the engine catch, idle. It must be time, past time, yet still she stands, frozen behind a sheet of ice.

I should reach out, tap her on the shoulder.

I could do more than conjure her memory.

No. Stop right there.

Rewind.

Let me not get ahead of myself.

My story must be told as simply as possible because there is nothing simple about it. An artificial intelligence, designed to draw inferences from seemingly random data, could scan its chronologies and coincidences to extract meaning. We humans struggle with anything more complicated than forward motion along a lonely axis.

The following narrative is therefore as linear as it was practicable to make it and written with the same rigour I was taught to apply to journalism. I have double- or triple-sourced details and fact-checked fallible memories as thoroughly as challenging circumstances, and a tight timetable, permitted. As a nod to that approach and for reasons that will become clear, I have called this book TIME/LIFE, though for a while I toyed with the title LIVE IN THE MOMENT, the name of a live album released by the band Gang of Four. Live can, of course, be pronounced in two different ways, to rhyme with give or dive, producing two different meanings, both appropriate to the subject matter, as is the ambiguity itself.

The jottings that preface each chapter should be treated with caution. These are partial in both senses of the word, fragmentary records of what I felt and thought, or thought I felt, as soon as I returned from the journey this book describes. Denied access to writing materials while away, I found myself seized by an urgent need to download words carried beyond term. To my surprise, much of the material that poured out of me related not to recent experience but the distant past.

The main text, though also autobiographical, is written with more care and in the third person. I did this to give myself a critical distance to people and events. Yes, this is a memoir, but I barely know my own mind, much less anybody else's.

Take Morgen and me. Three decades have merged us into a single unit. Together, we are more than the sum of ourselves. Even so, and this is our tragedy, we remain distinct. No matter how close a relationship appears, no person ever fully understands another. As for the passing years, they slice through the most resilient of bonds like secateurs through rose stems.

Time is implacable, but not, as you'll learn, inexorable, and although I recount events in the order I lived them, this may not be the sequence in which they occurred. Nor should you assume that the first or last stanzas of this story are any more significant than other passages. Certainly, this, my beginning, is neither particularly important nor relevant. It is merely a convenient place to start.

As for the ending, few autobiographies are spared the danger of a sequel, an additional chapter, a sudden reappraisal. Mine is an exception, and this foreword, for better or worse, the last section of the manuscript I shall complete. The conclusion I plan for this evening will prohibit any further input from me.

So, let me offer, right at the outset, a final thought — my last words, if you will. We live in vast ignorance. I hope my story, like love, might light it in a few casual places.

T he Time Traveller, as Elo Ó hAllmhuráin styled himself, held forth on everything from physics to feminism. His musings appeared profound, but rarely withstood scrutiny. Happily for him, scrutiny was also rare. For more than a decade, his had been a celebrated presence on broadcast media, the go-to for any producer tasked with reconciling a public-service remit for high-level debate with the competition for ratings. Ó hAllmhuráin always entertained, even as interviewers struggled to articulate his surname* or punctuate his answers with questions.

'Call me Elo,' he said, and they did, cosily. His contributions occasionally served up brain-stretching provocations. More often they were word salads, studded with borrowed ideas. Diehard fans reverently converted his statements into memes, white or yellow type set on galactic backdrops. *Science is the opposite of certainty*. Or: *In operating at the edge of what we know, we recognise how little we know*.

Any challenge to Ó hAllmhuráin, however mild, unleashed digital strikes against the heretics. Could he help it if his pleas for civility boosted the posts of his defenders? Sometimes he responded to prominent critics directly, with charm rather than offensives. Might he interest them in a rare trip to his sea stead, a sponsorship, or an intimate lunch? Yes indeed.

Many journalists emerged from these encounters as giddy as new lovers, but a few of the breed, mostly freelancers, continued to confront him with awkward facts. Tantalus smartphones and tablets remained beloved of wealthy liberals despite Ó hAllmhuráin's queasy politics, but their price point meant they could never justify their maker's claims of rendering carbon-spendthrift rivals obsolete. Nor were concerns about their other environmental impacts restricted to dirty manufacturing processes and the mining of such rare metals as Tantalus products still required.

---

* Elo Ó hAllmhuráin varied the pronunciation of his surname, see-sawing between 'O'Halloran' and 'Oh-Halve-Oh-Rhine'. For the purposes of this memoir, let's go with O'Halloran.

Ó hAllmhuráin didn't so much brush questions aside as bury them in avalanches of distraction. On the day the *Guardian* published a lengthy investigation into his empire, he posted a split-screen video to Fleet and the rest of his social-media feeds. In the left-hand frame, a shoal of plastic swirled like wrasse at the prow of his yacht. To the right, a clip from a recent advertising campaign for a legacy manufacturer saw silvery fish morph into sleek mobiles. 'Smartphones me arse,' Ó hAllmhuráin could be heard to say. 'Film the death of this planet on your old-fashioned mobile, but only if you don't mind contributing to it. And there's nothing smart about that.' He ended this message, short by his standards, with a phrase worn shiny with use: 'I call any product reliant on Coltan mining 'gnu technology' – because it's barely evolved from its type specimen.'

His competitors ignored the jibe, but a tech blog responded with estimates of the carbon expended on that single post, the processing power required to deliver it from Ó hAllmhuráin's Tantalus to his followers, hundreds of millions on Fleet alone, generating starbursts of further shares. The following day, *TIME*, which had named Ó hAllmhuráin its Person of the Year less than six months earlier, surprised its readers by publishing a guest column fulminating against him. 'Data centres these days are responsible for roughly the same level of global greenhouse emissions as air traffic. Elo is correct in pointing the finger at other forms of Big Tech, but in this he must include the damage wrought by his own activities, and that's even before we count the ways our societies are disfigured – and our democracies hideously subverted – by the matrix of smartphones and social media central to the Tantalus business model.'

The author, a former Tantulus insider, wound himself up to a final broadside. 'Don't worry, the Magus tells us. People of the future will develop carbon-capture capabilities and yet undreamt-of technologies to reduce or reverse climate change. He's probably right. Our descendants will be left no option if current generations shirk tough choices, seduced by the fantasies he peddles. The notion that technologists will fix the problems created by technology by developing more and better technologies is hokum, pure and simple and, for the planet Elo professes to love, deadly.'

Dory sighed and bookmarked the article. The manner of her departure from *TIME* still rankled, but her reaction in this instance reflected a wider unease about coverage of Ó hAllmhuráin. Even the rarer, critical pieces seemed unbalanced, formed in opposition to the sickly consensus and therefore defined by it. The *Guardian*'s long read, for example, mustered armies of sceptics to pour scorn on his latest initiative, while glossing over support in the scientific community for its foundational assumptions. As far as she knew, her own article for the *Strand* still marked the only serious attempt outside academic publishing to weigh Ó hAllmhuráin's claims, even if, ultimately, she rejected them.

Two lonely voices represented these significant perspectives to *Guardian* readers, and only in equivocal terms. The first, a cosmologist, enthused about the creation of an electromagnetic wormhole in a Barcelona laboratory, but added a caveat: science remained light years from creating a gravitational equivalent. The second, a theoretical physicist, sounded more tentative still. New findings on black holes might eventually prompt a revision of current understandings of spacetime, but decades of work would be needed to rule out likelier explanations for the results. The journalist didn't try to translate any of the terminology or clarify the key principles for non-specialist readers; Dory suspected he hadn't understood them himself. Nor did he give so much as a mention to another line of research, around quantum teleportation. He managed a little better with the earthbound detail, presenting evidence of Ó hAllmhuráin's over-leveraged acquisition of Fleet, poor working conditions there and at the tycoon's Montenegrin facilities, and the inevitable diversity and pay gaps right across his businesses. The piece also queried the security of data harvested from Ó hAllmhuráin's joint ventures with a number of governments in the Global South. More worrying were the whistleblower accounts alleging that this data, purportedly gathered to improve public health responses to the virus, really was, as Ó hAllmhuráin insisted, securely held – by quasi-official militias in some of those countries. There had long been concerns that information siphoned from *Morlock* players might be used around the world to surveil and repress.

So much for Ó hAllmhuráin's professions of free-speech absolutism. Say what you liked on Fleet or in *Morlock* chatrooms – but don't come crying to him about any repercussions. How Dory itched to ignore her brief and push him on these inconsistencies when they sat, toe-to-toe, on the TechCon platform.

Dory's duties would be minimal: to provide a quick, crowd-warming introduction – a formality because *everybody at TechCon adores Elo*, the producer had said, adding, 'We absolutely don't see this as a hostile interview.' Her accent transformed the word into *hostel*, an accommodating antonym of her intended meaning. Dory must also ensure the star attraction didn't get so carried away by his own eloquence that he forgot to make the major announcement he'd promised TechCon – or, as was his wont, overran. For a man obsessed with time – Ó hAllmhuráin capitalised the word in fleets and statements – he showed scant regard for its properties.

The thought prompted Dory to look at her screensaver, a skeuomorph of an old-fashioned watch. Ó hAllmhuráin's publicist had dashed her hopes of an evening of preparation and room service, summoning her to another briefing in one of the casino bars via a peremptory WhatsApp, but Dory's internal clock was scrambled after two flights across eight time zones. Could she grab a snack before heading downstairs? The view from the Porcelain Palace offered few clues. Las Vegas days flick on and off as if the sky were plugged into the same grid as the city. Desert and horizon had already merged into a darkness leavened only by the electric constellations of the Strip. She peered at the computer, realised it hadn't yet updated, checked the display on her iPhone. Damn.

A woman must eat, especially a woman out of her own time. Dory used to live for food, daydreaming of dishes consumed or yet to be, a dashi beaded with chili oil, a melting ribeye. Now she no longer experienced hunger, at least not of that kind, yet neither dared she go hungry. Skipping a meal invited excitable brain cells to trigger floods of serotonin that delivered not happiness, but a migraine. This wasn't a transaction she could risk. A rummage through the minibar revealed spirits, beer, chips and a box – crackers or nuts? In the few seconds it took to remove it, decipher the inscription, *intimacy kit*, and drop it back in its tray, the refrigerator charged her room. Better to try her luck downstairs.

The heart of the Porcelain Palace resides in its lower reaches, a series of twilit chambers that wink and repeat without visible end: tables, slots and bars; tables, slots and bars. Twice Dory passed the Last Chance before spotting its saloon-style sign between banks of roulette and blackjack: *Every hour is happy hour.* A smattering of customers seated at the bar, abstracted and solitary, belied that message. Usually she squirrelled away such observations for later service, descriptive colour for her writing or to entertain Morgen. Tonight, she had different priorities, clam chowder and a Virgin Mary. At a nearby roulette table, a foursome, women in sequins and men in holiday shirts, rotated their heads to the turn of a wheel. A fifth player hunched over his chips like a child defending a slice of cake.

The barman took her order, returning with a coaster, napkin-wrapped cutlery and a basket. At its centre nested a roll as shiny as the laminated menu and, fanned around it, packets of Saltines.

'Crackers.'

'Sorry?'

It took Dory a second to realise that the barman hadn't spoken.

'Crackers to bet against the house. He'll lose this spin, and another, then win again. That'll give him the confidence to play until he's totally banjaxed.'

The speaker, straddling the next stool, leant toward her, hand outstretched. 'Howya.'

Mirrored lenses reflected Dory's response in duplicate, a flash of recognition, a flare of irritation. 'I expected your publicist.'

Ó hAllmhuráin grinned, raising the twin Dorys heavenwards. Both frowned. Since when had that groove carved itself between her eyebrows? Instinctively Dory's hand moved to rearrange her fringe, stopping mid-flight to pretend an interest in the coaster.

'You wrote that I was the world's pre-eminent self-publicist,' he said. 'And you weren't wrong, no matter that you didn't mean it kindly.'

She recalled the comment, in the colour lede to her *Strand* piece. She had aimed, in a few pungent phrases, to convey Ó hAllmhuráin's vanity, his interventions in dramas and disasters, the dispatches from scenes of devastation, tumbling words freighted with emotion. Even still photography couldn't quieten him. His T-shirts often showcased messages along with a sculpted torso. This evening was no exception. *The future is already here, and I'm distributing it.* The Dorys grimaced.

'There's something I need to show you.' He gestured towards the solo player at the roulette table. 'See that yoke? What can you tell from looking at him?'

Not much, if she were honest. Suit, shirt, receding hairline. 'He's here on business. Maybe for TechCon.'

'Close but no cigar. He's in sales, probably life insurance. Something without meaning, at least for him.' Ó hAllmhuráin paused as the barman deposited Dory's chowder in front of her, then resumed. 'You and me, we're passionate about what we do. This guy doesn't care. Except right now. Now you can see his heart beating in his chest, fit to burst. He tastes it, the prospect of a different life. And a different life is exactly what's on the cards. He's about to lose his shirt, and his nags too.'

Now the man was pushing a stack of chips across the baize. Dory stared past him into the fathomless gloom of the casino.

'Like I say, betting against the house is a fool's errand. Amiright?' Once more Ó hAllmhuráin leant in, too close.

'Betting is a fool's errand unless you're too wealthy to feel your losses. Or when you're betting with other people's money – or lives.'

Ó hAllmhuráin nodded, ignoring, or missing, the barbs. 'It's all about the odds – and working out how to change them. Here's a safe bet. Dorian, if I may—'

'Dory,' she said, but he overrode the correction.

'Dorian. I bet you've spent hours prepping for our interview.'

'As I always would. Out of respect for the audience.'

'Are you after disrespecting your interviewees?' Laughter again, then a pivot to high solemnity. 'Tomorrow will be a big day. Together you and I will rewrite science, religion, human experience, the foundation of all knowledge.'

She sighed. 'Mr Ó hAllmhuráin, tomorrow we're going to sit on a stage at a tech convention. I'll ask questions, you'll roll out your usual schtick. That'll barely make headlines, much less history.'

'You're a hard case,' he said. 'All the better for our purposes. And by the way, call me Elo.'

They both heard it, the clack as the croupier raked in chips. The player's pile had halved.

'Suppose it were any old chat we'd be having. If preparation is a mark of respect, you wouldn't want to miss crucial information, now, would you? And that, Dorian, is why I'm here.' He stood, signed her bar bill and headed towards a blackjack table without a backwards glance.

Dory wrangled conflicting impulses. She ought to swallow a few mouthfuls of soup, but the situation, like the casino, offered options without choice. Sighing, she hoisted herself to her feet and followed him, every dragging step a small rebellion.

01:00

T *hey fascinate me, Dad's butterflies.* *Not in a good way. He thinks them beautiful, urges me to admire their wings, but always the bodies scream for attention. The similarities to people are inescapable, squat or elongated, hairy or smooth, delicate or, like Dad himself, robust. All dead. The pins bother me too.*

They don't feel pain, *Dad tells me, chuckling when I challenge him. Has he ever been a butterfly? No? Well, how does he know?*

'Is good question,' *he says. All these years in England and still he mangles the language. Mum corrects him, or, if she's in a good mood, mimics his accent.* 'What is wrrrrong wid you?' *Or* 'Vat a bik dok!'

Sometimes Dad engages with my concerns, tells me about life cycles and ecosystems, icy winters and sweltering summers. He arrived at this time and place by a roundabout route, from rural Poland to Haifa, onwards to Earl's Court and finally this grey town. Given an easier start, he might have been a naturalist. As it is, he can name every living thing that creeps or crawls or flies or sprouts. He rarely makes use of this knowledge, but perhaps he should. The extension he built in the months before my birth grows a yellow fungus that looks like ears or, if left untouched, unfurls into wings. Still, our house has a second toilet and a special place for a washing machine.

'You and me have pain receptors,' *he explains.* 'Butterfillies' – *he always adds a syllable* – 'are feeling only touch.' *At about my curious age, he started collecting them, learnt how to net his prey, squeeze out their little lives by pinching the thorax and mount them in display cases without tearing the gossamer or rubbing off the colour. The years have drained them of vibrancy.*

Is he aware of this transformation, or does recall replace what is lost? Each insect comes like his voice with a story of homeland, a snapshot of the past.

'Couldn't you just have watched them flying about, Dad?' *I wonder.*

'You see?' He points at one of the most boring specimens, fawn with black spots ringed in white. 'Very rare. On endanger list. Is Ripart's anomalous blue, Polyommatus ripartii.'

'It's not blue.'

'Exactly. Anomalous.' He pauses. 'They endanger because farming gets greedy, wants to go faster than nature. I killt him to save for future.'

Every day we made memories and as lightly discarded them. *Sometimes I hear those old songs, tinny and far away. Dad races me along a beach more mud than sand, lifts me on to the slippery blocks of the sea wall. By the time I am grown tall and he weak, my attention has scuttled from rockpools to the ebb and flow of the precinct. A gang of us roams the shops, crowds into cubicles, tries on ideas of who we might become. At night I fill notebooks with stories and poems. My heroines live in space-age cities and wear disposable catsuits. More rarely, they inhabit my own century and then they come entangled in the fronds of imagined histories.* See her palely loitering beside the dual carriageway, *I write.* Love shatters your windscreen.

Mum hovers at the margins, a coat on a velvet hanger, a drawer full of chiffon scarves. Only later, when Dad no longer leaves the front room, confined to a put-up cot, does she move to centre-stage. Invite your mates back to ours, *she'd say, though she wasn't reliably welcoming. You could tell the bad days by the smoke that wreathed the hallway and made a break for it when the front door opened – Caspar the Unfriendly Ghost.*

If she were in a benign mood, she'd offer us squares of dark chocolate none of us liked, and talk to us as contemporaries, if not equals. She preferred holding court to conversation. When she made me her confidante, I knew the arrangement wouldn't be reciprocal. Soon I acquired a listening face and other practical skills. Cooking and cleaning had never been her forte, or Dad's, but at least he'd tried. While his side of the family sat shiva, Mum moved into a studio flat with a tiny galley kitchen and a bed dented on both sides. I saw the place just once when I helped to carry her boxes inside. You don't mind, do you, *she said – statement, not question. Lest I did have it in me to protest, she began setting out the logic of her position in the stern-but-reasonable voice previously reserved for Dad. I'd shortly be away to college, and anyway, someone needed to show the house to potential buyers. ('Remember to bleach the* mould, spritz everywhere with Glade and make a cup of Nescafé just before they're due.') Plus, she didn't see the point of living with the dead.

In my numbed state, this made as much sense as anything else – which is to say, nothing made sense. Recollections of that time are fragmented, but there must have been a discussion about money. Whatever its outcome, I shopped as rarely as possible, not necessarily because of a lack of funds, though I'm pretty sure that was an issue, but in case somebody asked about Mum or – in a special voice – expressed sympathy. A value pack of porridge oats sustained me, the perfect preparation for student existence.

By the time a young couple came to see the house, I'd run out of coffee, but they moved, as if in a trance, through the freshened air, visualising futures in each unremarkable room. Later that same afternoon, Mum accepted their offer, and I began packing the few belongings that seemed worth keeping. Dad's brother would store them and put me up or – his little joke – up with me until I headed south. For some reason, he wanted Dad's butterfly collection.

My uncle did know to keep things light with me, which was helpful, but nothing compared to the relief of leaving that chilly little town. At university nobody looked at me with big eyes or deployed those special voices. Ignorance and incuriosity are the true comfort of strangers. My new friends were anyway resolved to live in the moment. We recited the lyrics to 'Hey Hey, My My' as if they were a manifesto for pleasure rather than a death wish. A commotion of parties and expeditions, punctuated on rare occasions by coursework and, in my case, cash-in-hand jobs at local hotels, left little time for reflection, but if you'd asked, I'd have told you I was happy. I Blu-Tacked a handmade poster to the wall of my room: a Brazilian poem about the mystery of endlessness.

It wasn't until term drew to a close that I checked in with Mum. After ten rings or more – an age, it felt, with so many students waiting their turn at the payphone – she picked up. Oh, she said, sounding distracted, it's you. Rejections sting more sharply if witnessed. I turned my back to the next in line, cupped the receiver and talked fast about train times and plans, perhaps a week at her flat – I could arrange the sofa cushions on the floor – and a night or two with my uncle. Finally Mum interrupted, as I somehow guessed she would. The new boyfriend is flying me to Malaga. Heaven knows I owe myself a break after all that business with your dad.

So many years I cradled this hurt, dandled it on my lap like the child I resolved in that moment never to have. And people call me clever.

Time can be plastic or precise, last an eternity or disappear in the blink of an eye. On the morning that simultaneously marks one of the beginnings and a key inflection point to this story, it demonstrated these properties in swift succession. At first and for what seemed a considerable while but probably lasted just seconds, the noise inserted itself into a dreamscape of predators and strange, elfin prey. Then, in a monstrous instant, it scattered them.

Dory fumbled for her mobile, pressed the speaker icon. *Where in hell was she?* The voice sounded familiar, but she struggled to place its owner or her current location. The pause stretched and hummed as she searched for a reply.

This could, in fact, be anywhere. Prints hung on the wall above her: the Eiffel Tower, reflected in a puddle; Crystal Palace, blurred and abstracted by sheeting rain. Next to her laptop, a telephone handset buzzed with frustration to be separated from its base. *Bellhop*, she read. *Housekeeping. Spa.* A hotel room, then. Perhaps the computer might yield clues. She prodded it into wakefulness. A series of questions. For the Ó hAllmhuráin interview. *Christ on a bike.*

The realisation jolted Dory upright. Just as swiftly, she regretted the movement. Everything hurt, and no wonder. Her back twisted to the curve of a chair, while her legs angled in another direction to wedge themselves in the footwell of a vanity table. She must have nodded off, but not before draping a towel over the mirror to block glimpses of a future she already knew – a woman, desolate, in the blue light of a screen.

Memories reconstituted themselves pixel by pixel: Ó hAllmhuráin's determination to make her believe the unbelievable; vignettes staged across the casino, a big win, a swingeing loss, another loss, each of his predictions predictably fulfilled. *I don't mean to ask you to accept anything without reasonable grounds*, he insisted.

Of course, she raised objections. *Incredible that you should waste time with these charades.* If he wanted to convince her, he should try showing her the science. Nobody granted the clamorous possibility of time travel would squander it on conjuring tricks. Anyway, what did her opinion matter? Hadn't he more than enough *disciples?* He shrugged. *How can a smart woman be so thick?* Tick, he pronounced it – and time was ticking away. When, hours later, he declared not defeat but a truce, Dory had hurried to her room.

Right up to this misspent evening she'd intended to hold her nose and get on with the job as agreed, maybe not with good grace, but efficiently. Corporate gigs would never be her natural element, her instinct to fillet rather than fluff, yet the costings from the clinic had dropped into her inbox in the same batch of emails as TechCon's invitation. The timing felt less a coincidence than a warning – scruples were now a luxury beyond her means. The problem with Ó hAllmhuráin's ill-judged intervention was that it reminded Dory that there was a cost to abandoning her principles too, supersized payday or not.

It was this realisation that had propelled her to the desk. If conscience dictated that she veer from TechCon's brief, perhaps she could still finesse it. Dory had fired up her computer, set to work concealing razors in toffee-apple questions. Too direct a challenge risked repercussions, jeopardising the all-important fee. Now, as she stared at her mobile, her imagined defence – that her well-prepared probing demonstrated how seriously she took the assignment – disintegrated. To fail in the most basic duty of a moderator, timekeeping, was *unprofessional*, her caller said, and Dory could only agree.

Belatedly Dory matched voice to owner: the TechCon producer, with a delivery that contradicted the urgency of her mission, each word standing in isolation: *No. Time. To. Waste.*

Dory tried to focus, but some part of her brain returned to a distant classroom and a physics teacher incandescent after finding magnesium hidden in the muzzle of a Bunsen burner. *Boys. And. Girls. Science. Is. Not. A. Game.*

She was distracted, too, by a conundrum. How could she have overslept when she barely slept? Insomnia had long defined her existence, the product of too many pre-dawn closes. Her move to an editing job had been, for want of a better expression, a lifestyle choice, guaranteeing less travel and a more regular schedule, if

in many ways a tougher one. It had been her responsibility to
shepherd the Europe, Middle East and Africa editions through to
completion, adhering to deadlines set not to London's convenience
but New York's. *Putting the magazine to bed* – that was the phrase.
Every week until her enforced departure she'd tucked up a new
issue, nice and snug.

The routine seemed to establish itself at chromosomal level. She
still remembered a time before *TIME*, when oblivion rushed in
like the tide to close over her head until morning. At some point,
sleep had become not a sea but a bathtub, her limbs at awkward
angles and the water growing tepid.

How she detested the small hours – a misnomer for time
bloated with despair at its own redundancy. The only mitigation
lay in giving it meaning. Silently she would slide from under the
duvet, careful not to disturb Morgen, creep downstairs, avoiding the second tread and the sixth, make a pot of Earl Grey
and settle down to work. This was why she was able to file so
many pieces and never miss a deadline. This was why she'd been
weary to the marrow even before the fates found crueller ways
to exhaust her.

Her fingers explored a furrow across her cheek where her head
had rested its weight on a hotel pen. The surrounding skin felt
spongy, as if the fluids in her body were pooling with gravity, blood
in a corpse.

Fluids. She needed tea, an ocean of it, hot and fragrant, not the
American stuff. There wasn't even a kettle in this room, just some
kind of coffee machine equipped with pods and levers. With that
realisation came another. At least a day had passed since any food
had passed her lips.

She ought to interrupt the producer, insist that a snack, a
sandwich perhaps, await her on site. The floor rocked as if she'd
been delivered to this moment by boat. *Can I just ask…* Too late.
The producer had disconnected.

Get. Dressed. Remember. Charger. Her mind mimicked the cadence
of the call. No time to print out her notes in the business centre,
if the Porcelain Palace even boasted such a workaday place. She'd
have to rely on memory.

Dory removed the towel from the mirror. Whatever the cut, suits made her look like she was about to demonstrate inflight safety procedures. If only she were on a plane, homeward bound, the day ahead behind her.

Needs must. Those needs had metastasised with Morgen's illness, leaving space neither for self-pity nor physical weakness. A shame Dory's body had missed the memo. Her stomach clenched as the express elevator enveloped her in a fug of cinnamon, then somersaulted as it raced to recoup lost minutes. The limo, by contrast, felt static, its windows tinted and tight against the morning.

'First visit to Vegas, ma'am?' the driver asked.

'I'm not feeling too good,' she said, and shut her eyes until a punch of desert air heralded their arrival.

'Follow me.' A runner, walkie-talkie at her waistband, ushered Dory through a loading bay full of sound stacks and lighting rigs and along a corridor, skirting a row of green rooms, each stocked with a breakfast basket. At the side of the stage, custody of Dory passed to a make-up artist. Always TechCon skewed male, yet in areas off-limits to attendees, women defended a narrow beachhead.

American fruit tasted of nothing, American pastries of sugar alone. Dory was past caring. *Might it be possible…?* A lipstick stilled her request, and she submitted without further interruption. *TIME* magazine had always urged her to inject colour into public appearances. Once, after getting up before the dawn chorus to participate in a US show, she'd taken a call from the publication's PR supremo. 'Darling,' he said, 'you looked like a black hole.'

She heard Ó hAllmhuráin before she spotted him. They hadn't tried to interfere with his complexion, but sunglasses supplied the missing contrast, bisecting his face with a strip of blue. Lounging against the prompt desk, he never once interrupted his call, accepting the ministrations of a sound technician, turning to offer a perch for the powerpack and transferring his Tantalus from one ear to the other to make room for the headset. 'Think how time travel will empower yer man in the street,' he said. 'Think how it will transform your job. Any geebag can come on your programme and talk shite about what they're going to do, but you'll be able to judge them on their actual actions. Deeds not words, as Nietzsche observed.'

A bolt of irritation splayed Dory's fingers. What a knob this man was. No way could she soft-pedal the interview.

When the latest batch of populists began lying their way to high office, journalism rushed to pathologise them. Dory held out against the tendency. To her mind, casual diagnoses offered bad actors excuses while stigmatising people with mental health issues. Even if Ó hAllmhuráin were a narcissist – and he certainly matched textbook descriptions – that did not give him a free pass. He seemed to her a creature of calculation rather than impulse, and better at faking authenticity than most of his kind. What havoc might he wreak in a world grown disastrously gullible?

At school, Dory had studied Hitler (twice), learnt to favour Cavaliers over rigid Roundheads, and to prize tolerance as an independent virtue rather than a quality defined by its context. She entered adulthood convinced that ideologues represented the greatest risk to humanity. Now she was losing her certainty about certainties. Again and again, men without guiding principles proved at least as destructive as fanatics, the messiness of reality no match for their simple slogans.

Often in interviews Ó hAllmhuráin teased a run at a presidency or prime ministership. (A citizen of four different nations, he could pick from a range of electoral targets.) Whether or not he got round to seeking political power, he already owned several presidents and vast stretches of the planet. His armies might be virtual, but they were true believers and hailed him as a saviour. Dory suspected he bought into the myth, too – the most dangerous delusion of all, because if you're God, the end will always justify your means. Whatever the nominal purpose of WEEN, it surely served his eternal quest: to dominate people, sectors, markets, countries. Behold his works, ye ninety-nine per cent, and despair.

TechCon gifted Dory a rare opportunity to reveal Ó hAllmhuráin for who and what he was. Subtle questions wouldn't cut it. Truth must be spoken to the power-hungry.

That principle came bundled with others. He didn't play fair. She would. She must advise him of her intentions. Dory had started towards him when someone blocked her way. *Kind. Of. You. To. Join. Us. Ms. Silver.*

Even teeth, all exactly alike, bared in what no primatologist would mistake for a grin, then remained on show. The producer spoke without once fully closing her lips. Dory must *keep within the taped boundaries*, she said, and make introductions *standing on the cross*. Proceedings would be livestreamed, so this choreography was *critical*. A clock onstage would count down the minutes. *You. Do. Know. How. To. Read. A. Clock. Don't. You.*

Make-up and sound converged, hands skating across Dory's freshly lacquered hair to position the headset, a diadem on a human sacrifice. Invasive fingers pushed a plastic bud into her ear, clipped its wire to the collar of her jacket. She flinched. The proximity of strangers still felt uncomfortable.

Quiet on cans please.

One minute to showtime.

A loud silence, then the opening notes of a walk-on theme.

Time, time, time.

Ó hAllmhuráin murmured something, saw Dory hadn't understood and bent down to her level. *Remember this moment. This is history in the making.*

30 seconds.

A stagehand held back the curtains.

You're gonna come back.

3.

2.

1.

As the music faded, Dory stepped into a column of light. She sensed rather than saw the crowd, mouths open for silage.

'Hello.'

The word cracked and split, lost its final vowel. Throat constricted, she persevered.

'We live in an age of technological wonder.'

Now she paused with intent. *Slow down.*

'We wonder at the transformational powers of technology. We wonder, too, about its unforeseen impacts. We wonder if technology is a force for good, for bad, or for both.'

She waited again. Still no sound from the unseen audience, just the throb of air conditioning.

'We trust tech to deliver us, whether from the inconveniences of shopping or thinking, writing thank-you notes or containing dangerous diseases, yet we also suspect it may be controlling us. We wonder if it will create jobs or take them away. We wonder if the letter that moved us to tears or the article that inspired us to protest or the picture that we understood as an expression of emotion is in fact the abnegation of these things, the sterile output of an artificial intelligence.

'We wonder if there's any value in wondering, given how far along these shining roads we've already travelled, our gaze on the horizon and never mind what's happening in our peripheral vision.

'We wonder whether politicians and regulators will ever succeed in subduing forces they barely comprehend, much less take a stand against corporations whose market capitalisation exceeds the GDP of many countries.'

She spotted the taped lines laid out for her and deliberately crossed them. Her earpiece squawked with anger.

'My name is Dory Silver, I'm a journalist, and that means my job is to wonder, in a directed kind of way, to ask the right questions and to pursue answers. Today I'm wondering about some of the issues I've just sketched out. I'm wondering, too, how the personalities, beliefs and priorities of technologists shape the products and services that in turn shape our futures, for better and, increasingly, very much for worse.'

Another squawk.

'Most importantly, I'm wondering about the man about to join me on this stage.'

Finally, a reaction in the auditorium, the shifting of excited bottoms, churchgoers preparing to sing 'Jerusalem'.

'A supernova, he is so fond of dazzling that it can be hard to make out the details. That's my task for the next three-quarters of an hour.

'You'll know him as a maker and creator; inventor of synthetic tantalum and the founder of not one but two tech unicorns. Underworld Inc, his first company, produces the top-selling

24

multi-player augmented reality game *Morlock*, now a franchise embracing a TV series, a run of live-action films and more than one dubious fashion trend. His second, Tantalus Systems, is famed for its eponymous Tantalus phones and tablets, and more recently branched into quantum computing.

'Nor are these achievements the only preoccupations of today's guest. His business interests – those we know about – encompass transit systems, smart cities, space exploration and the commercial exploitation of biomimicry and gene editing. He calls himself an effective altruist, also a libertarian social activist. Those last three words came together in his sudden bid for Fleet three years ago. In its aftermath, with the value of his companies diving, it appeared that his wings might finally melt. Instead he soared, even if Fleet languishes.

'He makes waves as the builder and absolute ruler of the world's largest sea stead. Several eminent art institutions around the world give house room to his photography, including London's National Portrait Gallery. Last summer came the announcement of his authorial début, a book on his favourite subject: himself. *The Time Between* has already broken global pre-sales records, and that's without a publication date. Originally expected to land this month, the memoir is on hold, reportedly so he can incorporate additional material on his Wormhole Electromagnetic Escape Nutation project, WEEN.

'Scientist, alchemist, philosopher, king – quite the Renaissance man. And of course, if time travel is possible, as he insists, perhaps that's exactly who he is: a man from the Renaissance.

'Please, put your hands together for Elo Ó hAllmhuráin.'

When Ó hAllmhuráin breached the darkness, thumbs through belt loops, his congregants at once became palpable, whooping, cheering, muddying the air with enthusiasm. The more he gestured for them to settle, the greater their ecstasy. He pressed his hands to his heart, then spread his arms, as if to embrace the room or ready himself for crucifixion. For a second, he appeared to glow, his famous pallor reflecting the footlights.

The delay gave Dory time to take stock. The backdrop was a huge rendering of the Tantalus logo, an apricot. Otherwise the designers had gone for a sci-fi aesthetic, more steampunk than *Amazing Stories*. At centre-stage squatted an odd-looking interview pod with integral seating, the size and shape of a skiff, but transparent.

Her headset directed her to the left-hand seat. The alternative was larger, a captain's chair flanked by a joystick and digital control panel. Everything else – seats and shelving – had been fashioned from the same material as the hull, clear as glass, yet radiating the spectral warmth of something that once lived.

She discovered a six-pack of mineral water beneath the chair, and quietly worked a finger through the shrinkwrap until she could extract a bottle. Not that any noise would have disturbed Ó hAllmhuráin, who by this point had moved to the outermost edge of the stage, bending over a sea of supplicant arms. What next? Crowd-surfing? At this rate, their interview would be over before it began.

The thought prompted her to consult the countdown clock embedded below the control panel, but its flashing numbers became no more meaningful with repetition: 25:25, 25:25, 25:25. Her iPhone had failed too. How odd. She could have sworn that a few hours' charge remained.

Only her watch proposed a time, if not the right one. Oh, to be home, all quiet but for the occasional complaint of a house unsettled by the Tube tunnels beneath its foundations. At this hour, living room and kitchen would be dark, her office too, only the bedroom illuminated, and not by choice. The council kept promising to retire the sodium lamp outside their window. Its light navigated its way around the curtains, picking out wardrobe, desk, books, bed, the incongruity of tubes and cylinders.

Dory batted away the image too late to prevent a swell of nausea. The stage lighting billowed. Beams, sodium orange, red and violet rippled across the clear base of the pod. She felt the colours as a series of vibrations, a sure sign of a migraine. *Every sliver of life becomes memory*, she told herself. *Every memory dissolves. This too shall pass.*

By way of confirmation, the applause finally petered out and Ó hAllmhuráin clambered aboard their platform. As he settled into the captain's chair, Dory arranged herself into a facsimile of interest, but he turned from her to the livestream camera.

'Dorian,' he said. 'Dorian Silver... Are you acquainted with the great Dorian Silver? Let me tell you I'm delighted to have secured her presence for this demonstration. And yes, I did say "demonstration". We're not here for the craic, but to touch the future. To reach out and touch it.'

He was taking over already. She must produce a comeback or surrender any shred of control.

'I was curious about why you'd requested my services. You're fully capable of interviewing yourself.'

'Dorian, as I told you last night...' He lowered his glasses, revealing those weird, feral eyes, and winked, actually winked, at the lens. 'You're a hard woman. And that...' He swivelled to look at her for the first time. 'That is the point of Dorian. God knows there are better journalists, better presenters, better people with whom to while away the hours – though God knows not many. I am a fan. Because Dorian has spent her life doing something meaningful – and that is not a sentiment you'll hear me utter in connection with many journalists. She questions. She is independent. She has a nose for shite and onions, and the tenacity to call it for what it is. Dorian Silver is a sceptic.'

His words cascaded, spilling first into a disquisition about scepticism (useful) and cynicism (destructive), then cutting a fresh course to the failures of journalism and his own dust-ups with the industry. Dory weighed another intervention but lacked the will or energy. Now he returned to her life story, painting a narrative she barely recognised, an arc of ambition and intent, stripped of all the happenstance that had done more to define her career than any planning. He lingered over her New York years, in particular the series of *TIME* covers on the Curasis scandal, casting Dory as a lonely truth-seeker. Her memories of the investigation thronged with stringers and freelancers, senior and top editors, subs and copyeditors, fact-checkers, the picture desk, the art department, the trio of in-house lawyers. She would always send up secular prayers for her pieces to land with the insouciant head of the legal department rather than his nervous juniors. Everything about her journalism had involved a team effort, collective decision-making, negotiations – at home, too.

At last, Ó hAllmhuráin appeared to be heading towards a conclusion of sorts. 'Alone among journalists, she has taken WEEN seriously. Her article posed a question about me: prophet or profiteer? And that,' he said, 'is why I told TechCon that I would appear only if Dorian Silver hosted the session.'

Bollocks, she thought. *Should've asked for more money.*

'When Dorian Silver believes in time travel, the world will believe in time travel.'

At this juncture, Dory did not believe in the current biddability of time. You may be dubious too – and quite right. Time travel is a staple of science fiction, not scientific fact. Even so, you're likely to be more persuasible than Dory. Few people take as much trouble as she to ground their disbeliefs with intensive research.

A degree in comparative literature with a side order of modern languages and a dissertation on the competing chronologies of Fernando Pessoa's *Livro do Desassossego* – the book of disquiet – were choices she had come to regret. Her mistake had been to opt for subjects that came easily instead of those that required effort. Nowadays she mistrusted nothing so profoundly as ease. Journalism forever placed her in rooms with people who flowed through life along pre-existing channels, their expensive educations masking deficits of talent. She saw whole societies poisoned by the false ideal of easy living, enshrining as their highest ambition not work but its avoidance and venerating fame as the surest route to that pinnacle.

She swam against these currents, applying herself to the areas and disciplines that came hardest to her. She subscribed to *Nature* and *Scientific American*, devoured popular science books, and eventually wrote one herself, on ageing. She specialised in politics and business, but when she covered the Curasis debacle, she could hardly test the company's fraudulent claims without first exploring molecular epidemiology and virus detection. Dory wrote with the confidence of someone who recognised the limits of her understanding and trusted to a hierarchy of good sources – that is to say, she lived in fear of being found out.

The commission to write about WEEN for the prestigious periodical *Strand* triggered every alarm bell. Theoretical physics made her brain hurt. There was only one solution: to lean on its most eminent practitioners. As a starting point, she tackled the better-known works of these intellectual giants, tangling most deeply with string theory and its unobserved dimensions. Stephen Hawking had long departed for a different brane, but two living legends, Peter Higgs and Lisa Randall, agreed to speak to her, Higgs gamely explaining the meaning of the god particle, while Randall managed to feign interest in Dory's sophomoric questions. Gravity, Randall told her, might not reside within our three-brane reality, instead travelling across spacetime to reach us in weakened form.

Ahead of Dory's meeting with Randall, she watched and re-watched an old clip of the scientist on *Charlie Rose*. When Rose suggested that researchers at Cern had disproved Einstein's famous equation, $E=MC^2$, Randall answered with a level of patience anyone other than a physicist would call infinite. This was an overexcitable interpretation, she said. 'There could be mysteries waiting to be found. But that doesn't negate what we know so far.'

If Randall stood by Einstein's formula and Hawking held that *the laws of physics do not allow time machines*, Dory made the informed choice to accept their analysis and trust to sober-sided consensus. That didn't mean science would never bend time, but any revolution foreshadowed by the Barcelona experiments remained more distant than Earendel.

Had you tried to tell her that she and Ó hAllmhuráin would shortly ride time like a waveform, a burst of neural responses would have taken a fraction of a second to assess and dismiss both message and messenger. Who knew how Ó hAllmhuráin had organised any of the nonsense at the Porcelain Palace, but where there's wealth, there's a way. Much easier to bribe a casino than to rewrite quantum mechanics.

Rainbows washed over the stationary vessel and its passengers. Dory spoke now, clear and calm. 'Mr Ó hAllmhuráin…'

'Call me Elo.'

'Not in a million years,' she said. 'As for time travel, I won't believe in it unless and until peer-reviewed science concludes not only that it is theoretically feasible, but confirms that it has measurably, objectively taken place, time after time, under laboratory conditions.'

He shrugged. 'You were always going to say that.' He turned again to the audience. 'Time is only a kind a space. We move through this element slowly, inching from one moment to the next, fearing what might come. And we are right to be frightened, because history is littered with disasters. What if we could make giant leaps across decades and centuries, harvest foreknowledge, change direction, avoid catastrophes?

'Well, we can. I am the world's first time traveller. Already I have visited futures, seen things you people wouldn't believe. Today I do so with a witness and companion. You've already got the measure of her. Dorian Silver is no lickarse. I repeat: when she believes in time travel, the world will believe in time travel.'

He reached out his hand, did something to the controls. At once, the vibrations and colours merged, and the pod shot forward, leaving a fragment of Dory's soul behind.

'Wrong place,' he exclaimed. 'Wrong time. Idiot machine.' Thump. Thump. Dory opened her eyes to find Ó hAllmhuráin banging the panel with the side of his hand. The perfumed air danced with each impact, its motes dispersing and regrouping. Nothing made sense, though every one of her senses instantly and passionately engaged.

A cherry tree shielded the pod, bowing to the majesty of its own blossom. Red and gold butterflies clustered along the boughs to warm their wings in the sun. Oh, what goodly creatures.

She opened her mouth to say something, slipped into darkness.

02:00

*H*ow the rich love Nature, or their conception of *her – a docile She, all mellow fruitfulness and legs* **akimbo.** *Observe as they walk their grand estates, each vista as pleasing and planned as the last, foliage clipped, wilderness tamed. Watch them taste of the organic apple.* Serpent tongues have told them that you are what you eat, and thus they must eat of the best.

Time, on the other hand… (See those dots? There she flies!) Well, she is their worst nightmare. Insensible to power and money, she guffaws as lifted eyebrows disappear into woven hairlines. Go ahead, *she teases,* pump poison into your faces, invest in snake oil. Whatever you do, I'll show you for a fool. *Like Saint Nick, she distributes gifts as she goes, breasts to men, beards to women and music to everybody, ensembles of groans and wheezes, rondos of sighs. Live long enough and you'll benefit from her generosity too.*

We used to be a well-matched couple, Morgen and I. *Despite Morgen's beauty, we even looked as if we belonged together. Morgen styled me and I submitted, provided that my red lines were observed: nothing restrictive of movement or that needed ironing, no flashy labels or sweatshop bargains, and absolutely no suits.*

Once in a while, when sadness overwhelms me, I lean into its embrace, scrolling through photos of happiness past. Here we are, clear-eyed and gussied up, Morgen's hand on my waist, our glasses charged to toast some marriage long dissolved. Now we're on a mountain ridge. It was Morgen's little joke to snap me in profile, my nose as sharp as the distant peaks. This picture of us in Paris gives me pause, recent enough that we've begun to transition into the comedy duo we would become, me a bird of prey, thin and beaky, my love softening to translucency like an onion. Morgen wears a favourite sweater, acid yellow, and a photoface, eyes narrowed as if facing not a camera but a gunfight.

Time never runs out of tricks — at least, until she runs out altogether. Who knew that birthdays become deathdays, annual reminders of lives lost. Who knew that buildings and belongings age with their owners, or that the march of our years could be measured in flaking plaster and the transformation of your sweater, now faded and filigreed by moths.

My sweet darling, do you remember when we decorated our living room, finally arranged everything just as we wanted, hung the pictures and the awards, three apiece? Two days later you cleared your throat, said 'Don't be angry' and informed me that the grey wasn't quite right. I didn't protest. Shall we hazard a guess that people who claim to enjoy the smell of fresh paint haven't lived with someone as sensitive to colours as you are?

As you were. I'm not sure if colours still speak to you. You have failed to remark on the mottled memory of a bubble bath I ran too deep or complain that the white ceiling and cornicing are greying while your grey walls — dove you called that shade, chosen after an agonisingly long process — are bleaching to bone. You don't seem to have noticed the fate of your sweater.

When did you cease to be the things that defined you? How did I let you drift away?

It's not as if I weren't on my guard. From our earliest days, I feared losing you.

Another memory: just six months into our relationship, I spotted a lesion on the nape of your neck, dark as the future, obviously a melanoma. Already I loved you too much to deprive you of a last untroubled sleep, so kept quiet, only to lie awake beside you, dreading the dawn and what crouched beyond it.

Such a strange reaction: I'm not neurotic, have often taken risks with my own life. Yours seemed more fragile, even then. Of course, when I looked at first light, I saw that the mark was just a smear of chocolate. You'd eaten a Mars Bar in bed.

'Silly sausage,' you laughed, folding me into arms that felt strong enough to protect us both.

Always I feared I would lose you, but never did I imagine losing you in such sad, slow increments. *Better, of course, than the terrible stillness to come. Death is irrevocable and non-negotiable. It does not mock us with dreams of miracles.*

Dreams. I carry all the dreams in the world.

Your specialists puncture every one. There's nothing more we can do, *they say. Protocols have been followed, treatment paths explored, boxes ticked. The only way is down.*

Not so.

I refuse to give up.

Love conquers all.

Where there's half-life, there's hope.

Faites vos jeux. Rien ne va plus.

S omething brushed against Dory's cheek, drifted across the bridge of her nose. Her ascent to consciousness had progressed in languid stages, like a diver moving up a shot line. Now she kicked hard for the surface, broke through, sneezed. The butterflies had quit the tree to flit in a haze of dandelion clocks. Rolling meadowlands stretched in every direction, thick with rosemary, scarlet columbine, rue, daisies and the yellow of dandelions not yet blown.

Dory's brain could neither accept the inputs nor ignore their physicality. An explanation circled once or twice before alighting on her arm. She gazed at its gorgeous wings, a little too bright, a tad too perfect. *Ah*. In the absence of a better idea, she'd go with this one. Ó hAllmhuráin must have used the pod to pitch them into *Morlock*, the latest Beta version, bumps and all.

This wouldn't be her first visit to a virtual universe. Over the years, Dory had explored realms real and imagined, admired their clever haptics, developed fleeting addictions to *Sim City* and *Second Life*. This, however, was something else, a fever dream, compulsive and intoxicating.

Even as her senses succumbed, her critical faculties fought back. Cutting-edge technology could serve the masses, but Ó hAllmhuráin used it to exploit them, peddling it like opioids. Whether Dory articulated that thought or simply demanded the immediate restoration of analogue reality, her words spiralled into empty air. Ó hAllmhuráin had vanished.

Alarmed, she leapt up, lost balance, sat back down. The manoeuvre dislodged an object from her waistband, black and smooth, a monolith in miniature. She ran a confused finger across its surface before, with greater caution, levering herself upright against the captain's chair. Beneath her feet, the pod pressed wildflowers and butterflies into a tableau of the simulated life it had extinguished.

For a while she stood and drank it in, this strange new world. Gradually the ringing in her ears disaggregated until she could distinguish component parts, glees of birds and the thrum of jade-winged insects careering between outsized mallows. A mouse skirred from a clump of panicgrass, froze when it spotted her, then made a dash for it. She ignored its trajectory, her attention drawn to the broken fronds where it had made its entry. A larger animal must have recently passed that way.

Ó hAllmhuráin. Had to be.

Find him. The thought hatched, part-formed and flapping, and after it, others, equally unfinished.

No. Wait. Think.

Many moons ago, she and her college friends had mastered *Galaxian*, monopolising the machine until the high scores became their roll call. If *Morlock* carried trace DNA from those smeary aliens, perhaps the teachings of that game also still applied. Later, as an editor, she would adopt the most counterintuitive as her mantra: *Who hesitates wins.* Time may be of the essence in covering breaking news, but judgement trumps raw speed.

Right now, Dory possessed neither capacity. Discombobulated she felt, as if taken apart and reassembled without essential bolts and screws. Her hands fumbled with something tangled in her hair. When the headset came loose, she recognised, finally, the little black box, its companion power pack. TechCon seemed remarkably distant, yesterday's nightmare, yet it must also be the present. For if Dory's assumptions were correct, she was still onstage, insensate and vulnerable, under the gape of the TechCon faithful. She shuddered. Whatever else she did, she had to locate Ó hAllmhuráin as a matter of urgency. Dory would play his game, but only to end it.

Colours continued to play tag across the hull of the machine, a little less vivid, perhaps, or only in comparison to the surrounding dazzle. After arranging the headset and power pack neatly, as if a sound technician might at any moment collect them, Dory added the earpiece to the pile and selected a new bottle of mineral water. Overheated plastic crackled in her grasp. Extraordinary these fine details of continuity, smell and touch.

Setting out along Ó hAllmhuráin's trail, she inhaled the pungency of the earth, freshness and decay, and felt the sun, unmediated by shade. Stems and roots tugged at every step, pitching her forward only to break her fall. Within minutes she lost her bearings, no longer sure of his direction or how to retrace her steps. The virtual might be harmless, but try telling that to her nervous system. She was panting, as if at altitude, and her scrapes and bruises hurt no less than the real sort. Worse, though, was the hunger – savage, as if she hadn't eaten in years.

Higher ground should help her to orientate, yet each small summit revealed only more of the same, undulating grasslands, the colours so saturated as to appear filtered. When she spotted a copse of trees, Dory's desires outpaced her to their shelter. She would turn the laws of this world to her advantage. Behold, beneath them, a hamper, already open, its cargo of latticed tarts laid out. And if a banquet is imaginary, why wait to be served? Dory sliced into a hypothetical pie, lifted a wedge, bit into buttery crust.

Brain food, she thought, and laughed aloud. *Hold it together.* Something, insect or plant, stung her into momentary sobriety. She barely had the strength to inspect the damage. Good that she did. A stinger protruded from her ankle, its tiny sac of venom still pumping.

Not much left in her reserves or the water bottle. Fewer choices. No option but to stumble on through this loveliness, praying to be saved from it. Finally, beyond the copse, she spied signs of habitation, or at least cultivation: a rough-hewn fence enclosing a field of barley so rich with other growth that from a distance it merged into the neighbouring meadow.

A path directed her around it and on to a wider lane pocked with hoof prints and what she took to be wheel marks. Barley gave way to asparagus, its spears pointing to the ridiculous blue of the sky. Dory snapped a plump stalk, devoured it tip to bottom, and another and another, marvelling at the intensity of flavour and how little she minded the grit. Next, she experimented with chewing on plumes of cavolo nero, gave up and wrestled a bunch of carrots from the copper-coloured soil. They tasted like summer.

Fear and exhaustion receded, and in their place something long absent stirred. A prelapsarian joy.

Up the lane she walked, a new lightness to her step even as the route steepened. At the crest of the longest climb, she turned back, searching for a glimpse of the pod. The copse, at least, was clearly visible. She could retrace her steps if necessary.

Ahead lay rougher terrain, a ravine hacked through bloodshot shale, bald but for succulents that stubbled gentler inclines with silver. The road took a cautious approach to the gradient, a tangent here, a switchback there, to reach, far below, a bridge across a creek. Even at this remove, she could hear the waters hiss and play.

Their volume increased as she descended, enveloping her in white noise. Eventually the trail contracted, its full width from overhang to precipice spanned by a single set of wheel ruts. Once, long ago, on the island of Flores, she had looked over the edge of a similar mountain road to discover a burned-out minibus, its skeletal driver fossilised in the act of escape. Now she clung to the bluff and almost failed to notice the ladder protruding above the outer verge.

Little about this construction inspired confidence: the gauge narrow; constituent parts delicate, cleats fixing the ladder to the rock as insubstantial as hairclips. Dory would try its strength before committing. But how? If she knelt on the escarpment, the rock too might break away. Eventually she lay on her belly and wriggled backwards to ease her legs over the edge, straightening once the rung held her weight.

Here goes.

If the metal protested, the song of the creek masked its complaints. Even so, Dory's nerves jangled. Such a long way down, and the cliff itself seemed friable. Gingerly, she leant back for a better view of her surroundings and got a first glimpse of what looked like a series of terraces incised into the ravine. Far below, on the uppermost of these, a tortoiseshell cat stretched in the lee of an upturned wheelbarrow. Its companion, brindled like a lynx, blinked up at her, licking a raised paw. His battle scars proclaimed him a tom. Life, or its perfect approximation.

Now Dory stopped, checked for obvious dangers. No other sounds penetrated the static of rushing water. Nothing moved but the ribcage of the sleeping cat and the tabby's tongue deploying across russet fur.

Every gamer knows to mistrust peace; it is the calm that heralds the storm, the minute to midnight. Fear hissed in Dory's ears like the creek. She wished she could deny it, but her accretion of minor injuries had challenged her understanding of digitised risks.

Nor should this have come as a surprise. Grief sickens us, stress weakens us, fear kills us. If you cut us virtually, do we not bleed? She examined a scratch on her wrist.

Who knew what coiled, ready to strike, at the ladder's base. From this angle, the belly of the escarpment obscured much of the terrace. Still, what else to do but follow rails and rungs to their conclusion? The voice in her head egged her on — *What's to lose?* — supplying an answer just as her feet made contact with the ground: *Nothing.*

The thought made her stagger. With a tail-twitch of contempt, the tabby wound through a fissure in a crag the colour of his coat. If only she could do the same. The wheelbarrow posed questions about its owners — when they might return, and how. Another sweep of the horizon confirmed two potential approaches: the ladder and a driveway emerging through a gap in the encircling cliffs two levels below her, perhaps linked to the same route she had just abandoned.

A chimaera birdwing caught her eye. As she turned to track its flight path, Dory gasped. Hewn into the rockface behind her stood a structure with blind windows and doors, columns rising smooth and seamless to an elegant portico. Above it, statues appeared to clamber up the slopes of a broken pediment.

She stepped back, the better to study narrative friezes across the upper stories. Might these carry clues to the civilisation that created them? Before the question crystallised, she scolded herself. Civilisation indeed! *Morlock* portended its decline and fall, the product of limited imaginations with unlimited funds.

Hard to ignore the grace of this particular setting, though. Harder still to remember that it consisted of nothing more than noughts and ones. This game was immersive in ways she wouldn't have dreamt possible. A splinter of verse resurfaced, bumping against her consciousness: *Something rich and strange.* A lament for a father.

For the first time in ages, just as she should focus on her own predicament, she mourned an old loss. How excited Dad would be to see the butterfillies.

Unnoticed, the tabby reappeared. He watched Dory cross the terrace, step into the shade of the portico, study the motifs around the doorway: wheat sheafs and roses. Only the windows and door lacked detail, blank stone, as if the designers couldn't be bothered to conceptualise an interior. Perhaps they intended the façade to be viewed from a distance. Which meant the ladder was a diversion.

Movement in the doorway smashed the hypothesis and sent Dory whirling to face whatever might emerge. The apparition that confronted her was wild-haired and wilder eyed, trousers torn at the knees, features stippled and streaked with red dust. She released her breath in a stream of profanities. The figure swore too, pixelating a little with each syllable.

A cat twined around its ankles. Glancing down, Dory saw the tabby. Automatically, she bent to stroke him, noting the precise differentiation between soft hairs and springy whiskers, before straightening to stretch the same hand towards the door. She tapped it as if testing a hotplate. The surface was cool.

Emboldened, Dory placed her palm on it, pushed. The material squeezed between her fingers, sprang back into shape when she removed the pressure. She tried again, this time with weight behind her shoulder, observing her image grimace with effort. The door stared back too, unmoved though not unmarked by their confrontation. Her hand had left a dust deposit, a streak across her reflection.

For the first time it occurred to her that the rules of this world might be reciprocal. She now knew herself to be vulnerable to injury. Maybe she could inflict it, too. Potentially helpful, but she didn't mean to damage this *temple*. She raised an elbow, wiped at the dust with her jacket sleeve, noticed she was making things worse. The streak, a rectangle, expanded, continued to do so without further intervention, filling the doorway, or – more precisely – emptying it. An oblong of sunlight picked out a mat, an iron boot-scraper, a stone floor, the edge of a richly patterned runner. Her hand met no resistance.

'Hello!'

The voice was barely audible above the rushing water. It took a second to recognise it as her own.

The cat brushed past her legs and down the corridor. Dory braced, took a tentative step forward, another, stopped to register a change. A dwindling of sound, then something louder, silence, as if someone had switched off the creek. The light had changed, too. No need to look behind her to understand what had happened, but she did so anyway.

From this side, the reconstituted door appeared neither stone nor mirror, but glass. Her instincts squabbled like lovers. Go. Stay. This might be a trap. *Oh for god's sake, Dory. Just do what you're going to do.* She remembered Morgen saying these words as they faced off in a hotel lobby after breaking news once more broke their plans.

They used to be regulars there. Couples whose work enforces lengthy separations must find coping mechanisms or founder. Absence makes the heart go wander. The traveller escapes responsibilities: the partner left behind might pine, but then adjusts to living without negotiations or compromises.

After a series of scratchy re-entries near the start of their relationship, Dory and Morgen reconvened on neutral territory. The hotel suited their purpose, far enough from London to avoid anyone they knew, and as comfortable as an armchair.

Their routine, if uninterrupted, never varied: the full English, extra black pudding for Morgen, followed by a circuit of the reservoir, shine or rain. Management supplied wet-weather gear for the latter eventuality. Whatever the season, Morgen would borrow Wellingtons, only to complain of sore arches. Now, in this alien vestibule, Dory discovered a similar provision, though a turbulence of reds, pinks, cyans and fluorescents at first disguised the utilitarian nature of the garments.

The boots stood neatly ordered like a Pantone chart, each shade correlated to the next. Above them hung coats organised to the same principle, the nearest sporting cerise wings and tail. Dory ran a hand over its neighbour, admiring its luminous scales, until a hand-painted sign snagged her attention: *Canto das Águas*.

Her eyes brimmed.

'What took you so long?'

The complaint issued from the end of the hall. Though she should be relieved to hear his voice, Dory needed a moment longer with her bittersweet memories.

Song of the water.

A few more beats and she capitulated, moving through to a vaulted space where Ó hAllmhuráin, pale as a Persian cat, occupied a recliner several sizes too small for him.

'OK,' she said. 'Enough now. Stop.'

'Stop what?'

'The game. *Morlock*. Whatever you want to call this.' Her gesture encompassed the room and the counterfeit landscape beyond its windows. The sky, she noted, had reddened.

'Is that what you think? Jaysus.' He straightened. 'I overestimated you.' Before she could reply, he held up a hand. 'To question is smart. To demand evidence is smart. To deny evidence and go on denying it…' A noise. Disgust or frustration. 'Wake up.'

For a second, she wondered if she might really be asleep. *Perchance to dream.* Had Ó hAllmhuráin drugged her? Everyone? Pumped hallucinogens through the TechCon air vents?

'Dorian,' he said. 'This is the future. The bastard machine took us to the wrong date and then refused to move. I just need to figure out a way to get us home.'

She had opened her mouth to argue when a silhouette flitted across the window, then another, then more, like a deceit of lapwings descending at dusk.

03:00

*T**he counsellor glances at her carriage clock, its malachite face flanked by brass pillars**. Should a woman who chooses a timepiece this ugly be trusted to dispense wisdom? Her website promises existential psychotherapy. To do is to be, yet here I am, stranded on her sofa. All the while she monitors that clock. Its chimes interrupt me mid-sentence, mid-thought. 'We'll pick this up next time,' she says, but* wait, what if there's no next time? *The unreliability of next times is what sent me to her. She smiles and the temperature drops. The open door of her consulting room affords a glimpse of another client, who turns away lest we know each other, by coincidence or because the cost of Clock Woman's services limits her potential customer base to the size of a Cotswold hamlet.*

To be honest – and therapy demands honesty – my expectations weren't high to begin with. She talks about healing, *but actions alone have the power to end this pain, deeds not words, as Nietzsche never said.*

Therapy valorises what we say over what we do. How often have I seen friends substitute counselling for the addictions that forced them to request help in the first place or seize on newly unearthed histories to excuse years of inexcusable behaviour. Still, I'd allowed myself to hope that these sessions would make me feel better, if only as a distraction. Instead, they leave me desolate. Morgen's brother, who urged this course, tries to convince me that discomfort is a sign of progress, memories bobbing to the surface of the bowl. I demur. We humans survive by making editorial choices, sanitising and shaping our narratives.

The grief never loosens its grip, but act for long enough as if nothing is wrong and distress subsides to a background noise, a distant river. Please don't deny me that comfort.

Nor do I have any desire to interrogate the past. Nostalgia rarely survives close inspection. Zoom in on any period and it resolves into pixels, the good, the bad, the banal, the beautiful, all mixed together, if in varying proportions.

It is my luck, and my sorrow, that so many lovely images repeat.

Morgen, unguarded, open.

Morgen in the morning, texting me a single letter, T. My love is awake and most days I will gladly stop, mid-sentence, mid-thought, and brew a fresh pot of tea, as requested.

Morgen playing truth or consequences.

Oh, here is one I would rather forget.

Morgen hurting, closed. Something I did, but I am not yet ready to confess and anyway, what good would it do?

Another pixel. If I cannot redeem myself at home, I will seek absolution through work, a piece on trafficking. So I find my way to a bar in Patpong, watch slender locals nuzzle red-faced foreigners. A few girls – they're horribly young – gather around, curious, because this is not a place for female tourists. I return their interest in kind, detached, taking mental notes. Does this anecdote provide me with a colour lede? Morgen used to tease me about my tendency to turn every experience into a story, with a beginning, a middle and an end.

They too have an arc in mind, these bar girls. They dream of being transported from this instant to a place of safety ever after. Most of their questions are about England, the men, the weather. One, though, asks about me, my name, do I have children, how old I am. 'Forty,' I reply. 'Me too,' she says. 'I'm fourteen too.' Minutes later, she lies on the podium, legs splayed, using her pelvic floor to draw on a cigarette and puff out smoke rings.

I describe this exchange to the counsellor to illustrate the dissociative culture of journalism, but she brushes the clue away and prospects for old wounds instead. Inevitably, she finds some. Give her a child until the age of seven and she will show you the madman. So what? I'm not here because of things Mum or Dad did or didn't do. It is the weight of now that presses me into the springs of Clock Woman's lumpy Chesterfield.

The present, what a gift. Time packages it in fancy paper, ties it with ribbon. Unwrap it – carefully, remember to recycle – lift the lid, peer inside. If you're lucky, you'll find contentment, or at least a glimmer of potential.

All I see is an empty box.

Breakfast consisted of a glass of red wine, two small flatbreads and a bowl of milk, its warmth and corona of foam suggesting a short route to table from goat or sheep. The location of any livestock remained a mystery. When Dory woke that first morning, surprised in equal measure by her surroundings and a delicious, alien drowsiness, the table was already laid. Their hosts sat with them, consumed the meal in delicate bites and sips, cleared the dishes, and all at once left, without fuss or farewell. They darted, these creatures, no trace of them outside, though Ó hAllmhuráin barrelled through the front door in their slipstream. His momentum propelled him as far as the cliff, where he halted, millimetres from the red rock, looking up and down and side to side.

Dory saw his mouth open, cupped hands to her ears to filter out the creek. It still swallowed most of his words, but their import was clear enough. *Ladder! Driveway! Gone!* The escarpment, now blank and unbroken, extended protective arms around the semicircle of descending terraces down to a diameter of wild water. Closer examination – Dory combed the lower reaches and Ó hAllmhuráin felt his way along the upper levels for concealed portals – confirmed their initial fears. They were trapped inside the compound. A cave at the base of the cliff, its maw just large enough to admit Dory, led to two connecting chambers, the first housing wash tubs and mangles, the second a winery.

At least the search gave her respite from Ó hAllmhuráin and his relentless fictions, his romance of time travel transforming into a paranoid thriller. Back in the building, the cats their only company, he beckoned her over, speaking in a stage whisper. When these *gobshites* next attempted a vanishing act, he would intercept them, hold one, maybe two at most, but that should slow the rest sufficiently for Dory to observe their means of departure. 'What if they've left for good?' she asked, more for the sake of argument than because she had considered the possibility. The idea immobilised both of them, characters in a stop-motion animation awaiting the next slide. Then

Ó hAllmhuráin moved again, a slow shake of his head. 'Always the bright side with you, Dorian.'

A casual observer might label the criticism a case of pot and kettle. Since landing in this strange place, Ó hAllmhuráin's bonhomie, always paper-thin, had deserted him, his artful dishevelment declining to ordinary messiness, skin glinting white and damp as the belly of a fish. As Dory moved away, he flopped on to a pair of recliners pushed together to accommodate his frame, a thing out of its element, no matter that the element was of his own creation.

His reluctant companion felt little surprise, less sympathy. PR-sanctioned accounts of Ó hAllmhuráin's life described him as a *self-made man*. As the term implies, this is a process not of becoming but constructing, often producing architecture that appears robust but lacks solid foundations.

Dory placed a cushion on the floor, propping her back against the wall. If Ó hAllmhuráin thought nothing of rearranging the doll-sized furniture to his needs, she would proceed gingerly, a good guest though her hosts were figments.

Meanwhile to urgent business. Ó hAllmhuráin's scheme wasn't exactly foolproof, and, anyway, how could she depend on him? He was the agent of this situation, his unravelling, she hoped, an act, a piece of gamesmanship. If not – well, Dory didn't want to think about that possibility, but what choice did she have? She felt weak as a kitten. Even now, after that glorious sleep and these few hours involving nothing more taxing than clambering to the lowest terrace and back, she could barely stand, much less risk attempting the one flight path left unexplored. She had spotted a huddle of stones at the midpoint of the creek. Though the waters roared a warning to anyone foolish enough to test their force, a leap to the first foothold might be manageable, if only she weren't so depleted.

Did her physical condition within the game signal gathering danger outside it? Events couldn't be developing in real time, or she and Ó hAllmhuráin would be properly sick, sustained only by a simulation of food and drink. A few days: that was the longest a person could go without water. What if they were not, as she had originally assumed, still in the pod on the TechCon stage, poised to regain consciousness under the gaze of a livestream, a gleeful Ó hAllmhuráin crowing that their whole crazy adventure had taken but a minute. 'We travelled through time!' she heard him cry. 'Wasn't that *deadly*?' Now a new image began to form, a second scenario, a glitch, their bodies vacant. She saw how the drama might have unfurled, a slow-dawning realisation, panic, an emptied auditorium, ambulances wailing them to a place of echoing footsteps and the three-note lament of bedside monitors.

A *demonstration*. That had been Ó hAllmhuráin's word for their headlong plunge into *Morlock*. Assault and battery. Kidnapping. Those were Dory's. Astonishing, in retrospect, that the producer had dared to criticise her professionalism. Dory looked forward to suing TechCon and its star.

That prospect briefly warmed her, but such an outcome depended on finding a way out of this nightmare. She set to working through hypotheses and implied risks. Not the risks to Morgen. Dory couldn't let her mind go to that realm of darkness; anyway, the agency staff would keep to their rota, however delayed her return. And if Dory never came back? Again, off bounds.

Focus on what you know, Dory muttered, then immediately distracted herself. In interviews Ó hAllmhuráin liked to quote Aristotle on the importance of reasoning from first principles. Finally, a point of potential agreement between them, yet the more Dory interrogated her situation on the basis of the few facts she possessed, the deeper her confusion. Not a single theory survived scrutiny. Why, for example, would Underworld's marketing team corral an audience to watch Ó hAllmhuráin and her twitch and frown their way through *Morlock* instead of asking prominent fans to try out the new version and supply testimonials? How did any of this relate to WEEN – or was the whole time-travel thing an elaborate smokescreen? Might *Morlock* be a testbed rather than an end-product? Surely there were psy-ops uses for a virtual environment of this sophistication. No need to waterboard when you can inflict grievous injury in another plane and leave no mark or evidence.

In a different context, this insight, sudden and unarguable, might have galvanised Dory to start chasing a potential story.

After all, the initial prompt for her Curasis investigation had been insubstantial, a mere *what if*. Ó hAllmhuráin's account of himself and his business activities cried out for a similarly forensic appraisal. Yet Dory's exhaustion was profound, mental as much as physical. Navigating this world of tiers required constant vigilance, endless second-guessing.

She wondered if Ó hAllmhuráin recalled the second part of Aristotle's observation, that *these things are perhaps the most difficult for men to grasp, for they are furthest removed from the senses*. The philosopher wasn't wrong. Any battle pitting lived experience against dry fact starts from a place of asymmetry. Ó hAllmhuráin alone existed outside this game, yet the humanish beings of *Morlock* seemed at least as credible. When first they manifested, a flicker outside the window, then flimsily embodied, she'd scoffed. Those large eyes and etiolated bodies; the strange skin; it was all too blatantly Roswellian. Yet by the time Dory sat down with them for their first communal meal yesterday evening, she found she wanted to swallow it all, not just the dishes, but the rough-hewn table, the light and shadows and scents, the substance of it. A tiny irregularity in the wood of the bench snagged her hand. She tasted familiar flavours, vegetal and earthy, and odder notes, something sweet to the point of decay, offset by a citrus sharpness. She even wondered if the local diet provided sufficient protein. No sooner did she formulate the thought than a platter of roast meat passed along the row, probably a hare, the animal's hind legs angled for a final leap to freedom. It reminded Dory of her uncle's whippet, Twiggy.

She had eaten what she was given, the servings small, but then again, so were the diners. Only at mealtimes had they perched for long enough to be studied, interacting little and wordlessly, though the room was full of words. A vast bookcase, floor to arched ceiling, lined the longest wall.

The facilities suggested that residents shared traits with humans. How detailed, Dory wondered, was *Morlock* programming? If she timed it right, could she surprise them sleeping in the serried dormitories of the upper floors? Might she find them abluting in the washroom with its communal baths? Did digital beings use digital toilets?

Ó hAllmhuráin raised his head. 'What's so funny?'

'Nothing,' she said.

Whether their hosts possessed unbodily functions – or even existed in virtual spaces not populated in that moment by *Morlock* players – who knew, but it would be worth finding out. If she pulled aside the green curtain to reveal Ó hAllmhuráin at the levers, she could call him out for the humbug she already knew him to be, force him to release her from the game. Meanwhile she wished he would shut up for more than a few minutes at a time. She grimaced. Life had spared her the business of dating, but friends sent regular dispatches from its frontlines. Ó hAllmhuráin might have stepped straight from one of these tales, a boor testing conversational gambits to see if anything landed. David Bowie's life and works? CRISPR gene editing? Right now, he was setting out his counterfactual take on Curasis and its fraudulent CEO.

This wouldn't be his first incursion into her areas of expertise, but at least he refrained from invading her space, a courtesy not extended to their hosts. Last night and again this morning at breakfast, he had gripped frail arms, demanded responses, barked abuse. Silence maddened him. He talked across it, did battle with it. 'If extinction is the rule and survival the exception, how come you lot survived?' A bark of exasperation, then 'Like pigeons', a truncated version of an earlier observation: 'You people are like pigeons. There must be young Mekons, but where?'

Mekons, he called them. Privately Dory devised a different nickname: the Apostles. Night and morning there had been twelve at table, whether the same dozen or a rotating cast, who could tell. Though striking, they were also strikingly similar, reinforcing her suspicions that the game's designers regarded them as minor characters. Why bother to fashion more than one gender or race? What need for backstories or distinct personalities?

In other contexts, their ornamentation – the shining robes, the garlands – might speak to individuality. Here it transformed them into a shimmer. Dory thought not of pigeons but hummingbirds, almost too quick to see, their colour itself an illusion created by light bouncing off their feathers. The comparison seemed particularly apt as she realised that they had returned, unremarked, flitting between kitchen and table. The creek should have announced their arrival, filling this room with music as the front door melted. Nor had Dory noticed the passage of time. Minutes ago, the sun hung directly overhead. Now it filled the long strip of window, its rays near horizontal and soft as a dying rose.

Ó hAllmhuráin, oblivious, kept up his barrage, wending predictably from Curasis to mRNA vaccines. She got up, a little stiffly, and moved to the kitchen counter, where one of the Apostles applied a scrubbing brush to a cairn's worth of what looked liked pebbles. Each pass of the bristles revealed root vegetables beneath the dirt, the skins redder than clay. Dory picked up a second brush and joined in the work, sensing rather than seeing a reaction, a sideways glance.

Dinner would serve up further such micro-expressions, a moue of amusement, a grimace so fleeting she might have imagined it, but then came something impossible to mistake. Ó hAllmhuráin's latest run of declaratory statements had coalesced into soliloquy. A solution to climate change was not the limit of his ambition but its shallows. His sea stead already modelled the global society he expected to emerge under his guidance, a libertarian meritocracy in which everyone flourished according to abilities equalised and enhanced by technology. 'There,' he said, waving an index finger, 'they will recognise no masters. There they will be free. This is the future.'

'No masters,' said Dory, 'apart from you. Anyway, I thought *this*' – she mirrored his gesture to indicate their surroundings – 'was the future.'

'Fockin' eejit,' he replied, without vigour. He removed his glasses to massage his forehead, closing inflamed eyes.

It was then that she saw it, as plain as the nose on that pallid face. An Apostle met her gaze, and, echoing Ó hAllmhuráin's gesture at TechCon, winked.

The next morning, building and terraces stood empty but for a curl of cats under the wheelbarrow. Dory's clothes, neatly folded on the little chair next to her cramped bed, had been laundered and mended, the table laid for two, and ladder and driveway restored to their original positions. So much for escape plans, though Ó hAllmhuráin acted as if the terraces might rearrange themselves at any second, chivvying Dory along as she sat down to flatbread and milk. 'There's no time!'

She ignored him, stronger after a second miraculous night's sleep, but still drained. If these meals nourished soul rather than body, she felt better for them, and the journey he now proposed – to the pod and beyond, wherever that might be, home or another looking-glass world – required every scrap of energy she could muster.

Before leaving they filled their old mineral water bottles, then descended to the drive. As she'd suspected, it met the lane two or three switchbacks below the head of the ladder, a longer climb, but gentler. From this level, they could see the bridge, its underside barely clearing the torrent, and, halfway across, a convoy of horses and riders.

Ó hAllmuráin launched a single word in their direction.

'I beg your pardon?'

He repeated it, though she had heard him all too clearly.

'Savages.'

With that he was off up the hillside, gulping air to expend it on yet another monologue. Consider the Mekons' inner life, or lack of it. Where was their ambition to do anything but sleep and eat and adorn themselves? Forget the Enlightenment. This was the Endarkenment, humanity decayed to a gaudy futility through a slow movement of degeneration, diminished in size and intelligence. All those books, *but did you see them reading?*

Little point, she knew, in wasting her own breath to pick apart this toxic slew. Instead, she would tell him about the wink, at once challenging his prejudices and needling him, an oddly satisfying prospect. 'Say that we aren't stuck in your game, or say that we are, but AI has taken over to a point that this universe is as complex and uncontrollable as the analogue world.'

Both watched a familiar phrase forming on Ó hAllmuráin's palette: *Dorian, this is the future.* She hurried on before he gave it voice.

'Say any of those things. Insist, if you will, that we're stuck in another century.'

An emphatic nod.

'You'd be wrong about your Mekons even so. Last night…'

Here she made a mistake, pausing to fill her lungs, and as she did so her thoughts strayed to those beautiful books. Printed in some kind of logogrammatic language, they were calfskin-bound with frontispieces and patterned endpapers. How it must have amused the game's designers to place old-fashioned, physical volumes in an imagined future.

Of course, Ó hAllmhuráin didn't let the lull go unpunished, talking over her as if to an invisible public. 'The Mekons enjoy the fruits of civilisation. Food, drink, flush toilets. Literacy, or its legacy. Advantages earlier generations cherished, fought for. Because without these things, life is just survival.' He gestured. 'Behold the aftermath of a great culture. Everywhere the remnants of innovation, and the Mekons grubbing about in the dust. Dorian, they wash by hand, drive carts instead of cars, break their backs in manual labour. Imagine you lived here. Mornings, you'd leave home through a door that dissolves and reconstitutes – almost certainly a form of quantum teleportation – yes, time travel. Evenings you'd return the same way. How could you rest until you figured out the science behind that portal and transferred this knowledge to other uses?'

The end of his sentence came out as a gasp, the gradient stilling his tongue as no interviewer could. Dory tuned into the wider soundscape, loose shale underfoot, the receding creek and, faint at first, a humming and twangling about her ears. From the summit, she identified a probable source, a baler, evidently steam-powered; and in the fields around it, lifeforms – horses harnessed to carts, goats with bells around bearded necks, and Apostles, picking and pruning, stacking and loading.

'Savages.' Ó hAllmhuráin, chest heaving, gave equal weight to each syllable.

He began to dictate a route to the pod – not the way Dory remembered, but she submitted; anything for a quieter life. The story of the wink could wait too. All the way down the hill and along the lane, Ó hAllmhuráin narrated their progress. *Denisovans could build a better road. The state of it.* A paddock of goats prompted

a sudden exclamation: *Don't you go looking at me with yer devil's eyes!*
The animals ignored his instruction, their horizontal pupils the
size and shape of the portal's smallest aperture, heads immobile
but for rotating lower jaws.

Dory ruminated too, on what she knew about Butterfly Effect
Systems. Hadn't she read, or maybe written, that such systems
permitted gamers to direct their own plotlines? If control can
be lost, surely it may also be seized. Ó hAllmhuráin promised to
pilot the pod back to TechCon, but what if he were lying? She
wondered if setting the destination might be as simple a case as
inputting date and time. Perhaps she could beat him to it. If so,
she'd have to be swift.

Right now, though, she was finding it tough merely to keep
pace. He had taken a sudden turn off the lane into the head-
height grasslands. She missed the root that lay across her path
like a tripwire, took a tumble. By the time she righted herself, the
landscape had swallowed him.

'Ó hAllmhuráin, wait up,' she called.

Rustling and a disembodied voice. 'Time waits for no man.'

Nor does a time machine. Dory bit back the observation.
No sooner had she located him than he stopped dead. Quickly
she covered the remaining distance to stand by his side, but even
before she saw the absence, she understood.

Later she would wonder about the hail of events that
followed. Had these been sequential rather than overwhelmingly
synchronous, might she have felt something, anything? Instead,
she observed.

The storm erupted from nowhere, lightning cracking like joints,
clouds boiling and splitting. Instantly, rain coursed down their
faces and into Ó hAllmhuráin's gaping mouth. He was bellowing,
a tethered goat, most meanings whipped away by the wind, but
one gaining clarity with repetition. *Who*, he demanded. *Who. Who.
Took. My. Time. Machine? Who?* Part goat, part owl. Dory suppressed
a sudden bubble of laughter, not that he would have noticed.
Knees buckling, he was folding in on himself.

It was his lower lip, jutting like a child's, that shocked her out of detachment. Morgen made that face too – whether in jest or distress, effective either way. *Don't do that to me*, Dory would beg. *You know I can't resist.* The lip had the capacity to resolve most disagreements.

These had been rare. A unit they were, partners, not least in negotiating the snake pits of their working lives. Dory learnt to beware forked tongues, whilst Morgen survived the poison of lesser talents. When first they met, Dory wondered at Morgen's apparent modesty. Later she came to recognise it as quiet confidence. Morgen's vision, pure and certain, left no room for doubt.

This solidity carried over into the rest of their lives. Morgen had been her rock in all the best ways, until she allowed herself to feel the relationship as stones in her pocket. One night she had said something terrible and saw Morgen's lip jut. In inflicting pain, she rediscovered tenderness, and in tenderness, remorse, *but too late, too late. Their innocence lost for ever, tears in rain.*

She began to cry – not for Ó hAllmhuráin, in pieces before her, but for Morgen. She hadn't really missed Morgen these past days – not in Vegas, not here. Now yearning tore at her heart, threatened to burst from her ribs. She wept for the Morgen of weddings and mountain walks and lying like spoons. She wept for herself, too, because she didn't much care that the pod had vanished. The home she longed for no longer existed.

In retreat, the squall stained everything sodium orange. She knelt next to Ó hAllmhuráin and for a while neither moved. Eventually she touched him on the shoulder. He was granite. It was then she knew: whatever the truth of their situation, he was no more in charge than she.

Taking action, however futile, felt better than doing nothing. Dory promised Ó hAllmhuráin that she would scour the area, as if there were the slightest chance they had mistaken another clearing for the landing site. The rain had done some preparatory work, beating down the grasses to waist height. She began working outwards in widening circles, a trick retrieved from her Hostile Environment Awareness Training. Completing the course had been a precondition of insurance for war zones, pure box-tickery, really. The instructors, a quintet of former paras, strutted and posed and blew things up. *Like a Deep Purple gig*, a Palestinian journalist whispered. Their sniggers earned a public dressing down. This was a serious business, life and death.

The journalist knew that well enough, bullet scars to his elbows and knees, and an obvious contempt for play-acting at war. On the second day, the paras singled him out, ambushing a convoy of jeeps, manhandling everyone to the ground, and subjecting him to a mock execution. The rest of the group, manacled and with burlap sacks over their heads, were forced to march across rough terrain, any complaints met with summary injustice. Only at the conclusion of the exercise did the paras explain its purpose. In conflicts, prisoners are at higher risk of being killed if they make trouble, whether by showing resistance or appearing too weak, a burden to their captors. Be the grey man, the paras said, the one they don't notice.

This was the sole lesson from the course that Dory consciously internalised, immediately recognising its application to journalism. It is always a challenge for reporters to be in a room without changing its dynamics. Be the grey man: that was the answer. Hard for a woman in environments teeming with grey men, but not impossible.

On her fifth and widest circuit now, she quickened her pace. It wasn't dark yet, but it was getting there, the mackerel sky streaked with coral. Only then did she notice an iridescence to the east, as if this world boasted a second sun. Refracted light or the glow of a distant city? She hurried back to the clearing to share her discovery, but Ó hAllmhuráin had gone. The ground alone bore testimony to earlier dramas: the imprint of the pod, a scatter of cherry blossom and, if you knew where to look, a fresh indentation where he had lain.

04:00

I **nnocence is a form of insanity.** *I read that somewhere. This afternoon, I'm lying across four laps in a minibus. A brace of heads emerges from the shoulders of the front passenger seat. Not sure who's at the wheel – none of my friends as yet has a driving licence. Even so, we regularly organise road trips, filling every seat of whichever vehicle we've been able to beg or borrow, then squeezing in a few more. We're old enough to understand that actions have consequences, young enough to sense that the consequences of inaction might be worse.*

This VW has seen better days, but I have not. Right now, I'm pretty much as happy as I've ever been, salt in my hair and on my skin, content to my bones. Carefree. Care free.

For the minibus is on the move, and don't we know it. Its suspension celebrates every flaw in the tarmac, and rust has breached the floor in two separate places. Look down and the road threads underneath us. I choose to watch the fugitive sky through a window framed in moss and silvered by a cobweb, its architect still cleaving to the glass. The sun clings on like the spider, resisting the end of this glorious day.

When evening prevails, it will be good too. A country pub, most likely, on the clifftops above a sea as tranquil as my heart. Someone brings me a whisky mixed with Crabbie's Green Ginger Wine, no ice, and I light a Rothman's. Mum and I have something in common after all. Still, this isn't a time to dwell on the past. My companions and I are living in the blithe moment and ahead of the curve. At a point in the future, smokers will be relegated to outdoor spaces and, later still, non-smokers too, but already my friends and I opt to sit on the terrace. Youth flows in our veins like Ready Brek. I doubt we feel the cold, though the temperature plummets as last orders approach.

Wedged at a table with integrated benches, the trestles blocking oblique exits, you need balance and determination to extricate yourself. Still, this must be my round, and anyway, only two of us have money. On top of our student grants, my flatmate Angela and I earn a decent whack restoring decency in the laundry of a seafront hotel, this town's popularity as a destination for dirty weekends embossed on the bed linen.

The extra cash is intended to finance a proper road trip next summer, across the Americas, before the formal commencement of my study year abroad and her final semesters here. Meanwhile we're minted. The hotel provides breakfast and lunch, and when the coast is clear we nick household supplies: toilet paper, sliced bread and individual containers of jam, Flora and Marmite. We started with bar work, but I sucked at it, all fingers and thumbs and generous measures, and neither of us were any good at humouring customers. Don't tell anyone, but the laundry isn't that bad. Angela teases me about how much I enjoy operating the steam press. The machine hyperventilates with excitement, three quick breaths to transform a tablecloth into a field of dreams. Fold, push, release: the alchemy is that simple. No meal served on such a crisp and snowy surface can ever be ordinary. We shall dine on Melba toast with curlicues of butter, chilled soup – Vichyssoise – followed by an elegant entrée, Sole Veronique perhaps, and, to finish, our just desserts, Baked Alaska. There in the laundry, hour upon hour, we build castles in the waterlogged air.

Only the canteen brings us back to a reality of sorts. At noon, scooping a portion of egg and chips from the chafers, we listen to our co-workers, all female. In these days before mobiles, one woman or another will spend her lunchbreak feeding the payphone. A child is always sick or a parent failing, the wages, princely for my purposes, barely adequate to household needs when everything goes as planned, much less in emergencies. Despite this, these women appear rich in ways I fear I'll never be, certain about what they think and feel.

Mostly they talk about mornings just gone, afternoons and evenings to come, and people, celebrities, family or petty, clock-watching suits and guests familiar to me only from genetic traces. Room 451 is today's topic. Earlier he called for housekeeping, held out a wrinkled scrap of flesh in place of a tip, complained he'd grown up without toys. I played with myself instead, *he declared.*

Incidents of this kind are like the weather, constant and generally unremarkable. Take my last-ever trip home. A damp day, suitcase heavy with memories, and the station concourse puddled. Dodging umbrellas, I committed to an escalator before noticing passengers below me scrambling against our downward trajectory. At the bottom of the stairs stood a man unzipped, his penis limp, as I supposed with shame, a pathetic phallacy.

If my younger self wonders why men do such things, she approaches it as a sociological question. It will be another year until a man gives her a lift, pulls a knife on her, makes her watch his scrabblings, and even then she won't learn – not yet.

The women in the canteen are already wise to the game. This morning 451 angled himself in the doorway so that the chambermaid had to brush past him to leave. The deputy general manager refuses to intervene. The guest is a regular customer, repeats this trick year in year out, harmless. Better toughen up if you want a career in hospitality.

The suggestion that the job is a step on the road to a better future riles everyone worse than 451's antics. Another maid drops a powerful word on to the table: organise.

This is thrilling. Instantly I leap to the barricades. So many people I will muster in support. Angela reads my mind, purses her lips. Fond though I am of her, she's strange that way, cautious, conservative. You'd think she would lead the charge, so much injustice she faces; I've heard the insults people throw at her. Anyway, I'm on the cusp of blurting out full-throated support for action when a receptionist kills the revolution with a single, contemptuous remark. This town, *she says,* is rammed with people who'd take your job – any job – without a moment's thought. Students.

Nobody looks our way, but I feel as exposed as 451, a guest passing through. That's me, then and always: a guest passing through.

Dory briefly considered striking out for the lights on the horizon but opted for caution. Shadows were falling, thick and deep, and instinct warned her to take shelter from them. The stirring of the grasses, innocent by day, acquired a menace. Once she even fancied that an animal, dull-white and stooped, ran across her path. Ó hAllmhuráin's whereabouts troubled her too. Had he departed of his own accord or been spirited away like the pod? Tamping down her unease, she began to retrace their earlier route, game-planning as she went. The final descent could be treacherous, and more so in the dark. Dory rejected in advance the option of the ladder, resolving to keep contact with the cliff, even at the risk of hitting her head on its overhangs.

As she cleared the summit, she realised this strategy was redundant. A flickering from the valley below drew borders between rock and night, guiding her way. Turning into the compound, she found its source, torches either side of the passage through the escarpment and bracketing the front entrance. How beautiful this place was, the carved figures of the pediments animated by the flames. As the door solidified behind her, she experienced not alarm but relief. A homecoming of sorts, this was, the building redolent of cooking, and Ó hAllmhuráin in his usual place on the Lilliputian recliners.

She felt, though she wouldn't admit this to anybody, much less Ó hAllmhuráin, pleased to see him. Had Dory been her usual self she might also have noted that he was far from his, mute throughout the meal but for a fleeting protest about his knife – *No more use than a spork*. As it was, she nodded off, came close to slumping on to her plate before a gentle intervention. Two Apostles shepherded her upstairs, made certain she was comfortable and drifted away. By then she had sailed in a different direction.

Back in the real world, Dory occasionally treated herself to what she dubbed a *soma holiday*, eight hours of over-the-counter oblivion. There was always a payback for this indulgence. The pills scrambled her writing, verbs to the end of clauses migrating, threads tangled. They suppressed dreams, too, another debit because the visions that rooted themselves in the shallow soil of her undrugged sleep could be epic and frequently made her laugh.

Morgen teased her — *you've been having fun without me again* — and it was true. The Dory of dreamworld cantered through shaggy-dog narratives with punning punchlines: *closed circuit TV* rendered as a rotunda of inward-facing screens or a German flower shop transposed to a corner of Hackney: oh, look, *Blumen Eck*. It wasn't all fun and games, though. Occasionally they came to her, the lovely dead, hugging her fiercely, speaking of times gone by. Then she would wake crying.

Tonight, in the compound, her dream gained a new dimension, more real to her than the world from which it plucked her. She flew, skimming the spires and towers of an uncanny city, dipping down towards waters that limited its sprawl, peeking into boats restless in the harbour. From here, she pivoted into canyons formed by buildings, encountered pedestrians, quicksilver Apostles and other species including her own. Close as she dared, she swooped, caught snatches of speech, mostly blurred but for two lines of Portuguese exchanged by lovers. For a moment, she mistook them for Morgen and herself in earlier incarnation, so similar did they look. *É urgente o amor*, exclaimed the Morgen-alike. *É urgente um barco no mar*, the Dory replied, face creased with joy.

If only she were able to land and speak to them, but there you have it, the curse concealed in the gift of flight. Once airborne, you're at the mercy of updrafts. The danger isn't plummeting to earth, but floating away, helpless and alone.

Dory awoke then, in tears but refreshed and, more than that, restored to clarity. She must find a way back to Morgen. Shame and guilt could divide as surely as any physical separation. What an idiot she'd been. And yes, she might not be able to save Morgen, or herself, yet in dreams and memories they walked side by side, Morgen's hand around hers. So lucky they had been to find each other. So lucky they still were. So lucky they would always be.

The day spread before Dory like a fresh tablecloth. Breakfast, she thought, then another trek to investigate whether the glow in the sky pointed to a city, uncanny or otherwise.

He was already there and dressed when she descended to the ground floor. Something about the look of him suggested he'd been there all night. 'Good morning, Elo,' she said, testing the last two syllables as if they might burn her tongue. He didn't respond. Impossible to tell whether the eyes behind the sunglasses were open or shut.

If the latter, he would see a communal area empty of life but for her, food on the table and an infusion on the stove, lemon verbena from its fragrance. Did Ó hAllmhuráin mark Dory's new lease of energy or the unexpected way she deployed it, pouring the liquid into mugs and bringing one to him? He gave no sign, nor did he touch her offering.

After a quick check on ladder and driveway – both in place – she ate and drank, cleared the dishes and looked for her water bottle, all the while alert for signs of movement from the end of the room. 'I'm planning to go out shortly,' she said, 'Do a bit of exploring. Want to come with me?'

Nothing. OK, then. Bottle filled, she turned to him one last time. 'I'm off.'

'Must be the weather.' The ghost of Ó hAllmhuráin, voice creaking with disuse.

She almost paused then to tell him where she was headed and why. Instead, she added the information to a lengthening list of topics to broach when the time was ripe.

Morning air settled on her shoulders, heavy with moisture from yesterday's storm or warning of another in the works. She wore it lightly, enjoying the flex of her calves, the sensation of joints moving without complaint. Her breathing felt easy too. Dory thought of the phrase Morgen used in the days after the transfusions: *They've given me the blood of young soldiers.* At the last minute she altered course, turning down the lane towards the bridge. She would take advantage of her replenished strength to check the view from the opposite side of the gorge before pursuing the now familiar route to the landing site.

The road tacked up the red rockface to meet the skyline. From the peak, agricultural lands spread below her in pleasing patterns, but she barely glanced at them, her gaze caught and held by an incongruity. Straight ahead of her, a pyramid rose from fields of golden rape.

Something about the colossus unnerved her – not merely its size, but a half-memory, or a false one, déjà vu. She nevertheless hurried towards it, the details coming into focus as she drew near, rectangles she had mistaken for stone blocks revealed as empty frames. The pyramid's upper reaches were skeletal, great struts supporting a cross-hatching of narrower beams to converge in the heavens. Here and there, and with more frequency towards the base, panels of onyx-coloured glass hid metal and concrete bones.

The rape plants grew brighter than she had ever seen, and taller, halfway up the high wicket fencing that protected the site. Through the bars, she glimpsed four vast and trunkless legs standing proud of the yellow flowers, and, in their shadows, a pharaonic head, beard and nemes azure striped.

She knew then what this building was supposed to be – just days ago had tried to spot its analogue original from the window of her commuter flight to TechCon, an amputee reaching for the stump of what had been.

Years ago, she had come to Las Vegas as a tourist, later returning to research her book on ageing. The area was, after all, a global centre of what practitioners called age management and a distinguished biologist she interviewed for the same project labelled 'hooey'. Dory understood the industry as something else again, a secular religion promising, if not life everlasting, its nearest alternative.

Vegas introduced her to the church's patron saints – how many she wasn't quite sure. These doctors were harder to tell apart than the Apostles, their surgically enhanced unifaces expressionless, brows pulled tight above noses chiselled to extinction. They sang from the same hymn sheet, too, each informing Dory that her physical condition was *suboptimal*; she could dramatically improve her longevity by following their patented courses, hormones, proprietary supplements.

By day she consorted with the clones, at night bathed in the eternal brightness of the Strip. She knew enough of the city's bloody history, its unsustainable present, that she might have resisted its charms if Morgen hadn't surprised her by stealing away from a tour to join her there.

Morgen's passions, unlike Dory's, were never hedged with misgivings. Twice in a row they dined at the Rosewood Grille at Morgen's request. Dory liked lobsters well enough, but these giant beasts demanded effort. She ate only the tail meat and claws, refused to bother with messier excavations. Morgen left not a shred of sweet flesh in any part of the shell, sucking on legs and licking fingers. *Oh my love, gorgeous in a plastic bib.*

After the first blowout, they crossed to the Mirage, then took a cab to the Luxor. Morgen revelled in its artificiality, urging her to stop analysing the experience and just enjoy it. They filed through a recreation of Tutankhamun's tomb ('on Paiute burial grounds,' she said, earning amused side-eye), watched guests ferried from check-in to the lifts along a Stygian river, and of course had a go on the slot machines. Less predictably, they won, cherries all the way, wealthier when they got back to their room than when they'd set out on their high-spending evening. Their hotel was old-school, faded. In Vegas, history moves at variable speeds.

That would appear to be the case in *Morlock* too, but Dory presumed nothing in the simulacrum post-dated anything else, no matter how box-fresh or weathered. She watched a pair of jade scarabs bumble past, sighed. The wicket gate was padlocked, its posts too spindly to carry her weight, the spikes daunting. She could give up, yet the pyramid exerted a strange pull. What lay within? Long-dead fruit machines or living memories, facsimiles of decay or rows of razors, eternally sharpened by pyramid power?

If only she had a razor to slice through the fence or, like Occam's, hack away distractions. Simple solutions are always the best. As she discarded the idea of improvising a tool, the gate swung open, padlock gaping with shock. Her enthusiasm for exploration as suddenly blunted, Dory forced herself to go inside.

The pyramid transported her to an unexpected time and place, Donegal. Dory had travelled there for a story about the drivers and costs of a global banking crisis. *There's nothing ordinary about these properties*: that had been the developers' marketing pitch for Luggnagg Hills, and they weren't wrong. Most houses on the ghost estate stood empty, but for the wildlife that reclaimed them, foxes and rats. 'Won't you take a little walk?' asked one of the few human residents, showing her into what should be his kitchen. When she complied, the floor tilted crazily. It was a dream of gracious living without foundations, built directly on top of a brook.

Now a broken slab of the pyramid rocked and pivoted with her every step like the ghost estate kitchen. The Styx had carved a new route through the lobby, leaving the tourist boats grounded. Dory wouldn't look up, not yet. The height of the atrium had dizzied her even when its floor felt solid.

Sandwich boards and freestanding placards marked a path through the debris. *To the exhibits*, she read, and *Museum this way / zum Museum / para o Museu*. Another sign, water-damaged, proved harder to decipher. *Odd worlds? Old worlds?*

Cautiously she followed the arrows up a fractured staircase to a mezzanine, yelped as she came face-to-partial-face with a figure carrying a flap of his own skin, white teeth grinning in flayed skull. On a table next to him, a human foetus contemplated the hole where its umbilical cord should be. A third body had been preserved in the act of running, as if its owner hoped to outpace death or seize the red-and-white life preserver hanging on the wall.

Dory stared at the exhibits, willed her heart to slow, moved along the row to examine a series of glass display cases. Many objects meant nothing to her, an entire vitrine filled like Morgen's Mystery Drawer with a tangle of cables and connectors. A trio of cases housed a more familiar collection, a Motorola Car Radiotelephone, hand-held bricks, StarTACs and Alcatel Clamshells. Keyboards evolved then disappeared, screens shrank, only to expand. An iPhone, rigidly persistent, faced a Tantalus, and linked through lengths and breadths of time, an Apple Watch versus an Apriköt.

The smallest items looked like implantable devices – sigils, perhaps – though Dory couldn't think why such high tech would have been grouped with a pile of old TV control panels. The cabinet stood open. She reached in, picked up one of the remotes, tested its weight, was replacing it when the next display case snagged her attention.

Magazines and books, foxed and stained, seemed to have been grouped by colour. *L'Etranger* lay uneasily with *12 Rules for Life*, Angela Saini and David Graeber propped each other up. The last volume forced another noise from Dory: *huh*. Its cover showed a machine much like the pod, the image bracketed by the title and author's name: *TIME/LIFE: A memoir by Dory Silver*. The case resisted her every effort to prise it open.

05:00

Gather your ticket stubs while you may. The future will tether you like a farmyard animal. *My uncle tells us this and we follow his advice, not that we understand. Still, carpe diem! Though Laker Airways recently went bust and old-style carriers charge an arm and a leg, there are other options, Magic Bus, slow boats, fast planes. We're open to all of it. Courier companies offer cheap flights, sometimes even pay us to fly. In return we route via second and third countries, dropping off parcels and forms in the recesses of airports civilians normally don't see. It's the perfect mode of transport for people like us, without baggage or fixed destinations, travelling hopefully. Since João and I cannot make our sun stand still, we make him run, from São Paulo to Paris and then, just as he settles over Europe for the summer, we're off again, to Jakarta.*

That city unnerves us, too similar to Sampa, the shanty towns collecting like plaque at the base of a gleaming white snarl of skyscrapers. We leave after a few days, riding eastwards across the archipelago on a procession of buses and rackety commuter aircraft, consumed with each other and the bright and changing world. In Yogya, we are scooped up by a clutch of bored expats, who invite us to cocktails at a grand Dutch colonial mansion. So cheap, *says an Englishwoman, waving her Manhattan at a receiving line of uniformed waitstaff. In Kuta Beach, already shop-soiled by the tourism that will swerve neighbouring islands for a while yet, we encounter another breed of foreigner. Faded Xeroxes on public notice boards carry portraits of prisoners marooned in the local jail on drugs charges. They beg for books, cigarettes, conversation, a sense that someone, anyone, cares. Sadly, we have no time to spare; Lombok is calling and, after that, the Gilis. On Gili Air, we eat magic mushrooms and snorkel over technicolour reefs.*

Soon we're on the move again, to mountainous Flores. The journey to Maumere introduces us to Roman, a priest whose brother also serves a higher order, as an army commander in East Timor. Roman lights one clove cigarette from another and warns us against assuming ourselves welcome in the remoter reaches of this landmass. Though Islam and Catholicism battle for the townsfolk, the people of the interior practise older faiths. We must take care to arrive by daylight, lest anyone mistakes us for ghosts and tries to kill us deader.

The prospect should concern me. Instead, I am captivated.

Flores isn't meant to be our last stop. We have plans to see the dragons of Komodo, find a route to Sulawesi and then, who knows, another island, another country, so much to explore. First there's a volcano to climb, Kelimutu.

The manager of the losmen *advises us to set out at four in the morning to be sure of reaching the summit by daybreak. Such precision strikes us as unusual in a place where the question* What time does the bus depart? *most often elicits a pleasing but impracticable response:* jam karet, *rubber time. The manager insists:* For Kelimutu, time is of the essence. *The sharper the angle of the sun's rays, the more vivid will be its trio of crater lakes, each a different colour to the other and from one day to the next. This volcano is not extinct, merely sleeping, its snores releasing ever-changing combinations of chemicals into the water.*

At dawn we reach the summit, discover that Tiwu ata Mbupu, *the Lake of the Old, often turquoise, is midnight blue, while mustard streaks inflect the green waters of* Tiwu Nuwa Muri Koo Fai, *the Lake of Young Men and Young Women.* Our lake, João calls it. No, *I demur,* this one is yours and mine: Tiwu Ata Polo, *the Enchanted Lake, glowing red as a garnet.*

Has João ever looked back on this moment and despaired? Probably not, for most memories lose their pigment in the wash of everyday existence. Only trauma is indelible. Years later, despite such happiness with Morgen, I still feel what happened as a day-old bruise. João and I are back at the losmen, *laughing to find ourselves compelled after the exertions of the seven-hour hike to celebrate our aching bodies by combining them again. Desire is strong in us. He has only to sit alongside me for the fine hairs on my arms to rise and bend towards him. I have never before known passion like this.*

A knock and, without decent pause, the manager enters. As we scramble to cover our nakedness, he tells João he is needed. The Canadian is sick, very sick. Come please, Dr Neves.

We chatted to Wade on our first day here. He seemed disengaged, but we've encountered too many travellers from Canada and the Antipodes to read much into that. Something about the vastness of their home countries makes them approach travel not as a pleasurable occupation, but a series of tasks to check off, parcels to deliver, forms to complete.

Wade's companions stand at the foot of his bed, watching him convulse and foam. I cannot add value, but try anyway, grab a flailing limb. João pushes me aside, puts his head to Wade's chest, prizes open an eye. He tells the manager that Wade needs immediate medical attention. Is there a vehicle, a hospital? The seminary in Maumere has basic facilities, but nothing that could cope with this kind of emergency, likely cerebral malaria.

Imagine if we grasped the significance of events as we lived them, rather than in their non-negotiable aftermath. *Who wouldn't try to tamper with outcomes?*

The next minutes reroute my life.

A three-wheeler arrives. João squats on its open platform next to the patient. As we kiss goodbye, my hand slips into his rucksack, retrieves and palms his passport. You can check out any time you like, Doctor João, but you can never leave.

Of course, oblivious as I am, I do no such thing. *João tells me to follow on, soon as I can, to Labuan Bajo. We'll reconvene at the guest house we've already circled in our copy of* Lonely Planet *and from there resume our adventure. I smile, kiss him again, and go back into the* losmen *before he is out of sight.*

The next day, I arrive at the guest house and ask for him. The mother and son who run the place confer. Perhaps they haven't understood my phrasebook Bahasa, or could this be the wrong lodging? I check the name again. As I do so, the son addresses me in English. The young doctor has left. He went to the airport with the dying man. Are you the wife? He gave us a letter for you.

João's handwriting is unmistakable. After I returned to England for the last year of my degree, his letters pursued me, sometimes two a day, once even three, on blue airmail paper, sheet after sheet, both sides covered to the margins with his cramped, closed script. There were instructions, not to forget him or his language, our language now; to stay true; to prepare for a life in Belo Horizonte. He would describe scenes from the hospital or share news of his family, his new niece, his elder brother, and occasionally of the national transition to democracy.

His cousin, Tancredo Neves, has thrown his hat into the ring to be Governor of Minas Gerais. João approved the move but refrained from a public endorsement. He had his own ambitions to tend.

The letter he wrote in Labuan Bajo proves shorter than any sent during that year apart, concise and merciless.

Chuchu,

By the time you read this, I'll be on my way to Brazil.

You will probably be angry at me, and you have every right to be. I didn't dare to tell you I was leaving for the same reason that I cannot be with you. You are too different from me, *paixão da minha vida*, too strong, because the normal things don't matter to you. If I had tried to talk to you about this face-to-face, you'd have laughed and then kissed me. That's what you always do when I try to have serious conversations with you.

Remember on Kelimutu, at the red lake. You told me we should pray to the spirits and I complied, with all my heart: I want to be a neurologist, I said, to buy a nice house in Funcionários, raise a family. To do all of this with you. Then it was your turn to make a wish, and you made a joke instead.

['Hear me, spirits of the lake. My heart's desire is a cheese and pickle sandwich.' *These are the words that broke us, that day on the edge of the crater, and you know the funniest thing? It wasn't even a joke, not really. Throughout the climb, as we admire redwood and casuarinas and listen to the cackling of birds and monkeys, I am fantasising about a sandwich.*]

In that moment, I recognised a truth that I have tried my hardest to ignore: there can be no long-term future for us. If we travelled around the globe, flew to the moon and back, you still wouldn't be ready to settle down. I'm not sure you ever will. You made a joke in place of a wish because to you home is an abstraction — love too, I think. Believe me when I say there is nothing I want more than for you to be part of the life I see stretching ahead, but this is not to be. I must find someone who shares my dreams. You must decide what your dreams are.

Forgive me.

My love, always.

Your João

Not my João, but somebody's João. *Three years later, I see her in news footage, walking with him in Tancredo Neves' cortège. João's cousin has not only succeeded in his bid to become Governor but gone on to win Brazil's presidency. His premature death renders him immortal, a new Tiradentes, father to the nation, a martyr, too, albeit to diverticulitis or a tumour (accounts vary) rather than the Portuguese.*

Mrs João wears black, including a chic little hat with a veil that allows me to believe her plain underneath, or better yet, cold. It may be my imagination, but João himself looks defeated, a man not sharing dreams but surrendering them.

None of this helps. Only time and Morgen will do that, and the former takes quite a while to work its charms. After João abandons me, I remain at the guest house for a further week, caught in a cycle of crying and retching. When, finally, I make it to the town centre, I buy a postcard of Kelimutu, inscribe it to João at his family home in Minas Gerais, add a message he should recognise. 'Why, this is hell, nor am I out of it.' *Back in in São Paulo, we saw* Richard Burton *and* Elizabeth Taylor *in a movie version of* Dr Faustus. *A star-crossed couple playing star-crossed lovers.*

That night I go to a tourist bar and pick up a German called Dieter. He has tombstone teeth and an earnest determination to disprove stereotypes about Germans. 'Two Germans walk across the bridge. One falls into the water. The other is called Jürgen,' *he says. Then, in case I've missed the point,* 'This is funny.'

Sex with him is satisfyingly unpleasant, an endorsement of my misery, but Dieter can't believe his luck and persuades me to come with him and his friends to Komodo the following day – the trip I had discussed with João. The boat deposits us on the scrubby island with a guide who carries a stick lest the dragons take an interest in us.

This seems unlikely. The giant lizards lie about like rolls of industrial flooring until the guide puts down his burlap sack and extracts from its interior a small goat, noose around her slender neck, Tiradentes on the gallows. She rolls her eyes, pulling against the restraint, while he loops the other end over a post and retreats to safety.

I don't need to watch to know what happens next.

Dory, who could have murdered a sandwich right about now, was thinking about her dad. *Terrible food,* he used to say, dishing up the tea, *and so little of it.* His efforts weren't actually bad, just a bit samey – fish fingers and beans, baked potatoes and beans, sausages and beans. The cuisine on offer at the compound was of a higher standard altogether, but there really was so little of it. Hunger shook Dory awake in the morning, tapped her on the shoulder before she finished breakfast and lodged petitions every few minutes for the rest of the day, docile only for the barest of hours after the evening meal.

Throughout her life and right up until the past miserable months, her appetite had been feral. *You'll get fat,* her mother warned, but she never did. Mum was right about Dory's table manners, though. Fortunately, Morgen didn't mind, sharing Dory's love of eating, if not her metabolism. They dined like kings, and often as messily. Not that they restricted themselves to Michelin-starred restaurants. Artistry creates distance. A person stranded on a desert island doesn't crave *îles flottantes.* In this moment, Dory yearned to bite into aged cheddar and Branston between two thick, and thickly buttered, slices of sourdough.

A swallowtail interrupted her reverie, alighting on a warm flagstone and opening its batwings. She recognised the type, even knew its name, a pipevine. There had to be some compensation for a childhood spent in the company of its dead relatives. The light lent an oil-sheen to the Halloween colours, black with an edge of white plus seven orange spots per underside. A fortnight's worth, the time elapsed since she and Ó hAllmhuráin arrived in this place.

Odd how fast the sands run when you're not racing against them. The sun rose and set on her intentions to search for the skyline city. Each morning she would check that the object she stole from the museum remained in its hiding place. Otherwise she sat, as now, amid piles of books, gathering wool or, more rarely, information. No amount of staring at logograms revealed their meaning, though a repeating character resembled nothing so much as a hummingbird. The illustrations provided more data. Her so-called memoir in the museum had prompted her to search the library for further references to the pod, and soon she found them. Several books depicted it on what appeared to be a dais of some kind. In other renderings it flew, whether through clement weather or, in one image, a hail of butterflies. Pilot and passenger tended to be easily identifiable, if interchangeable. Sometimes Dory occupied the driving seat, with Elo demoted to the smaller chair. She spotted similar images in the friezes that decorated the building.

When darkness fell, she moved inside, shelved the books, ate whatever supper the Apostles provided, hungered, slept – oh, these sleeps – and always she pondered, theorised, waited. She couldn't say for what.

The pyramid had changed everything. Which made no sense.

What she saw and experienced in the giant carcass of the Vegas hotel should have slotted neatly into her working hypothesis. *Morlock*'s designers or AIs were certainly more than capable of personalising the game to incorporate the histories, hopes and fears of its players in exactly such a way. Most of us career through the digital universe like comets, trailing plumes of data and metadata that, once captured, reveal more about us than we ourselves know.

Dory had paid for the Vegas trip with her credit card, described the Vegas trip in her book on ageing. *Morlock* would be aware that she was a writer, could easily have compiled a dossier on her up to and including her decades with Morgen, who, as a public figure, had been widely if inaccurately chronicled. The game also possessed the ability to track the rough and tumble of recent years, not that Dory ever opened up about Morgen's health, but through tiny modulations in her behaviour over time.

So *Morlock* remained the simplest explanation, every zeptosecond from TechCon onwards (if not before?) a programmed dream. Dory had seen preposterous things. Melting doors. Evanescent rock formations. Gates that sprang open.

And yet, she came back from the pyramid a believer. Somehow, she had accepted this world at face value.

It wasn't that she dismissed the possibility that every scrap of it might yet prove virtual. Rather she understood the dreamscape and its inhabitants to be as real as any other experience, within whatever terms and realms they existed. Life, but not as she knew it.

This perspective shift prompted others. Whereas for years she had forced the pace of events, always trying to steal a march on a deadline, now she returned to an incarnation of herself long dormant. She knew she had to get back to Morgen, structured her research to that purpose, but that didn't mean shutting out the world around her. Every day, she bathed in the song of the river and the breeze that carried it, feeling each ripple as if through a new skin. This place, this magical place, was changing her, sloughing off old defences, a renewal, not a flaying.

Elo — she accepted the name — had undergone a greater transformation still. He spoke in an unfamiliar voice and tone. Only occasionally did the official version reassert itself, for example, when she yawned during one of his reminiscences. *Did she not realise that most people would kill to spend quality time with him?* He followed that up with a command: *Bring me a cup of that filthy herbal stuff.* When she complied and he as swiftly thanked her, it was clear how far both had travelled.

He also listened, if mostly to himself. Since the Apostles remained mute and she kept her thoughts to herself, this struck Dory as fair enough. Another development: she found herself deliberately drawing him out rather than shutting him down. His subject matter had shifted to what might be his true origin story.

While the public Elo left her cold, the gap between the construct and the authentic person interested her. Years back she'd identified a similar disjunction in an artist, an *enfant* turned *vieux terrible* driven to produce works at monumental scale and almost too hyperactive to submit to interview. More than a few of the overachievers journalism subsequently flung in her path suffered from variants of this syndrome. She recalled a Tory politician — you'll know the one, used the alias 'Marty McFly' — promising career in tatters after falling for a honeytrap, his weakness, despite tabloid sniggering, a desire of a different sort, to act as saviour with the young escorts he hired.

TIME liked to exploit Dory's contact book even after she took a desk job, and shortly before her exit dispatched her to interrogate one of Morgen's sometime collaborators, a pop megastar. From a distance, he appeared the sort of whom Mum used to say that *if he were a bar of chocolate, he'd eat himself.* Up close, he proved as fragile as a butterfly's wing. In a parallel universe, he might have led a life of quiet contentment. In this one, he self-medicated on adulation, waking one day to find himself pinioned by the dependencies he'd been compelled to create, no escape, for ever on show.

Those prone to the complex were, to a man, male. The women Dory profiled sensed the dissonance between their public identities and the mewling nub of their real selves at least as keenly as did their male counterparts, but they admitted to these anxieties, sometimes even to journalists. Elo and his ilk deflected, compulsively seeking attention of the kind that sees without seeing.

In many circumstances, the instinct served Elo well. Here it didn't. Deprived of the means to manufacture a diversion and absent his usual adoring audience, he initially went into overdrive, then lapsed into depression. More recently still, he looked in the only direction that offered safety: the remote past. It wasn't that things had been easy for him, but rather the opposite. He had prevailed, would do so again.

Dory listened as Elo began retracing old routes, kicking the kerb on Bushy Park or hefting his satchel the length of Zion Road. A first pair of glasses inserted a barrier between the young boy and the world, while giving him an air of astonishment at its vagaries. It took several attempts before opticians fine-tuned the prescription. In the meanwhile, and though close work caused him physical pain, he started dismantling things and, less frequently, reassembled them, his toys, a toilet cistern, once and dangerously, the cooker. He also taught himself to read. The family house was full of books. His Ma was a great reader, so people said, and not with approbation.

Iris Nuttall had set tongues wagging the instant she and Elo's Da, Barney O'Halloran, stepped out together. She was sophisticated. He was not. His parents opposed the union, summoning priests and family friends to declare the marriage destined to fail all parties involved – spouses, children and God. Had the O'Hallorans welcomed Iris, she might have made compromises. Instead, she refused a *Ne Temere* and saddled her firstborn – identical twins – with outlandish names: William and Harry. The twins attended a Church of Ireland school, Mount Temple, among its first intake. Third son, Robert – christened at Zion Parish Church and rechristened Ello Ello Ello by his brothers because of his resemblance to Sergeant Slipper in the *Beano* – was something of a brainbox, so Iris encouraged him to sit the exams for Blackrock College. He won a full scholarship and dropped an L. Elo was on his way.

'Where did he come from?' Barney asked Iris, but knew the answer.

The Holy Ghost order who ran the school held rugby as a faith, second only to religion. Despite Elo's heft – pushing six foot as he entered his teens and yet to trade white pudding and fried bread for protein and personal trainers – he proved a dismal prop. That was lucky, given stories of what went on in the showers. Generally, the priests left him alone and his classmates ignored him, neither beguiled by his eccentricities nor sufficiently irked by them to bully him, though once, under a stained-glass window celebrating the seven gifts – wisdom, understanding, counsel, fortitude, knowledge, piety and fear of the Lord – an older boy called him an *awful dryshite* and ordered him to keep his distance.

Elo did. In a later encounter onstage at the World Economic Forum in Davos, that fellow pupil, now matured into Bob Geldof, claimed to remember him. He might have been telling the truth. Elo's pallor marked him out, and by sixteen so did his academic record: the youngest Dubliner ever to win a scholarship to Stanford. The *Irish Times* ran a photo of him holding up the offer letter and squinting at the camera, less Sergeant Slipper than Piggy in *Lord of the Flies*, if the character survived to put on a growth spurt. As Barney once observed, the child fell out of the ugly tree and hit every branch on the way down.

You wouldn't find that cutting or other early images of Elo in online searches. His first start-up wasn't Underworld, despite the claims of his press teams, but an online reputation business, MemoryHole, itself long consigned to deliberate obscurity, the better to do its job for the publicity-shy super-rich. Elo originally wrote its foundational programme to expunge his own history from the public record. In the mean time and over several years, surgeons expertly crafted a new face for him, square of jaw and straight of nose, only the colouring unchanged and those unmistakable eyes.

Dory, who knew nothing of this, felt sympathy, even kinship, as Elo described his departure from Dublin. He hadn't been comfortable in his skin, and she related to that. He left home at a tender age, as she did, compelled to put miles between himself and those who could hurt him most. She too had arrived at university not only the baby of her year but a misfit. There the parallels ended. She learnt to survive by mimicking the behaviours expected of her. There had been bad days, of course, still were – bouts of self loathing after she did or said something so jarring that people saw her for what she was. Morgen had identified her difference the moment they met, acknowledged it with affectionate teasing – *How's the weather on your planet?* – and miraculously loved her all the same.

An outsider eye is useful in journalism – less danger of getting too close to the organisations and people you're covering – but so is empathy. Dory hoped herself capable of that too, despite being – another of Morgen's labels – a space oddity. She had more in common with Elo and the hollow men she profiled for *TIME* than anyone but Morgen suspected; she saw their flawed humanity and understood what drove them. If only it drove them to better decisions. The key difference between Dory and these titans – apart from her abject failure to found a tech unicorn, run a country or sell out stadiums – lay in their coping mechanisms. She was most at ease observing from the sidelines – or better yet, disappearing entirely: *the grey man.* Dory couldn't imagine any of these men managing this trick, or wanting to do so. Their instinct was not to blend in but stand out.

Articles about Elo typically missed this essential truth. It wasn't his head for numbers that defined him, nor his gift for conceiving other worlds, but his unwavering determination to conquer the world he hadn't designed.

Today, as he reached a turning point in his autobiography, Dory found herself gripped. There he was, about to embark for San Francisco, his future already bright in conventional terms. The

Stanford degree should enable him to earn decent money working in the field then still known as IT, or maybe teach. Life was showering him with opportunities and experiences. He had never left Ireland before, never flown before. Iris took the first leg of the journey with him, ferry and train and an extra night at an Earl's Court B&B so they could sightsee. Heathrow fascinated her son in a way no jumble of old buildings could. Several times he rode a travellator to the end, disembarked and rode back the other way. Now, on the approach to JFK, an earlier feat of technology came into view, Liberty. *Give me your tired, your poor / Your huddled masses yearning to breathe free.* In that instant, Elo told Dory, he decided to be a colossus, bigger than any previous immigrant to this country, the jolly green giant included. Far below him, sun bounced off the waters of the Hudson as she raised her arm in salute.

The American dream isn't crabbed by reality, not least because it's fiction, but red tape does fall from the skies with its tickertape. A stewardess leant across the row to hand Elo a landing card and customs declaration. *Sir* must complete both parts and pass through immigration before catching his connecting flight. Reaching into his rucksack, he discovered that his Bic had disgorged its ink like a frightened squid. His neighbour, a Brooklynite, dabbed at his passport and complimented him on being Irish. Such a great country it was, punching way above its size in terms of global influence. The literature! The music! The enterprise! The charm! She added, *In America, you Irish are royalty.* Though the young man stared out the window as if he couldn't hear her, he would turn up at Stanford with a hokey accent and homespun vocabulary almost as foreign to him as the State of California. The Gaelic spelling of his surname made its début in his Stanford matriculation forms.

Elo settled into his dorm, ignored his roommates, and made no attempt to join fraternities or societies. Why bother, for he contained multitudes. Anyway, he sought acolytes, not friends; followers, not companions. In his freshman year Elo was in the common area, watching an episode of *Star Trek*, loosely based on *Lord of the Flies*, when a single piece of dialogue lifted him off the sofa with its power. Humans, Mr Spock observes, have a superpower all their own: to believe what they choose and exclude anything painful. Well, Robert O'Halloran chose to believe in science and Elo Ó hAllmhuráin, not necessarily in that order.

His Ma accepted the metamorphosis, his brothers and sister could get stuffed with their sly ribbing and anyway, he who succeeds laughs longest. If Barney had views on the matter, he played them close to his chest. He was one of those men who speak in bursts, garrulous only when selling or if drink had been taken. A sales representative for Dunnes Stores, he was often away on the road, or so he claimed, though unbeknownst to Iris, he'd hooked up with a Cork woman and sired a second brood. The truth emerged years later, when one of Barney's drinking companions delivered a tell-all eulogy. Elo wasn't there, his Da having provided insufficient notice of his funeral for him to attend.

Elo found out about his half-siblings during a fireside chat about poverty with Geldof and fellow global Irishman, Bono, in the Swiss resort of Davos. As they wrapped up with few questions from the audience, the microphone passed to a tabloid journalist, who congratulated Elo on his expanding family. 'Seriously?' he asked her. 'Which of my girlfriends has popped?'

Once the journalist resolved the confusion, and after Elo assured Bono that he felt fine, the tabloid got its quote. 'Good on Da. Better to boldly go into that other world, in the full glory of some passion, than fade and wither dismally with age,' Elo said, reaching for James Joyce and tripping over a bigger influence. 'Also, tell my new relations that if it's a slice of my money they're after, they can g'way on.'

You'd be hard pressed to think of two people less alike than Elo and Morgen. Any superficial similarity crumbled under analysis, much as humour will. So, yes, both lived in the public gaze, but one sought it, while for the other it was a by-product rather than a goal, occasionally useful, often an irritant. Morgen's quiet clarity read as the inverse of Elo's effusions and explosions, and their physical differences could scarcely be more conspicuous. So why on earth was Dory struggling to distinguish one from the other?

A minute earlier, she had finally told Elo about the illustrations. *See*, she said, *here we are.*

'The Mekons predicted this?' He paced, sat down again. 'I don't get it. I just don't get it.' Lifting each book in turn to peer at the drawings, he paused at the picture of the machine engulfed in butterflies. 'That's not me. That's your squeeze.'

No. Dory protested but once Elo pointed out the likeness, she couldn't unsee it, the cross-hatching not shadows, as she had imagined, but the engraver's shorthand for skin that used to shine from the inside, now dulled to taupe. Illness had shrunk her beloved's universe to a bed, first in the hospital, now at home. 'I door you,' Morgen used to say. 'I window you,' she'd reply, pushing up the sash to admit lifegiving rays. These days even that small dispensation was denied. An antimetabolite prescribed to dampen the sarcoidosis triggered an allergy to sunlight, forcing them to live like vampires (if the undead live).

None of the doctors could say exactly what role heredity played in the disorder or responses to drugs or why sarcoidosis and the virus had combined to such powerful effect. Despite advances in genomics, humans would take another few centuries to read each other like books. In the mean time, genes expressed themselves in unforeseeable ways, and in Morgen's family they ran riot. There were autoimmune conditions and heart problems, straight hair and black wires growing from their heads, chin dimples and faces smooth as pomegranates. Morgen's older brother might as well be a carbon copy of their father, their younger sister the picture of their mother. Morgen resembled neither parent, a changeling with green eyes.

Angular, critics called Morgen's music, and it had been an apt description of the musician too. No longer. Steroids blurred the beauty. It was the inverse of Elo's transformation, a face losing definition, but for one defining feature. Morgen's eyes, like Elo's, resisted modification.

'I envy you.'

Elo's comment interrupted her descent into sadness. 'What for?'

'You and your rockstar. Indecent to stay together for so many years.' Elo laughed. 'Bride Number Five gave me my marching orders the day before TechCon. She says I should marry myself.'

'Morgen isn't a rockstar.'

This was reflex. Both she and Morgen tended to bat away the phrase, Morgen more of a musician's musician than a household name, but Dory anyway wasn't sure how best to react. Not too long ago her uncensored response to a similar admission had fractured not only her relationship with the speaker, but Morgen's. A filmmaker it had been, their friend of many years, and over those years the partner of as many women, all exquisite and exquisitely disengaged from the things that interested him. That evening, his latest paramour attempted conversation with Dory. 'It must be interesting to have a job,' she said. The filmmaker, cupping a balloon glass, sighed loudly. A while and two brandies later, he declared to Dory that this liaison would die like its predecessors. He yearned for what she and Morgen had, the closeness, the companionship, but how to find true love in a shallow world? 'Try going out with someone maybe at least half your age,' she replied. Even to her ears, it sounded brutal.

Elo's tastes were more Catholic than the filmmaker's, his women short or tall, fair or brunette, and some in their thirties. None were dullards. Truth be told, neither were the filmmaker's. The problem in every case was simply one of timing, of lives hopelessly out of sync.

'Are you upset?' Dory eventually asked Elo. She meant about the death of his marriage, but he answered a different question, his mind back on the pod drawings. 'We have to find my machine.'

She'd been waiting for the right time to discuss her plans with him. Always she preferred to let research run its natural course before ordering her findings into an article or book, absorbing details until she became so heavy with knowledge that there was no option but to expel it. You never knew how long the gestation would be or when the waters might break. When they did, there was no going back. Once, after spending more than two years trailing a future king, a man every bit as alien to this planet as she, and more inclined to melancholy, Dory suddenly hit her research limit. 'I can't wait to stop thinking about you,' she had blurted. 'Understandable,' replied the morose monarch-in-waiting.

Several times she had overridden a similar impulse with Elo. The Elo she first encountered would have demanded immediate action, also dictating the form that action should take. Now she must take a chance. She was full to bursting, if not with hard data, then with suppositions, possibilities, and none of the usual ways to pin them down.

Dory had mined every source in and around the compound. The Apostles resisted engagement. The volumes themselves had yielded as many clues as she had been able to decode, and quite a few more that she couldn't. Their pages contained a number of recognisable figures, Herakles and Cerberus, Anansi the spider, the azure dragon and vermillion bird, logograms of guillotines and a symbol that might be a Star of David. What help was any of this?

The things best to know are first principles and causes. Thank you, Aristotle. Here, then, was her paltry collection of facts and conclusions.

The Apostles posed no obvious impediment to escape. Apart from the single instance of vanishing drive and ladder, Dory and Elo roamed free. On the other hand, and lacking alternative suspects, she assumed these beings to be implicated in the disappearance of the pod.

As for Elo, he was fundamentally untrustworthy and, for the same reason, predictable. In any situation, he would put himself first. For as long as their interests coincided, she could work with him, alert to the possibility of double-dealing.

So her next step must be to get him on board. She would tell him about the distant glow, propose an expedition. Without knowing why the pod had been taken, the question of where it might be remained hopelessly open. The city, if it existed at all, could prove red herring or pink elephant, but cities tend to offer more and better insights into civilisations than rural areas such as this.

As for the risks of leaving the compound, well, Dory hadn't seen any evidence of predators. She recalled the white thing that lolloped across her path as she returned to the compound at night, but the mind plays tricks in the dark.

She and Elo should anyway set out early, making the most of daylight. There were known dangers, cliff edges, overhangs, impossible grasslands, sloughs of despond where natural springs bubbled up through the clay. The Apostles dammed and directed some of these, sank wells in other places. Water bottles could be replenished. Food supplies for the journey were more problematic. A cold store at the back of the winery contained rounds of cheese and jars of preserves. Provided that at each of the next few breakfasts she and Elo kept back a flatbread apiece – her stomach clenched with anticipatory hunger at the thought – they could put together a couple of sandwiches.

Elo was looking at her expectantly, a child waiting for the lesson to start. Dory wondered how swiftly his old behaviours would reassert themselves once they got back to Vegas. That day was coming. She had to keep faith in the future, or, more accurately, the past. Even so, she felt a tiny scratch of regret at the prospect of leaving this place. Its tranquillity, the song of the water – she would do her best to carry them with her.

06:00

*T*__hese are halcyon days for journalism.__ *The digital revolution is changing every process for the better. We cut and paste disordered thoughts without a mess of scissors and glue, correct errors without recourse to Tippex. No more pleading with the research department for access to a database that churns out long-dead articles in pointillistic characters, nor, when denied (because these searches cost the earth), staring at microfiche until our eyes bleed. Information is cheap, and the Internet contains multitudes. Though I still use printers' marks, these are for my reference alone. The logogrammatic language is vanishing into obsolescence with the typesetters who developed it.*

Sometimes I regale the newsroom with tales of a forgotten world, copy tasters and copytakers, or the hours and effort it took to set up a single interview BGE – before the Google era. Not that identifying potential interviewees got you far. The next hurdle was to discover their contact numbers, then stay on the case until someone picked up the phone or remembered to restock the fax machine.

Smiling as if remembering a lively family wedding, I describe a photographer using the boot of his car as a darkroom, so absorbed in his task that he barely flinches when a Molotov cocktail shatters at our feet. There is nothing, *I say,* that technology has not made easier for our profession.

Oh, but my audience is restive. These golden lads and girls are primed to recognise luck only in the moment it takes flight. It falls to me, a veteran, to try to waken them so they might catch that bird, cup it with both hands. I fail. Though words are my business, none have edges sharp enough. We never had it so good, *I say, voice thick with passion. The few reporters still listening look at the floor, embarrassed.*

If nobody else can see the truth, I am dazzled by it. The world is brighter by the day. TIME *assigns different colours to different job functions. My recent ascent to the charmed circle of* top editors *turns my on-screen edits from sodium orange to blue.*

That we journalists spend more time at our desks is the price of progress. The website prefers all-you-can-eat buffets to haute cuisine, volume over quality, speed rather than accuracy. The beauty of online is that mistakes can be rectified after a piece goes live. Move fast and fix things, that's our new motto.

At pitch meetings, reporters keep proposing topics they've seen covered by competing publications. Whilst our craft involves adding value to existing stories, we should always break our own exclusives too, so I urge my charges to leave the office. Get a feel for trends, develop contacts, I tell them, but some, like eternal flames, never go out.

At first, I blame the self-absorption of rising generations. The media loves to write off entire cohorts, and unconsciously I've bought into our own distorting caricature of millennials. Like much fake news – a term not yet in circulation – the trope contains a grain of truth, though no more. Job applicants used to list the ways they could serve TIME. *These days, they're as apt to state the ways in which* TIME *could aid their personal development.*

I don't consider how difficult it must be to come of age amid a clamour of virtual voices or that these newer pressures intersect with the old, nor do I understand why junior staffers seem to prize work-life balance above their jobs. Who becomes a reporter expecting a predictable routine? Admittedly, my team hasn't got the time to report stories properly, much less kick off their shoes and kick back. Data, until recently in short supply, is firehosing us. A lot of knowledge, it seems, is a dangerous thing.

Editors face fresh challenges too. From the moment we bite into the apple of content management systems, metrics trump instincts. I can tell you not only which stories attract more eyeballs, but the exact point at which those eyeballs lose interest. Obviously we transfer our learnings to the print product, and anyway, there's a famine going on. The dearth of display advertising diminishes the magazine until it is little more than an iconic cover and a few boilerplate features, skin and bone. Those features shrink, from around five thousand words for a major story to a bare fifteen hundred, while online articles, though technically free from length-limiting dictates, decline into collections of headlines, standfirst and keywords.

We become experts at search engine optimisation. For years to come, a brief dispatch entitled 'Japan's Booming Sex Niche: Elder Porn' will cycle through TIME*'s top ten most-read list, subsiding only to bob up again. Sex sells,* *but online advertising will never rack up the revenues print used to generate. Meanwhile, subscriptions and newsstand sales plummet. Why would anybody pay to read in hard copy what they can browse for free?*

The only viable strategy is to attract more eyeballs. Proprietors take that to mean punchier (controversial) pieces, celebrities, quotable figures. Those populists are always good for a laugh. Italy's Silvio Berlusconi establishes a template that others follow, stealing the spotlight from worthier opponents. Reliable go-tos outside the political sphere include Morrissey, Elon Musk, the Donald and Elo Ó hAllmhuráin.

Thank god for new media which brings our work to wider audiences. TIME *is growing its reach on the infant socials Facebook, Twitter, Fleet and Flickr, posting links to stories, and pushing staff to develop what management has taken to calling our* personal brands. *Not that I need pushing. These platforms promise a better future, distributing megaphones to the Green Wave, the Arab Spring, lifting the powerless, unchaining the oppressed.*

Stop looking at me like that.

How should I have raised the alarm about the beginning of the end of the world when I didn't even spot the beginning of the end of TIME*?*

It was dusk when they reached the edge of the grass-lands. Before them the ground fell away to create a natural moat, rising again to the base of the city walls. Anyone on the ramparts would spot them as soon as they broke cover. What to do? Retreat wasn't an option; their supplies were exhausted and so were they.

'Look,' said Dory, pointing as figures emerged from lofty gates to cross the drawbridge in loose military formation.

'Hey, maybe we should walk out with our hands up.' Ó hAll-mhuráin spoke with the high-rising intonation of Southern California. Dory didn't notice. She was assessing his suggestion and finding herself in agreement.

If they seemed more in tune than usual, it probably helped that they had spent the past hours discovering overlapping tastes in music. *Well,* Dory mused approvingly at one point, how *unexpectedly leftfield.* Unbeknownst to her, in that synchronous instant Elo entertained a similar thought before dismissing it. Obviously she was merely ventriloquising Morgen's opinions.

Shared passions for bands or musicians are no guarantee of wider harmonies, as Dory should have known. The journalist who speeded her departure from *TIME* – let's call him Chuck, though that's nothing like his real name – declared over their first and only lunch that David Bowie was his idol. While Dory didn't do hero-worship, she came close to making an exception for Bowie. *Ziggy Stardust* had been the second LP she ever bought, her constant companion until *Aladdin Sane* came along. That album marked a quantum leap for Bowie and for music. Chuck concurred. This would be their sole point of convergence over the coming eighteen months, apart from the job Dory had and he coveted.

Only after her ousting, as lawyers fought to establish different plotlines for the same cast of characters, did Dory learn of the campaign Chuck had waged, badmouthing her to juniors and creeping through the deep-carpeted executive floors of the TIME/LIFE building to pour poison into gullible ears. She hadn't grasped the threat he posed, though she couldn't miss his hostility.

Her attempts to pacify him – showering his work with appreciative comments and offering him increased responsibility within the team – merely fuelled his rage. It was a clenched fury, neck muscles stiffening in her presence. He had a special voice for her, too, the kind people usually reserve for the freshly bereaved or the very young.

Hers was an unwinnable war, but one night she triumphed in battle. At a dinner hosted by friends of Morgen, Bowie took the neighbouring seat. As usual, she observed from the edges of the conversation, joining in only when she felt she might add value. That moment came after a drummer, a rare female of the species, spoke of the harassment she'd endured on tour. Her tale sparked a wider discussion about the music business. It was then that Dory spoke up. There were parallels with journalism, she said. Men in both industries tended to give themselves a free pass, paying lip service to egalitarian views while exempting themselves from the standards they demanded of others. Creativity, you see, cannot be straitjacketed.

This, Dory continued, would be bad enough if their targets alone were affected, but culture shapes public opinion. Toxins in the system pollute the output. History is not made by great men.

Bowie engaged with this provocation, adding his own examples and encouraging Dory to expand on the theme. She had already downed a beer or two, and soon she was regaling the assembled company with tales of Chuck. How good it felt to vent. Bowie egged her on.

She came away from the evening with a photograph of herself and Bowie she considered posting on her socials like a raised middle finger. Tempting, but Dory decided against it. Always she kept her life with Morgen private. When finally she uploaded the image to Instagram, Bowie was dead and Chuck no more than a dot in her rear-view mirror.

'Dorian!' Elo's whisper brought her hurtling back to their present. 'They're coming.'

He was right. In pairs, the squaddies marched. Their trajectory would bring them to this hiding place within seconds. She acted on impulse. 'Over here,' she called. 'We're over here.' Hands in the air, she stepped from the shelter of the long grass. A heartbeat later, Elo followed, arms also aloft.

Sometimes it's difficult to remember flurries of events, even for journalists trained to do so. This sequence Dory would never forget. Time was too short and nightfall too close to register finer details, but the approaching squaddies possessed a heft and variety that distinguished them from the Apostles. Humans! As she emerged, their reactions appeared as closely coordinated as any military drill. All fifteen stopped dead and threw up their hands.

Ages it seemed to last, the stand-off that followed, everyone with arms stretched to the heavens.

Eventually Elo spoke: 'Are you taking the mickey, or what?'

'Hey,' said one of the lead squaddies, 'we're totally not. Like great that you're here.'

'Were you expecting us?' Dory asked, not that this seemed particularly important, but it was the only sentence her brain produced.

A second squaddie – camouflage trousers a size too big, a fish pendant around her neck – answered in a voice Dory associated with childhood. 'Well hell-lo.'

It took a few seconds to place. *Leslie Phillips*. Dory's arms dropped to her side. The squaddies mirrored the move.

'Gorgeous to meet you both. Shall we toddle?' the squaddie inquired.

'Whaaaat?' Elo had yet to recover the power of speech.

'It would be like awesome if you'd come with us.' Squaddie number one, pure Valley.

'I have questions,' said Dory.

'Don't we all, poppet. Don't we all.'

The city turned out to be a Tardis, bigger than it looked from the outside. Crenelated walls lent it the air of an Italian hill town, an impression reinforced by narrow streets, the buildings leaning inwards to whisper about the strangers in their midst. Up steep inclines and cut-throughs the procession wound, Dory and Elo hemmed in by the squaddies and petitioning them for explanations and answers. *Take a chill pill*, the squaddies replied. And *ding dong*.

'They're as annoying as the Mekons,' growled Elo.

'More so,' said Dory.

Neither wondered if their new acquaintances might pose a danger. Later Dory would marvel at how easily she and Elo submitted.

They climbed past loggias and courtyards, everything enclosed but for the sudden release of squares. Orange lamps shed just enough light to reveal how far they were from Umbria, the architecture reliant on a combination of sandstone and a material both lucent and lucid, recalling the long window and dissolving door back at the compound.

Wherever Dory looked, she glimpsed movement, reflections chasing across surfaces, a rippling of life too, hominids of at least two kinds, humans and Apostles, the former strolling or gathered in the squares, the latter perching or darting. A three-wheeler overtook their group, quiet as a sigh, and then a flock of Apostles, descending in size to little more than knee-high.

'Look,' Dory said to Elo, 'young Mekons.'

He didn't reply. They had stopped just below the apex of the citadel, only a cathedral and the night sky ahead. To their left, a snubnosed tower blocked the stars, its bulk alien to the gentle townscape. Even so, nothing about this aspect prepared Dory for the interior. The building pulled the same trick as the city, larger by far than its poker face let on.

They entered not at its base, but the midpoint of an enormous atrium, lozenge-shaped like an upended Zeppelin, and striated with ramps, footbridges and narrow-gauge rails. Bubble lifts plied the tracks without visible means of support or propulsion. Theirs spat out a bar of Brian Eno, clammed shut and shot upwards before scooting sideways to dock.

The change of direction threw Elo against Dory. Now he seemed in no hurry to move. 'You smell,' she said, and he did, the ammonia tang of a skate past its sell-by date. The scent trailed him into a room you might find in a designer hotel, its every functional feature concealed. Violet and rose uplighters accentuated a theatrical gloom. Dory had just begun a more detailed assessment – *FFS, only one bed* – when the darkness intensified. Sure enough, the lift bay was contracting. Within seconds, nothing remained but a tiny O of surprise, a mouth without a body. She felt around it, pushed and prodded, but nothing yielded.

'Curiouser and curiouser,' said Elo, unruffled. He sat on the bed, bounced, lay back, bounced again, starfished to emphasise ownership. 'Decent mattress.'

A door opened in a different wall, cutting short Dory's protest and admitting a squaddie, her cart laden with chafing dishes. Once again, Dory found herself transported to the past, this time to the staff canteen of a seafront hotel. She had barely got her feet under the memory of a Formica table before Elo's voice dragged her back.

'Hundreds of years of progress, and what did that produce?' he said. 'Trick walls and a hostess trolley.'

He probably wouldn't have expected a response, much less the one he got. 'Apologies for the delay,' said the squaddie, positioning the cart in the middle of the room. It was a member of the original crew, she of the *Carry On* voice and baggy fatigues. 'The Doctor will join you tomorrow. In the mean time, make yourselves comfortable. I'm sure you're tired and hungry.'

She did something to a third wall, creating yet another doorway. 'You'll find a second bedroom and bathroom through here, and a well-stocked minibar.' She pointed to a handset on the bedside table. 'If you want anything else, just pick up the phone and ask.'

'Ah sure,' Elo replied, 'if only that were true.' Dory found herself wondering if it might be.

Nodding as if satisfied, the squaddie hitched up her waistband and stepped through the first wall, not even bothering to wait for it to fully dematerialise.

The suite, though comfortable, lacked windows. Dory, like a child on a journey, grappled with a single thought: *Are we there yet?* She hoped time was racing. Despite the exertions of the day and the fullest stomach in – what? – weeks, her insomnia had returned, too much to process, legions of questions assailing her and no opposing army of answers. The Doctor? Who? Elo shrugged, but as they ate he did manage to tailor some of the new data to his old assumptions. This world, he said, had evidently developed two divergent classes or races, the Mekons clearly drones, while humans – he called the peoples of the citadel Tyranids – remained the superior strain, inventors and keepers of technology.

Irritated by this deduction and determined to rest, Dory retreated to the second bedroom, lay flat, practised circular breathing. When that didn't work, she tried to relax by degrees, from the tips of her toes to her metatarsals and thence to her ankles, giving up when her knees refused to play ball. A buzzing disturbed her too, whether from an external electrical fault or her own wiring.

After a fitful doze and a period spent staring at the ceiling, she got up, paced, explored her limited realm. The air still carried traces of the peculiar meal the squaddie had delivered, an elaborate moulded savoury, shrimps dancing in aspic; Scotch eggs smothered in curry sauce; chicken Kyiv; cheesecake topped with tinned mandarins. The bathroom reeked of synthetic lemon. Shower, sink and toilet, apparently fashioned from a lump of the same clear substance as the pod, flaunted their pipework. Sources of illumination, by contrast, hid in recesses or behind screens. Dory made the mistake of standing on the bed to examine an uplighter, curious if the bulb were coloured or the effect was achieved with a gel. The answer was neither. Its pink beam felt like a skewer to the skull.

Chastened and with spots flitting before her eyes, she tiptoed into the neighbouring room, noting that the trolley and any debris from dinner had been cleared. Elo, dead to the world, stuttered and roared like an outboard motor. How had she slept through his racket night after night at the compound? How could he sleep through so much as one of his own snores?

If only the new day would come. She and Elo still carried mobiles and, on occasion, checked them, as if the screens might spring to life. Funny how hard the habit is to break, even after you've learnt to tell the hours by the sun and moon, count minutes and seconds in breaths or hunger pangs or the dances of butterflies, which speed as the end of the afternoon approaches. In this suite, all such markers were banished.

Perhaps the spyhole might offer clues. She approached with caution, temples still throbbing from her encounter with the pink beam. Reassured by the white rays filtering through the aperture, she put her eye to it, only to stumble backwards as the wall grinned and gaped. In an instant, perhaps less, nothing but nothingness remained.

Morning had indeed broken, bright shards of light dropping from a mullioned roof far above and bouncing off the plaza storeys below. On first glimpse, the building had recalled a scene from *Metropolis*. From this height, she revised her judgement. The place could be an atrium hotel, except that its rooms gave straight on to the void.

Dory loathed atrium architecture. How exciting it must have been for the Victorians to see the first glass domes and steel-frame towers rise up, faint and fair. All too soon that era passed, a dream, its legacy metastasising into my-building-is-bigger-than-yours bombast. Surely developers of the future would have corrected course?

She moved forward again, testing her nerve and a different kind of resolve. In the last year, whenever she crossed a Thames bridge or waited for the Elizabeth Line, Dory toyed with the idea of an accident, swift and ambiguous, not that she would ever act on the impulse. That would be cruel to bystanders and worse for Morgen, no longer fully Morgen but Morgen enough to recognise yet another betrayal.

Right now, however, Morgen knew nothing of Dory's whereabouts. Whether she and Elo remained physically onstage at TechCon or had disappeared in a blaze of colour, they must be presumed victims of a misfired stunt. *If Dory falls unwitnessed in a parallel universe, does she make a ripple?* So easy it would be to take a running jump into the updraft. And then? A moment of weightlessness, the illusion of flight.

Long ago, on assignment to a strange city, she had woken to a commotion, peering down from the gallery of her atrium hotel to a scuttle of people around the breakfast bar and, at their centre, a pietà. A security guard cradled his legs. The rest of his earthly remains lay across the salvers, arms outstretched, broken head haloed in Fruit Loops. The scene disturbed her, and not only for obvious reasons. Somehow, she had seen all of this before, foreseen it, his swan dive, the aftermath.

News crews quickly blocked the lobby exit. The man was known in the area, a politician. Had Dory witnessed his final moments? No, she lied, and this exchange too triggered a powerful sense of déjà vu.

'The actual *fock*?'

Rough hands on her shoulders, an arm across her chest and suddenly she fell backwards on to the bed, one of Elo's legs beneath her. He extricated himself and glared at her.

'In the name of all that's holy, what are you playing at?'

His voice had returned to Ireland, or maybe it always wandered like this, but it carried a new element, concern. Immediately she attempted to reassure him.

'I was just looking,' she said.

Elo had sounded sincere when he claimed not to know of a doctor, but the moment the delegation arrived, Dory saw his expression curdle. Recognition, and something else. Fear.

'Apologies for keeping you waiting.' Two squaddies flanked a figure, adult though her voice occupied the helium register of a child. 'Ms Silver, Mr Ó hAllmhuráin, welcome to Guerglas and the Chancellery. This conversation may take some time. Perhaps you would prefer to sit?'

Their interlocutor was already seated, on a vehicle similar to the three-wheelers they had seen on the streets. Dory took a corner of the bed, leaving space for Elo, but he remained standing.

'Where is it?'

'Always you are in such a hurry, Mr Ó hAllmhuráin.'

She moved alongside Dory, hand outstretched. 'Perhaps a formal introduction is in order. I am Doctor Roweena Falou.' She glanced at Elo. 'As Mr Ó hAllmhuráin knows.'

Dory watched Elo subside as a cartoon character melts to a puddle. The woman trained her attention back on Dory. 'This must have been quite a difficult experience for you. You appear to be coping well.'

'Thank you.' Dory dabbed at tears that sprang, unasked, to her eyes, threatening to contradict the assessment.

'Tell me,' the Doctor continued, 'what you understand of recent events. What troubles you most?'

Where to begin.

Dory knew the rules of storytelling. She ought to open with events onstage at TechCon, proceed to a paragraph summarising the scope of her tale, move to a well-paced exposition of the past weeks, analyse the challenges to her assumption, list her conclusions and perhaps end with a thought-provoking epigrammatic sentence, a kicker. This would give her account structure and clarity. The sentences that burst forth followed none of these rules.

'I'm at sea,' Dory said. 'I'm happier and sadder and more alive than I've been in years, and I have no idea why or what to believe any more.'

'Yes,' said Doctor Roweena. 'Temporal shifts will do that to you.'

Looking back (or forward), Dory would identify this as the point of no return. Though she knew next to nothing about the Doctor, instinctively she believed her. The weight and thrust of empirical evidence, reinforced not just by Elo but this second, apparently credible voice, finally pushed her beyond the threshold of reasonable doubt. The idea still made no sense, yet it made more sense than anything else. Dorian Silver believed in time travel.

II

07:00

I'***m singing while Angela sets the table.*** *She won't let me help because the angle of a fork matters. Not yet thirty, and already she has matching crockery, linen napkins and her first baby on the way.*

'What's that?' she asks. She means the song.

'Gang of Four,' I reply, wandering over to the sideboard where spirits and mixers line up to impress. Imagine so much choice and not a single dusty bottle of airport ouzo. This is adulthood. 'I think I'll have another gin,' I carol. She watches me out of the corner of her eye, concerned that I'll mess up her curation before the other guests arrive.

We've all got opinions, but where do they come from? Who planted them, the seeds that in Angela grew into pink plates with gilt edging and in my body failed to germinate? Our worldview, aligned in many respects, diverges on such matters to breaking point. Not that she's my only critic. There's Mum, of course, a fine one to talk, plus a run of bitter exes.

'You're like a bloke,' a soon-to-be ex-lover growled at me recently, and this wasn't light years away from the reality. Had I been born in a different age to a wardrobe of possible identities, I might have tried on a few, though never that rigid costume labelled man*. Girlhood didn't quite fit either, womanhood arguably less so. Last summer, on a Naxos beach, overdressed among nudists in a bikini bottom, I ouched across hot sand to buy a bottle of retsina, only for the bar owner to mistake me for a boy. While my shape, or lack of shape, has shaped me, I reject the idea of destiny, biological or social. What infuriated the lover was my answer to his question 'Where do you see yourself in ten years' time?' Perhaps he expected me to paint a fantasy of a common future, or at*

least express a desire for the rite of passage that people term settling down, when, often, they mean merely settling. 'I imagine,' I said, 'that I'll be on this sofa, staring at that crack in the ceiling and thinking, "I must do something about that."'

One look at my kitchen should have warned him to run for the hills. At this point, I have yet to discover my obsession with food, and the fridge contains only bottles of beer and some taramasalata, pinker than Angela's plates and crusted.

Her kitchen is immaculate like the rest of her house. It's the child who will break her. Tonight, she's urging me to hurry up and have babies of my own. Misery loves company, I joke, but I'm worried she might be planning to matchmake. Several times she's mentioned a lawyer who's coming to dinner. Sure enough, he's a singleton, specialising in divorce and funny on the topic. He's also gay, though I'm pretty sure she doesn't realise this. Angela smiles across the candlelight at our instant rapport. Not that our conversation would earn her approval. We're discussing why the lawyer is growing rich on failure. Marriage between a man and a woman is not part of the natural order, but a construct developed in response to specific circumstances. The nuclear family, a more recent invention, is already breaking down, successful only in economies that reliably provide enough work for male breadwinners, and even then their wives keep refusing to play the game.

After dessert and a cheese board, Angela, her disgusting husband – another story – and the couples with children fade, but the night is young. The lawyer and I head to a party at an Islington warehouse. Invitations have been issued to residents of that page of the London A–Z. Though neither of us fit this requirement, we're confident of blagging our way in.

Who knows whether Morgen believes me. Perhaps nobody does, but on my life – or Morgen's, more valuable by far – what I am about to tell you is true. When first we kissed, a scant hour after meeting there, a shooting star blazed across the sky above, bright enough to cut through the city's sodium haze, and faster than any aircraft. The world receded to a distant hum, an ebb and flow of revellers, a thrum of music and conversation, just the two of us, leaning against the balcony railing.

We rarely spot turning points – the actions or inactions that reroute our lives – until they're behind us. This one I recognised in the miraculous moment of it. Holding Morgen, inhaling Morgen, felt like coming home.

Within weeks we were living together, within months close in ways I still find surprising. Always I'd insisted on boundaries, separate finances, clear understandings. Never again would I leave myself vulnerable as I had with João, but this was more than an excess of caution. I neither expected a life partner nor sought one. My days and head were full of dreams and deadlines. Probably it helped that Morgen travelled as much as I did. Time was on our side, yes it was, creating a life of farewells, reunions and snatched moments. We slipped into a lovely familiarity without losing any of the excitement or forcing the pace.

What luxury it was to come together in the pre-digital age. Later I would witness friends attempting to navigate dating websites, then apps, deciding to meet or not to meet potential partners based on instant assessments of long-term prospects. Sara – not her name, and anyway she's an everywoman in this context, a cipher – decides she'll risk a date with John (also more symbol than man). They agree on a café, less commitment than a restaurant, and daytime is better than tawdry evening for such encounters. The wooden chair scrapes across the pitted floor as Sara takes her seat, already inspecting John. He looks older than his photo. Is that the indentation of a ring on the third finger of his left hand? What secrets lurk in his past and present that might derail their future? Oh, but look at his T-shirt – vintage Iron Maiden. This date will be torture. Before she's ordered a cup of tea, Sara has plotted her escape.

Events move faster still on reality TV. Once Morgen sickened, we became addicted to these technicolour universes, especially the dating shows, formats in which strangers couple and time gallops, every hour a week, every week a year. Where are we in our relationship, *the participants would ask, minutes after first introductions. Such fun to observe these tender unions emerge in a blaze of glory like hothouse flowers or butterflies, then as swiftly die.*

A few months ago, we watched two series back to back, Morgen under the sheets and me on top, careful not to disturb the drip and aware of Morgen fading in and out. Not that it's hard to get back up to speed when you miss a bit. Wake up after a long doze and nothing much will have changed, despite the accelerated timeframes. If Morgen seems befuddled, that's because these buffed and polished beings all look and sound alike. And it is confusing, so-and-so kissing whatchamacallit on the terrace while pursuing thingamabob, leaving whosit crying rivers of mascara. Morgen sometimes musters a laugh at my expositions. It's a sound that moves me like music.

97

Companionship, you see, is the most precious component of love, its quiet core. Yes, passion is addictive, romance joyful, and your wedding might count, as ours did, among the happiest of days. Even so, it's the moments you don't preserve in photographs, celebrate in poetry or describe in novels that really matter. These are unremarkable and unique, utterly commonplace and completely irreplaceable. Nothing is better than the deep, deep peace of the double bed, even when that bed is surrounded by the machines that are keeping your sweetheart alive.

T he stories Elo and Doctor Roweena told that day consisted of the same foundational ingredient and came out as different as *Omelette Arnold Bennett* and *Baked Alaska*. As sure as eggs is eggs, Elo would always make himself the hero of any tale, but in this instance, he sounded plausible, enough detail and none of the flourishes that decorate lies. How to square that with Doctor Roweena's version? She portrayed him as a *carpet-bagger*, using that archaic word along with others more modern and as pointed as knives. Dory, who had begun to see Elo's vulnerability, perhaps feel a smidgeon of sympathy for him, found herself again unmoored.

For hours he and the Doctor went at it, Elo setting out a timeline of events, Roweena slicing through it line by line, rearranging the pieces to make different meanings. The process reminded Dory of the way David Bowie had produced lyrics, chopping texts into confetti to forge new combinations, a technique borrowed from the American writer William S. Burroughs, who himself adapted it from dadaism.

She wasn't sure why the Doctor had anything left to ask, given how much she already claimed to know. That the pod would arrive at these precise coordinates of time and space had not only been anticipated, Roweena said, but engineered by her. As yet, she refrained from listing the charges against Elo, but insisted his crimes were of the highest order. For all her softening towards Elo, Dory couldn't claim to be surprised. He had a history of moving fast and breaking things, and people, in pursuit of his goals.

'Mr Ó hAllmhuráin,' Roweena chided him now in that fluting voice of hers, 'you took something that didn't belong to you, and never mind the consequences.'

'Roweena,' said Elo, 'What happened wasn't my fault.'

'Mr Ó hAllmhuráin, ignorance is no defence under the law.'

'Not ignorance,' he said. 'The opposite. A calculation of the greater good.'

It is probably worth reproducing, in full, Elo's initial statement. Like William S. Burroughs, Elo would change his testimony several times.

One night, in Mexico City, Burroughs shot dead his partner Joan Vollmer in front of their four-year-old son. The writer blamed a drinking game gone wrong (he had aimed for a glass balanced on Vollmer's head), then revised the story. He had dropped the gun, causing it to misfire. He later developed an excuse involving a potential purchaser of the gun, who asked Burroughs to demonstrate the weapon. Ultimately, Burroughs received a two-year suspended sentence, also election to the American Academy of Arts and Letters and France's Ordre des Arts et des Lettres.

If Elo expected to get away with murder, he was only following the prompts of his own culture. In this universe, he would find no such tolerance. Perhaps it was this dawning realisation that prompted him to keep embroidering his depositions. In any case, as Dory could have told you, truth is a complicated beast. As a journalist, it was her duty to hunt it down, corral it with details and the corroboration of witnesses. How should she square this mission with a phenomenon that not infrequently saw interviewees of high integrity misstate or mangle their telling of events, while inveterate liars spoke honestly? Memory is unreliable. Recollections may vary.

Not only that, but each one of us perceives the world differently. Take colour. We can agree, you and I, that the sky on a summer's day is blue, but are we sure we mean the same thing by *blue*? That was a question Dory and Morgen debated one night on the steps of a theatre. Both had been struck by a scene in the German play they'd just seen, *Danton's Death*, in which the lead character challenges the idea that people ever really know each other.

One of Morgen's best-known songs explored this theme. While Dory agreed with the broad idea – that all of us view the world through our own prejudices and filters – she argued that science disproved certain notions of subjectivity. Take colours. Although there might be variations in the structures of our eyes, most of us have more or less the same numbers of photoreceptors, rods and cones, and are therefore likely to experience colours the same way.

There are obvious exceptions, of course, people with colour vision deficiencies or, more rarely, tetrachromats, lucky individuals, all women, born not with the usual three classes of cone, but four, and as a result able to perceive colours unimaginable to the rest of the population.

'That's you, my love,' Morgen replied. 'Always seeing what others cannot.'

Elo's tale opened on a morning when the blue struggled to emerge from grey. Often along this coastline the clouds forget their place in the natural order, displaying a side of themselves that only gods or spacemen ought to see. On this date they behaved as they should, high in the sky and dreary. Still, nothing could dull the beauty of this spot, the promontory a prototype for sea-stead construction, as wild and ragged as if the waters had carved it.

He sometimes slept in the office, a phrase at dingy odds with the apartment on the roof of the main block. He deliberately fostered the misapprehension among his wives or girlfriends that the accommodation consisted of little more than a put-up bed in a single room. Anything to keep them away. Tantalus HQ, designed like the rest of the campus by sustainable architects Obi 3, wasn't just a workplace but the physical projection of his innermost thoughts. Women had no business there.

It was a smart building, if not smart enough. Obi 3 had conceived the apartment as a cylinder, with a strip of window performing a full 360-degree loop around the circumference. Light-sensitive glass darkened as the sun climbed above the horizon, returning to absolute clarity only at dusk. The problem arose in weather like this, bright enough to trigger the response but too murky to warrant it, even for a resident who wore protective lenses. The founders of Obi 3, either siblings or a couple – hard to tell, and invariably clad in matching Buzz Rickson's – had talked a good game about architecture meshing with nature. They were right, especially in an environment rich with salt and marine birds. Now, as Elo gazed at Bair Island, a seagull reminded him of the sort of glitch that bedevils technological progress, delivering a gelatinous smear across the panorama. He turned towards Palo Alto and Menlo Park, wishing for a BB gun and windows that opened.

This was the time of day Elo set aside for the project of living long enough to live for ever. He must survive until the singularity. Though he disliked the protocols, more than twenty of them before he even paused for a beaker of green tea infused with creatine and collagen, the programme had already made a difference, his biological clock in measurable reverse. The issue, as always, was time. His had exquisite value and the regimen took up too much of it. Already he'd sacked the lead doctor, mainly for her failure to speed the effects and prune the process, but he also disliked her flippancy and that stupid Eastern European accent. 'I didn't get the hell out of Ireland to live on cabbage,' he complained during one of their consultations. 'This diet is doing my head in. It's bor-ring.'

'Is good,' she'd replied. 'If we can't make you to living longer, we making you feel like you living longer.'

The new doctor knew his place, but had yet to improve on his predecessor's results.

Sighing, Elo set down the beaker and was about to embark on the first of two sessions on the Isokinetic Accelerator when his Tantalus rang – or rather, giggled. His youngest children must have tampered with the settings. The caller would be HOG. Few people had this number and fewer still dared to use it.

'What's the story?'

'Something's come up, boss.'

Fred Waterford was already waiting downstairs, modelling the skill set that underpinned his unstoppable rise within the organisation: always on call, self-effacing in dealings with Elo and menacing towards everyone else. Supposedly he had a wife and family, but nobody ever saw them. Neither did he, so the joke went – not that anyone dared tell it to his face. All employees across Tantalus, Underworld, Fleet and a constellation of smaller initiatives bore job titles that appealed to Elo's sense of humour. They were User Experience Drones Class 2 or Finance Grunts Third Tier, Growth Hackeroonies or Discontent Managers, Lab Rats or Systems Anals. Waterford, Elo's right-hand man, bore a unique designation – HOG

– an acronym for Hand of God. 'I can manage without just about any of yous, except for HOG,' Elo would say as encouragement to other staffers to raise their game.

HOG opened the door of the DB5 for his boss, then settled into the passenger seat, silently braced against Elo's driving. Always Elo mangled the gears, and that offended HOG, not that he would show it. The car was as much of a movie star as any of the actors that shared her screentime in *Goldfinger*, and belonged to a collection which included a yellow Rolls Royce Phantom from *The Great Gatsby* and a Model T Ford used at different times by Laurel and Hardy and Coco the Clown. Elo should only ever drive his clown car, thought HOG – *Toot, toot! Blaaarp!* A catastrophe of screeching shifts and a near-miss later, they pulled up on the tarmac next to the boss's jet. Thence it was smoother sailing, ninety minutes, and Ancient Egypt appeared on the horizon, jostling New York. There she was, too, Elo's talisman, half the size of the original and lifting her lamp beside the golden doors of a casino. Liberty.

A limousine met them at the steps of the plane and soon they were heading not into Las Vegas but away from it, towards Death Valley. Long before travellers reach that desolate place, the landscape foreshadows what is to come, the sands turning from gold to grey, a valley of ashes, the loneliest place on earth. Another person, passing intermittent signs of life, bungalows and an occasional church or convenience store, might wonder who had washed up in such a wilderness and why. Elo never troubled himself with other people's life choices. He closed his eyes behind his amber Ray-Bans – the wrong shades for the desert but this morning had been *focking funereal* – stirring only as the limo drew on to the forecourt of a garage.

The property, like the others along the route, stood in isolation, brick-built and filthy, two red pumps standing sentinel out front, its windows boarded or so caked with grime that they might as well be. Elo took one look at the situation and started cussing out the driver. What kind of *donkey* fails to top up the tank before collecting passengers? Now HOG exercised his rare licence to interrupt, cutting across the invective. *No, boss*, he told Elo, *this is our destination*.

A trio of men loitered outside the workshop, two of them Elo's employees and the third a garage owner named Wilson, in overalls, leaning against the rusted carcass of a Dodge. The moment Wilson pulled back the wooden doors, Elo understood why HOG had insisted on him making the journey. The space lacked artificial lighting, its fluorescents long spent, and the dust kicked up by their entrance dimming any illumination the day provided. A vehicle lift loomed out of the darkness, an empty bier. None of this mattered. The thing lit itself, glowing and oscillating, colours pursuing each other like eager dreams. The tarpaulin that had masked it lay in a heap on the floor. Elo exhaled, as if he'd been holding his breath in anticipation of just such a moment. Then, slowly, he walked over to it, his magical boat aground on an ashy shore.

They brought the machine back to Tantalus. What else were they to do? Elo's voice grew querulous under Doctor Roweena's impassive gaze. Yes, indeed, he kept the find secret, as any responsible technologist would, gagging the garage owner with fistfuls of NDAs backed by a home visit from HOG. He needed time to figure out what they were dealing with. In the mean time, Elo instructed that a section of the campus be cleared, aborting a start-up incubator to do so, and pulling personnel off multiple teams and workstreams, including Fleet, which promptly suffered an outage. This must take priority.

From the beginning, his highly paid experts hemmed and equivocated, the Rats shifty, the Anals full of hot air. Even so there was consensus. Irrespective of field or specialism, everyone who studied the boat confirmed that it represented something new to science. Its constituent materials alone defied classification. The banks of levers seemed to promise functionality, but nobody could persuade the machine to do anything more than pulse prettily.

One afternoon, amid all this chin-scratching, a pair of oddballs arrived at the gates. Tantalus had their *ship*, they told security. They looked eccentric and not particularly clean, but that phrase might have triggered recognition if the presence of the mysterious machine were not a secret shared on a need-to-know basis. Who knew that Elo's Imperial Royal Guardsmen, the IRGs, needed to know. Because the IRGs weren't in the loop, they waved the visitors away, only for them to return hours later, politely insistent. Rebuffed again, the strange strangers set up camp on the verge of the approach road, making themselves scarce when Tantalus called the cops, but resurfacing as soon as they left. After several days, their vigil prompted enough chatter to alert HOG, who decided to check them out.

It was raining as he drew up alongside the encampment, so he stayed in the yellow Roller and wound down the window.

'This here is private property, folks,' he growled.

The woman had a peculiar little voice.

'We too wish to talk about private property. You have our ship. And, for the record, this land belongs to San Mateo County.'

HOG noticed a daisy chain around her neck – *Jesus, a hippy* – but unlike his underlings, he recognised the potential significance of her words. *OK,* he said, still gravel-voiced, *climb in.* He'd better find out what these jokers knew, and whether they might help decode the weird boat thing.

No need to trouble the boss with any of this as yet.

Somewhere around this point, Doctor Roweena interrupted, not with a challenge to Elo, but for lunch, another aspic mould and a pyramid of white bread triangles filled with sandwich spread. Dory and Elo ate in silence. The Doctor took nothing for herself. Perhaps eating wasn't an option. Roweena and her chair appeared to be a unified entity, connected at various junctures; more recently Dory spotted a ridge under Roweena's clothing that, though subtle, could be a J-tube. Only a few months ago, Morgen had undergone a jejunostomy – the greatest insult yet, that such a gourmet be denied the pleasures of taste. We start life on milk and pap, only to end it on pap and milk, but by now Morgen could not tolerate so much as baby food, all ability to smell long gone too. People in bodies that function like clockwork imagine pain to be the worst of all fates. While

Morgen endured an ever-changing palette of physical torments, these absences hurt more.

An abrasive person, or one plugged into the world rather than monitors, might have raged at the nurse who construed impaired senses as a bonus. 'Cheer up,' she urged Morgen. 'At least you don't get jealous when your wife makes herself dinner.' Morgen simply nodded. It was Dory who snapped – *What a stupid thing to say*! – and anyway, Morgen's illness meant she rarely entered the kitchen, and then only to grab a pitta bread and a spoonful of taramasalata (old habits) or microwave a ready meal. *Whereas for Morgen not to be able to wake up and smell the tea…* She was shouting now, tears in her eyes. Quickly she regained control and excused herself. Things had been trying of late. The nurse accepted the apology but remained fluffed up like a pigeon.

The virus first showed itself in that very same kitchen. Back then it was an Eden, Dory and Morgen blissfully ignorant of their impending expulsion. *This batch of Earl Grey is a bit blah*, Morgen had said, *almost no bergamot*. Further symptoms came later, and even then, Dory didn't recognise them as signs of illness. Detached, Morgen seemed, and of course that was the problem, the bonds of earth loosening, the glorious spirit beginning to float away.

Had Dory understood what was going on, might she have spared Morgen the worst of the damage? Only later did she discover that their GP had provisionally diagnosed pneumonia and urged Morgen to go straight to hospital. Of course, nobody knew about this illness yet, apart from officials involved in its cover-up. Stories were emerging – a city on the opposite side of the world locked down, an implacable disease – but then, as now, the authorities insisted on timelines that denied early victims accurate diagnoses and, for the unluckiest, their correct cause of death. It was like that with the aftermath of the virus too, millions across the world suffering serious long-term effects but little formal recognition of this toll.

Morgen resisted the GP's advice and continued to bat away Dory's worries, pretending even as oxygen levels dropped that nothing was wrong. *The album won't finish itself, you know.* One day Dory came home to find her beloved slumped in a chair, conscious but cyanotic. (*We can agree, Morgen, that you are blue, but do we see blue the same way?*) Finally, Dory did what she should have done weeks earlier and called an ambulance.

Months after this initial hospitalisation, Dory asked one of the specialists if swifter intervention could have led to better outcomes. He answered her with caution and kindness. Difficult to say. At that juncture they still knew so little about this disease and its shapeshifting ways. Morgen's underlying conditions would certainly have complicated matters. Also, he added, Dory had good reason to be distracted. Her mum had died just a few days after Morgen's admission.

When Morgen was first installed in ICU, Dory didn't grasp the implications, and anyway she focused on the few positives, the convenience of Mum and Morgen both in the same London hospital, St Thomas's, and the strange kinship of the family room, everyone there for similar reasons and interacting with an honesty close friends would struggle to replicate. One woman had kept a bedside vigil every day for three months to that point, and would continue to do so until the ban on hospital visitors. Her spouse died a day after her banishment.

Oh, but Dory and Morgen were the lucky ones. Their friend Andy Gill, a madly innovative musician and founder of the band Gang of Four, succumbed in the first wave. He too ended up in St Thomas's, a different corner of ICU. A long stretch of whitewashed concrete dividing the hospital grounds from the Thames walkway became a memorial to the pandemic dead, every day hearts added to represent the lovely dead, Gill and tens of thousands more, until the wall ran along the river as red as an artery.

Eventually Dory would map her life and Morgen's on to the history Elo and Doctor Roweena were contending. While she watched Mum die and Morgen sicken, Elo had initiated the sequence of events that brought them to this room.

'Shall we?' asked the Doctor.

Elo had given up on the mushy sandwiches. 'What is this,' he demanded, suddenly aggressive, 'an interrogation?'

'No,' she replied. 'An accounting.'

When Elo learnt about the strangers, they'd already enjoyed his hospitality for the worst part of a week. HOG messaged rather than calling, deploying the standard phrase, *something's come up*, and proposing that he brief the boss in the rooftop apartment. Thus far, the need-to-know circle aware of the visitors locked in a data-storage facility extended only to himself and Darth, the head of the IRGs, and HOG didn't intend to expand it beyond the addition of Elo in case radical action were needed.

He waited until certain the boss would have finished his morning routine before texting, poised to ascend as soon as his summons came. Today the boss must be fidgety, his response so fast it almost caught up with the outgoing message and the scene in the apartment far from tranquil. Papers lay scattered across the minimalist décor while Elo paced, half his face hidden behind oversized sunglasses, black ones – never an encouraging sign, even though the weather had brightened.

'I want to hear good news,' he said as his consigliere exited the elevator.

'Got it,' said HOG.

'My point or the good news?'

'Both.'

HOG quickly ran through the story, omitting the IRG's failure to pick up on the potential significance of the arrivals. He also glossed over the reception he had given the pair, describing his one-sided exchanges with them as *friendly chats*. And so they were. Not a lank hair on their greasy heads had been touched. If lights had been left on throughout their stay, well, that was an oversight. If music had been played at ear-splitting volume, that was just part of the service. Who wouldn't want to listen to Warp 24/7?

To be fair, as HOG was not, the guests hadn't complained. The problem resided not in what they said but what they didn't. So far, the strangers had given up just a handful of details: their names, Doctor Roweena and Professor Zachary; and a reason for their presence that stretched credulity. They were, the Professor said, bioethical historicists on a research trip. OK, that part HOG could buy. They had the air of people who spent time with their noses in books, unattractively dishevelled. But then their story got weird. They claimed to have travelled from the distant future.

In any other circumstances, this would have earned a rabbit punch, but HOG restrained himself. Wild theories about the boat were taking root. HOG was of the personal opinion that the Chinese or the Israelis had something to do with this, the set-up too advanced for the Russians, but the consensus among Elo's experts and with the boss himself had shifted towards extraterrestrials. In that context, time travel seemed as reasonable an explanation as any, so he laid it out.

The boss clearly agreed, no longer pacing the room but quivering like a sighthound sensing a squirrel, then letting loose about branes and black holes and quantum teleportation, only to stopper the flow with a peremptory, 'Well, what are you waiting for?'

HOG, who recognised this mood, was already stepping into the elevator, on his way to fetch the visitors.

Never ignore first impressions. The more sophisticated civilisations become, the greater their tendency to downgrade older systems of signalling, micro-expressions, odours, body language, yet all of these are useful pointers to character and intention. That Elo didn't think much of Doctor Roweena and Professor Zachary on meeting them was neither here nor there, because he didn't think much of anyone. The Doctor, however, made a mistake. She recoiled from Elo as she had from HOG, but deliberately suppressed her response. That left her undefended against his treachery, if faithful to her calling. Bioethical historicists of the future, like journalists of the past, aspire to be neutral observers. It is not their business to like or dislike the subjects of their work.

Dory grasped this parallel as soon as Doctor Roweena sketched out the project that had brought her and the Professor to the Nevada desert. Although one of many pieces of the puzzle that she inserted into Elo's account of events, the Doctor's description of that first encounter might be the most significant. The two sets of people who faced each other in Elo's swanky living room stood

109

either side of a rift in understanding so profound that a star may as well have died right there between them.

The Doctor and the Professor had come to learn, they explained, part of a team researching the past with a view to avoiding its mistakes. Unlike our era's casual approach to history, its future practice had been shaped by the near extinction of all the living beings of the planet and the slow and painstaking work of recovery that followed. While our century bows to the myth of progress and worships at the altar of growth, the peoples of Doctor Roweena's time – human or otherwise – abjure this religion.

Long ago Dory spent an evening at a club, squeezed between supermodels and actresses and a public thinker so famous in his native France that he was known by only three initials. She had hoped to tempt him into unpacking his views on how to balance the aspirations of emerging nations with old economies. Instead, snowy shirt open to the sternum, he joined in a game of Bunny Ears.

Raised voices interrupted her reverie, Elo losing patience, talking over the Doctor. In Roweena's version of events, HOG had threatened, in front of Elo, to drop them in the Bay. No, Elo was insisting, HOG was a rough diamond but would never have said such a thing. Elo himself had been solicitous, enquiring whether his guests had everything required for comfort.

'We did not,' said the Doctor. 'We needed our ship.'

Dory recognised in their otherwise contradictory accounts the outlines of a good cop/bad cop routine, but the Doctor still seemed mystified by the dynamic between these men, and more so by everything that had followed. She came back at Elo with a flurry of objections, but in essence they all boiled down to the one anguished question: why had he been so intent on running before he could walk?

A mark of a successful society isn't how advanced its technologies are, but which it chooses to deploy and how. This was the point that to the Doctor appeared self-evident and to Elo ungraspable. It wasn't that he rejected it outright, but rather that it slipped through his fingers like mercury. Even now, when his decision to pilot the ship without a full knowledge of its properties had beached him in the future, this understanding eluded him. At the time of his first confrontation with Doctor Roweena, his failures to date, though disastrous to other people, had left him unscathed. Why should this be different? His sole focus was to master and exploit the science that powered the machine.

This *yoke* could be *epoch-making*, he enthused.

'Yes,' the Professor answered. 'Potentially'.

Elo hailed its potential to *change the course of history*, and the Doctor nodded.

'Unfortunately.'

The response didn't compute. 'The earth is heading towards ecological disaster, amiright?'

She nodded again.

'And your time machine can make a difference.'

'Yes,' she said, 'but what kind of difference?'

HOG, whose only query about the machine thus far had been to ask about its kinetic potential, could see this exchange was getting precisely nowhere. He didn't pretend to fathom the crap that obsessed Elo, wormholes and cosmic strings, but the movie *12 Monkeys* had taught him that eliminating present danger could perfect the future.

'Hey lady,' he growled at Doctor Roweena, 'I get it. If the boss changes the course of the future, you might not be born. But believe me, if you keep stonewalling, you'll wish that you'd never been born.'

Doctor Roweena looked at him, her gaze level. 'Time travelling can lead to such outcomes, but only in rare circumstances. The greatest danger to the individual resides in meeting oneself.'

08:00

*M*y watchstrap disintegrated, so we've travelled to the Big Smog. *Morgen and I are staying with friends in Topanga Canyon, hiking, reading, chatting in the hot tub or the pool, no clockwatching necessary. Even so, I insist on finding a replacement. Seems that I'm comfortable lounging around without a stitch of clothing, but feel naked without Dad's Omega on my wrist.*

Deadlines rule my life, even if there aren't any. Nevertheless, when some while into the future, Apple launches a smartwatch and, a week later, Tantalus unveils a sleeker rival, the Apriköt, I'll be too bloody minded to wear either. Belatedly I'm asking the right questions. Why gift corporations the data or oblige the authorities by donning a tracker? The additional functions these devices offer aren't worth the hidden transactions. Time is the sole measure that really matters, except in a few specific situations. The only wearable technology I will ever embrace apart from the Omega is my dive computer. Oh, and for twenty-four hours a Holter monitor, after the virus finds a second way to break my heart.

Dad's watch is large on me, as it became on him, but pleasingly simple, just the twelve, three, six and nine written as numerals and the other hours and increments shown in a sunburst of platinum. The fastening is the traditional kind too – lugs that can be unscrewed to secure a leather band. In Macy's, I choose a new strap, fairly neutral, black mock crocodile, and Morgen, who dislikes air-conditioning, heads straight to the counter to ask the assistant to fit it for me.

'I would love to help you,' she says, 'but I can't.'

We look at her, perplexed, Morgen's mouth already twitching.

'My boyfriend left me, and he took myself.'

'Your shelf?' Morgen, who is trying to make me laugh, nearly succeeds, but we are both old hands at this game.

'Myself,' she explains. 'My. Self. He took myself and now I can't use my hands.'

'How does that work?' Morgen asks. 'Did you wake up one morning to find your hands had gone on strike?'

'Yes, it was morning,' she answers, dreamily. 'I looked in the mirror and myself had gone.'

'Awful. Are you expecting yourself to come back?'

'I am,' she says. 'My shaman tells me I'll come home one day and find myself at the kitchen table.'

It's about ten years since our Topanga sojourn, and for once Morgen and I have plotted a full-scale holiday. Though we are in the habit of meeting up here, there and everywhere, our mini-breaks are almost always organised off the back of existing travel for work. When you both have jobs that send you spinning around the globe, home becomes your favourite destination.

This year Morgen has been recording with one of the founders of the Brazilian band Legião Urbana, while I've been reporting a cover story on the international drugs business. A significant emerging player in the trade is a São Paulo-based gang, Primeiro Comando da Capital, PCC. When Morgen and I realise that our missions will bring us to Brazil at the same time, we resolve to seize the opportunity. Couples whose time is not their own are forced to get by with scraps of each other. We're blessed in that way, our work despite its pressures comparatively flexible, and Morgen answers to nobody.

All that is required for us to make time is time. One night, we sit down together, compare diaries and itineraries and then, crucially, block off the dates. Maybe we're a little drunk on Cloudy Bay. Why not disappear for a whole month, we exclaim, intoxicated by the possibility. Of course, my commitments soon whittle away a chunk of days – I am, after all, still an employee – and Morgen is restless about an album, always a new album. Never mind. A fortnight is an eternity for us. This will be a proper break, I say. The tragedy is that I'm right.

The thing that coils, fangs bared, could have struck us anywhere, though Morgen insists on invoking the past while I will repeat until I'm blue in the face that this is exactly what João represents, no more. He is ancient history, a ghost. Plus, Morgen and I have travelled to and within this country more than

*once since those long-ago days, together and separately, and always, until now,
without incident.*

*If I'm on edge, it's because of the drugs story. Imprisoned leaders of PCC
have been using mobile phones to direct a wave of violence from their São
Paulo prison cells, police and thieves gunned down in the streets, bystanders
too. One of my contacts, the boss of a smaller cartel, is hiding out in
Heliopolis, a neighbourhood that started as a favela and never rose above its
beginnings, just crusted over like a scab. The morning of the interview, his
henchman meets me at its ragged border to lead me through the warren of
dirt paths and corrugated iron. Once we are hours deep into this hellscape,
he wheels around.* Ainda não tá com medo, mina? *he asks –* Are you
scared yet, lady? *A candid answer would be,* Yes, but too far gone to
turn back. *The story of my life.* I'm fine, *I say.*

*It's not exactly a lie. Any residual tension that mars the first days in Bahia
shouldn't be a big deal. Just as I've learnt to cope with Morgen slinking back
from tours and mussing our bed like a feral cat marking territory, so Morgen
is used to the crunchy aftermath of some of my assignments. It can take
me a while to decompress. That's why we've developed our routines, always
a bit of luxury to ease potential friction – in this case a boutique hotel in
Salvador. Once a convent, it is decorated in what the information booklet by
our bed describes as* colonial style, *each painting and bejewelled knick-
knack a reminder that the church acted both as an arm of imperialism and an
extractive empire in its own right.*

*Within these cloistered walls, nuns prayed and the Dutch surrendered after
defeat by Portuguese forces. Morgen capitulates too, agreeing to an early night
though Salvador is alive with music. The second day goes better – I relax sufficiently to eat, drink and make merry, for tomorrow we die. As we might. When,
the next morning, we pick up a hire car to drive to Lençóis, we fail to grasp that
the route winds through wilderness, no petrol stations or food shops. The car
is running on fumes by the time we pull up at Hotel Canto das Águas. Many
couples would be arguing by now. Though grim-faced, we don't blame each other.*

*Our skirmish relates to the accommodation we've been allocated – little
more than a cupboard and facing away from the waters that give the hotel its
name. Their song permeates every corner of the building, loud enough that we
raise our voices even once we stop arguing. Morgen chides me for choosing the
cheapest room rather than the best. Happily, the manager promises to move us
tomorrow. Just one suboptimal night and everything will be right as rain.*

The food turns out to be good, too – always a relief. Nothing can plunge us into depression faster than dodgy cooking. We intend to stay in Lençóis for a few days before heading off into the surrounding national park, Chapada Diamantina, diamond plateau. *Morgen's asthma, though not yet exacerbated by sarcoidosis, rules out hiking. Instead, this will be a guided tour on horseback. Over dinner, we rekindle excitement for the idea and dawn finds us wrapped in each other in the small bed in the small room.*

Our new quarters lift our mood still further, a suite with a private veranda above a series of chutes and falls. We sit here for hours watching hummingbirds streaking across the horizon like the star on the night we met. Butterflies alight next to us, sunning peacock wings.

Some years from now, when Morgen lies gravely ill, something prompts me to search Google Earth for the hotel. The proprietors have zhuzhed it up since our stay. In summer months the waters could dry to a trickle, but the additions, a swimming pool and water slide, turquoise against the aberrant green of an imported lawn, must make them sing year-round.

Briefly I wonder if the hotel had to seek planning permission. If so, they could have argued that their changes reflect local history. After all, insults to the Lençóis landscape are fully in keeping with its past. For hundreds of years, Europeans dug and furrowed this area in a quest for gold, diamonds and, in the nineteenth century, minerals to power their industrial revolutions. Then came a new invasion, mining corporations with heavy machinery, diesel pumps and dredgers. Once they had stripped what they could find, tourism took root in the churned soil, leaving fewer marks, just the odd Coke can in the rapids or white flowers of toilet tissue snagged on the bushes.

Foreigners love this place. The hotel manager tells Morgen that musician Jimmy Page has a house nearby. 'I'll run away if I spot him,' my love says, and I laugh. Page failing to recognise Morgen, even in flight, seems about as likely as me mistaking a hummingbird for a hawk.

Before we set out on our trail ride, we undertake shorter excursions on foot or, once we procure petrol, drive to local beauty spots. Further upstream, great slabs of limestone form the banks and conduit for the singing waters and the enterprises enabled by their flow, local residents wading thigh-high to wash their clothes or pan for diamonds smaller than tear drops. At Poço do Diabo, devil's pool, we venture in up to our necks, though Morgen takes some coaxing. Another day we admire, from its base, a table mountain called Morro do Pai Inácio. Legend relates that a slave who dared to love the daughter of his master scaled it in a bid to evade vengeance, only to find himself cornered. Fortunately, he carried an umbrella. Smiling down at his pursuers, he raised it and floated away to safety.

We are seeking shelter too, but by grounding, our feet planted in the dusty soil and arms about each other. This is why people take holidays. For me, there is an added benefit to time with Morgen. My love makes me a better person, always has, always will. The alchemical formula is mysterious and also simple. Morgen sees me, and despite this, and to my eternal amazement, cherishes me. This, in turn, encourages me to do what I can to merit my extraordinary good fortune. Then there's the generosity of love itself. We have so much of it that we easily spare some for the rest of the world.

It's ironic, really. Had we loved a little less well I might not have stabbed Morgen through the heart.

The horses crop grass, a pleasing sound. *They aren't tied, don't need to be, reins left to dangle, but apparently that's enough to make them feel tethered. It's called ground-tying, our guide Caio informs us. What happens if something spooks them and they bolt? We're a long way from anywhere. Caio grins. 'Then we eat each other or die.'*

We've stopped beneath a copse of gnarled trees next to a lake that looks older still, bloody and primordial. Caio could be the son or kid brother of the gang member who led me through Heliopolis, round of face, wiry of body and near-identical tattoos, the kind you give yourself in prison with a needle and biro ink or ash. There the similarity ends. Our guide talks ten to the dozen, Portuguese mixing with American English, and a grin that first appeared when he took in our limited horsemanship, and is currently directed at Morgen.

'Little bastards! Uh!' Morgen is performing a strange dance.

'What is it?' I call. The moment we arrived Caio and I dived into the lake, while Morgen still hovers at its edge, hip deep.

My love yelps again and we swim towards the sound, worried now. We needn't have been. Morgen's legs are silvered with tiny fish.

'Lunchtime,' says Caio. 'Yum, yum.'

'Get them off me!' pleads Morgen, and I do.

We camp that night on a stretch of flat rock, Morgen swathed not only against the chill but also the memory of those carnivorous fish. *I'm the one who lies awake, of course, and when I finally drop off, it's into an element far shallower than the lake, just enough to birth a beast of a dream.*

It pins me down with a force that stops me from breathing, crushes me behind glass. The shapes are difficult to decipher in the dark, white and stooped. Then one of the creatures approaches, regards me with red, unblinking eyes, a thing that has grown without light. We are deep underground.

The monster turns away, wordless, yet somehow, I understand. My fate, my future, must wait as I bear witness. Although I try to call out, the warning sticks in my throat. My dearest darling, fly! *The glass divides us, silences me. All I can do is watch as they crowd around Morgen, touching and prodding, squeezing and compressing, forcing life from its secret places, not just the lungs but the blood and the cells.*

Morgen, I love you. I door you. I window you. *The glass denies me even these well-worn assurances or the comfort of a goodbye. In twelve minutes it is over. Morgen reclines, a poet or a saint, still perfect, still Morgen, but pale, so pale, eyelids not quite shut. The emerald of those beautiful irises shines through for the very last time.*

Oh, Morgen, I cannot live without you.

That realisation or a nightjar wakes me, and I stare at the cold constellations above our campsite. Over time, I've seen a lot of death — just a few days ago, in São Paulo, a boy discarded like a broken suitcase, too many bullet wounds to tell which one killed him. After similar experiences, and worse, my employers offered me counselling, tried to insist, but what's the point? It's other people who need fixing, not me. Most of you are in denial, whereas in routinely confronting the act and inevitability of dying, I embrace my own mortality, laugh at it. Why else would I be drawn to danger, wreck-diving, helicopters wheeling above battlefields, tanks speeding across oil fields outside Basra? Nothing scares me because one way or another we all must die and, in that instant, become nothing, less than nothing, a mess littering a pavement or blocking a bed.

Once, sitting with Morgen at the hospital, days before wards closed to visitors, a patient in the adjacent alcove suddenly drowned in her own fluids. The monitors changed their tune and acquired a rhythm section, running feet and the squeak of castors on linoleum. There were other noises too, the perfunctory application of electricity to a heart already stilled, but it was obvious she'd gone. Her husband arrived, panting and crying. He'd only been in the family room; such cruelty – there day in, day out and she chooses the one moment he isn't tethering her to earth to sneak away. We heard the nurses escort him back to the waiting area for sweet tea. Minutes later a different set of wheels rattled across the floor, brakes deployed, a thump, thump and the drone of a zip, and there she was, shuddering past us, embarking on her final journey in a black body bag.

I watched without feeling. Her time had come, as it comes to everyone. What a feat of dissociation. It's not death I should fear, but life without its glorious reason for living. Once again the sentence forms, shimmers in the air: I cannot live without you, Morgen.

A pause, and a second string of words joins this phrase, aching syllable by aching syllable: And. So. I. Must.

It made sense at the time.

T he first rule of time travel is that you don't talk about time travel. Doctor Roweena and Professor Zachary resisted every method of interrogation thrown at them, from gentle persuasion to gut-twisting threats. Elo drew the line at actual violence lest damage to the receptacles of knowledge accidentally cut off access to that most valuable of commodities. Instead, HOG reinforced his regime of intimidation with sensory assaults, depriving the guests of freedom, light and all but a single protein bar per day. To his surprise, they tended not to finish it, as if such meagre rations exceeded requirements. He'd begun to wonder whether Elo might sanction waterboarding when, without warning, the Professor appeared to crack.

Everyone had gathered in the laboratory for the regular briefing, opened, as every morning, by Elo with a speech to rally the troops. *Before them stood the key to a brighter future. The keyholders –* he gestured in the direction of Doctor Roweena and Professor Zachary *– could surely hasten their progress, but with or without their help, Team Tantalus was bound to prevail.* So certain was he of this outcome that over the past forty-eight hours he had restructured his businesses and lined up the necessary financial instruments to launch a new company within the corporate group. OK, so they might not yet know exactly how wormholes facilitated time travel, and there were as many questions about M-theory and superstrings as antimatter, but the waveforms involved in this process could not be of the mechanical variety, for they existed in spacetime without a medium to propagate them. 'Gentlemen,' he said, 'and lady...' – noticing only in that moment the absence of any female other than the Doctor – 'I give you the Wormhole Electromagnetic Escape Nutation project, WEEN. And don't you smirk,' he said, pointing to her. 'The name has nothing to do with you.'

Silence, then a movement from the corner. Her colleague.

'You seem to be struggling with the science,' the Professor said. 'Would you like me to take you for a spin?'

'You what?'

The Professor repeated his offer.

119

'Do bears shit in the woods?' said Elo, interest trumping anger at the public insult.

'Yes,' said Doctor Roweena.

He disliked many things about the visitors, but this in particular got his goat. They were literal as well as didactic. His days of accepting lectures from anyone were long past, much less from people who wouldn't recognise a figure of speech if it got up and gave them a haircut. The woman was the worst. She'd gone off on a jag yesterday, zero relevance to the task in hand, something about the relationship between reproduction and longevity. 'Everything,' she said, 'is a trade-off. Animals that live longer reproduce less.'

What *rawmaish*, as Da used to say. Elo carried boyhood memories of his pet mice refusing to mate and then eating such young as they did produce while the O'Hallorans' next-door neighbours bred like rabbits. To date his own progeny numbered thirteen, at least officially – the full Last Supper, as a talk-show host recently joked.

Still, the Professor had his attention.

'A spin where?' he asked.

'The past holds too many unknowns,' said Zachary, 'but if we select coordinates far enough into the future to eliminate risk to you, and with sufficient distance to our own time to protect us, there shouldn't be a problem. What about March 22, 2233? Or a period after our time – 3535, for example?'

'How far can the machine take us?'

'That isn't the right question, Mr Ó hAllmhuráin,' the Doctor replied, and Elo's hackles rose again.

'What,' he said, speaking slowly as if to a child, and her voice really was that of a toddler, 'might you consider to be the right question?'

'The point is not what our ship can do, but what you would wish the exercise to achieve,' she continued. 'In theory there are no limits to its range other than those we impose for prudence. Each deployment raises existential hazards not only to passengers but to life past, present and future, in this brane and others.'

'It would be bad if we met ourselves,' Elo offered, remembering their earlier conversation.

'Yes,' the Professor agreed. 'We must avoid that eventuality and the many zones and dimensions uncharted or already assessed as deadly. Also, we do our very best not to create new stubs. That way madness lies.'

They discussed logistics. The laboratory, if used as the launchpad, must be cleared of anything – and anyone – breakable. Though the ship would be programmed to return to the exact place of departure, with the time of re-entry set to zero plus three rontoseconds, ripples of cosmic inflation could knock the craft off its trajectory. While pure time wasn't susceptible to such disruptions, spacetime could be. The machine had been known to turn up as a much as a metre from its target. For that reason, they usually deployed in the open air, and never with audiences. Elo's insistence on secrecy ruled out the first of those protocols, so they must prepare accordingly.

Then there was the question of who would travel; on this, Elo and the visitors swiftly locked horns. He wanted HOG along for the ride, but the ship wasn't equipped to carry a third person. The solution seemed simple. He, Elo, would steer the ship. They just needed to teach him how to do it. The Professor told him this would not be possible. The machine responded only to people it recognised, and pilot training, much like that between a guide dog and handler or a dressage horse and rider, took time – intense, detailed and psychophysical.

In the end, Elo blinked first, needing several days to reach that point and presenting the decision not so much as a climbdown as a reframing. Many of Elo's best ideas – the development of synthetic tantalum, for example, or the ways in which extended reality could augment mental health provision – hadn't been his at all, until, suddenly, they were. So it was with his rare course corrections. *Ridiculous to bring HOG,* he protested, as if the Professor, not he, pushed for his lieutenant's inclusion. *Someone had to stay behind to mind the shop.* When the Doctor observed that Elo would only be absent for three rontoseconds, he talked over her, issuing a flurry of instructions.

Thus it was decided, and the next day he took the passenger seat. After a reluctant HOG left the lab with Roweena and the rest of the team, the Professor produced something from his trouser pocket, slotting it into a gap next to the levers. Clearly the IRG had failed to search him thoroughly. Heads would roll. Out in the corridor, some of those heads waited, oblivious. Then everyone felt a vibration and heard Elo's voice, strained and strange.

'You'd better come in,' he said, so they did. The machine sat on the same spot, its colours fierce. Elo, paler than ever, slumped in the captain's chair. Of the Professor there was no sign.

Doctor Roweena sat very still as Elo told this part of the story, her expression unreadable but her posture eloquent. For all she had shown them courtesy, she radiated anger, and something else too. It takes one to know one, and Dory recognised the grief that held the Doctor rigid.

In Elo's version of events, the early part of his travels with the Professor had passed without incident, if an experience that blew his mind and fused every synapse could be described in such terms. Time streams by too quickly to perceive the changing world outside the ship, but for some reason an occasional scene imprints, as if caught in the pop of a flashbulb. His campus shot upwards like a triffid, blocked the light, only to be replaced by an outbreak of geodesic domes. Water reared as a wave, then rose like a saviour, gave way to an electric storm or a battle – hard to tell, but the sky burned. Afterwards came, in blinding succession, a darkness, a brightness, a verdancy, each image punctuated by a sleep of sorts. On his sixth or seventh awakening the Professor spoke to him. 'This is the far future, close to the limit of our mapping. As you see, much repair work has been completed.'

Elo looked about. They faced the Bay, Bair Island to their left but to the right not a trace of Palo Alto, and around him nothing of the empire he had nurtured into life – nor any buildings, for that matter. Sky and sea sparkled, variations on an unfamiliar blue. Above them birds circled. *Bloody gulls.* Grass grew long and lush, and among it poppies of the brightest scarlet he had ever seen.

'We can leave the ship if you like,' said Professor Zachary, 'but we should not venture any distance.'

'San Francisco.' Elo's throat was dry. 'Can we go there?'

'Too far,' the Professor said. 'Also, the city no longer exists.'

'Quake?'

The Professor shook his head, no, but failed to offer an alternative explanation.

At that moment, the earth tilted on its axis and Elo gripped the sides of the machine. He wouldn't be sure when recalling their short sojourn at these coordinates whether the rocking sensation came from within, a form of motion sickness, or – a sudden thought – if the underpinnings of the artificial land built out into the Bay had eroded. His one absolute certainty, in the instant and as he retold the experience, first on his return to the laboratory and later in the suite with Doctor Roweena and Dory, was that he hated this future – not that he could put this reaction into words. Had he possessed a modicum of self awareness or a narrator to sift through his mess of impulses, he might have compared the sensation to staring at the night sky, though that comparison would fail too. While night skies remind most people of their insignificance in the grand flow of time, Elo regarded stars as resources to be mined in due course. Now, however, surveying a scene in which every one of his achievements had either been expunged or compromised, he felt, in his bones and stomach, the brute force of transience.

What Elo did manage to articulate was this: for whatever reason, he sensed mortal danger. Rather than exit the ship as invited, he leant across Professor Zachary to grab the joystick. It was reflex, pure and uncontrollable. He intended no harm. Anyway, why did the machine react? *It should have taken its instructions only from the Professor.* He sounded almost plaintive whenever he uttered this defence.

Where next they came to rest, the colours had inverted, sky red and ground a roiling cobalt. Because they weren't resting at all, but sinking, into seas that stretched in every direction. Already the machine might have submerged, except that it had landed on a large rock, almost as red as the heavens, its otherwise smooth surface flecked with algae and barnacles. When the Professor spoke, his words were drowned by a terrible screaming, as if of a giant gull. They looked up and saw a white butterfly bearing down on them, wingspan wider than Elo's smallest jet. *Christ!* Nor was their rock a rock at all. All around them, red carapaces broke surface, some rising higher as many legs churned water, or tails flipped bodies to near vertical. At once a giant claw extended, caught the butterfly as easily as if it were a dandelion clock, pulled it down into the waves and thence out of sight. Relief died in seconds. As Elo reached to swat a fly that tickled his cheek, his hand encountered a length of steel cable. He sensed what it was, but turned anyway, coming face to shiny face with one of the lobster creatures. Hard to tell if the eye at the end of the antenna focused on the occupants of the machine, but the claws clacked and snapped with unmistakable menace. This time it was the Professor who acted, detaching a small panel to input new data. Before he could finish the task, they were reversing through light years at the speed of negative matter.

'Even then, at the dawn of time travel, ships understood the importance of home,' Doctor Roweena said, directing her gaze towards Dory. 'They are no less intelligent than you or I, and' – though she didn't indicate Elo, she might as well have done – 'more so than others.'

'I couldn't have known,' he said.

'Precisely,' the Doctor replied. 'Even children are wise enough to be wary of things they know that they do not know. As a scientist, you should also respect the boundaries of knowledge, the unknown unknowns. We cannot expand those boundaries without risk, but we mitigate through the application of process.'

Earlier, Elo had summarised for Roweena the content of the briefings she and the Professor had inflicted on him ahead of his ride to the future; their numerous warnings that the machine was not only sentient but emotional, and of the disorienting effects of time travel. Lest this proved too complicated to retain in an emergency, they boiled it down to a single, implacable rule: touch nothing.

Dory, so gripped by the horror of the tale that her usual hunger alarms failed to ring, started when the wall dissolved to admit the hostess trolley.

'You should rest and refresh yourselves,' said the Doctor.

Though Dory disliked a cliffhanger and had done little more these past many hours than listen, she acknowledged that a break would be welcome. Also, the scent wafting from the trolley stirred memories of Dad in the kitchen – only one fancy dish in his repertoire, Boeuf Bourguignon, always served with mash, and cooked with real wine. He would open the spigot of the wine box, take a slug, wink at Dory, and whisper not to tell Mum 'or hell is to pay'.

She got up from the bed, stretched, walked over to the trolley. The first casserole indeed contained a beef stew of some sort, mushrooms and shallots emerging from the gravy like rocks from the sea. Elo bent down to inspect the dessert on the second tier and sighed. 'Gur cake.'

Next to the cake – actually a form of pastry, divided into squares – sat an artic roll, frozen hard enough to use as a weapon, and with a protective ring of sharp-cut strawberries. Elo meanwhile picked up the serving spoon and began digging about in a second casserole.

'Dublin coddle.' He sounded happy. 'It's like the chefs have got inside my head.'

'They have – not that they are chefs.' The Doctor, matter of fact. 'You eat what you are. This is not a particularly beneficial technology, but comes as a by-product of the language system, without which I alone would be able to communicate with you.'

She turned again to Dory.

'I believe there are flaws and glitches, for which my sincere apologies. The programme tends to place undue weight on early life experiences.'

Like psychotherapists, Dory thought. Her hunger ebbed.

09:00

***T**hey say you become a fully fledged adult when your parents die.* In different ways, Morgen and I disprove that rule – both orphaned, yet neither of us ready to put away childish things. Staunch and gentle and evolved though Morgen is, my love even now retains the wonder of the very young, plus a vulnerability simultaneously precious and alarming. Imagine surviving decades in the music industry without growing a protective shell. Though truth to tell – and I really am trying to be honest, despite every instinct to the contrary – the business has never inflicted more than surface wounds. Love alone tears Morgen apart, again and again, for a former best friend and bandmate turned tormentor, and for me. I am able to inflict exquisite pain, and one night in Chapada Diamantina, I exercise this power.

Before I confess, a thought experiment: let me turn back the clocks to a point before our choices were constrained. What if, instead of remaining children, Morgen and I had bred them? Would I still have tipped us into crisis?

Starting a family wasn't always out of the question, despite the logistical challenges. Our biologies may have ruled out natural conception, but nature can be circumvented. Plus, there are always children seeking homes – unwanted girls, infants with complex needs. Balancing caregiving with our existing commitments would have exacted a toll on the quality of our work, and probably on our relationship, but we'd have muddled through. People do.

We discussed the concept more than once, Morgen keen, but not sufficiently convinced to insist. My terms were harsh. I agreed neither to carry nor cradle, merely to offer support, financial and practical. Nor could I guarantee affection for any offspring. To soften the edges of these negotiations, we developed a series of jokes and private memes, a fantasy brood, each child ridiculously named in rock tradition: Contraflow, Crackle and Ambrosia. (Morgen, the eternal foodie,

126

used to take a guilty pleasure in tinned rice pudding.) Somehow, we never reached a firm conclusion, always diverted by a new project, a fresh excitement, and then the moment passed. Time isn't, as commonly understood, a river, but a dream house, seemingly vast, a place of doorways and corridors. Too late, you realise that the doors lock behind you and those strips you mistook for carpets are travellators. There is no turning back.

Ageing walks beside you, while illness prods you onwards until all your options are exhausted. I remember Dad, on his cot, denied the most basic of choices, too weak to adjust the angle of his body. How he hated it, this dignified man, needing help with what health visitors euphemistically termed 'personal care'. I tried to make him understand that it made me feel better to make him feel better. So it is with Morgen. The application of a warm towel is a kiss, the emptying of a bedpan the tightest of hugs, especially for those of us guarded in our emotions.

Medical science kept Dad alive until it didn't. It will keep Morgen alive until it doesn't. Yet what price a miracle that rather than ending suffering extends it? I used to watch Dad, knowing it would be kinder if all movement ceased, yet overwhelmed with relief to detect the faint beat of his I ♥ Kraków *T-shirt.*

As for Morgen, try though I may, I cannot accept the way our dream house has rearranged itself. Surely some corner, an attic or a hidden stairwell, must harbour salvation. When Morgen first sickened and the doctors warned that any recovery would be partial at best, the evening news reported that Gang of Four's Andy Gill had died. Months later, I wrote an email of condolence to his widow explaining why Morgen would be unable to do so. She replied wishing us well and urging me to seek more and better medical opinions. Andy's original prognosis had been similarly gloomy, permanent impairment. 'People keep telling me "Andy wouldn't have wanted to live that way,"' she wrote, 'but I think he'd be furious to be dead.'

It was her email that persuaded me to look into II, *the Ignis Institute, and yes, I'm perfectly aware that a journalist who dissected 'alternative' medicines and life-extension technologies in a popular-science book and wrote a series in* TIME *exposing one of the worst snake-oil peddlers should attack such a place rather than patronising it. How much easier to be a critic when you've no skin in the game.*

Ignis himself is more lizard than snake, hooded eyes and a dewlap that catches in his starched collar when he turns his head. Unlike some of these so-called doctors, he does have a pedigree, and he also hedges rather than

127

overpromising. The treatment is experimental, the results unpredictable; hope, but not as we know it, Jim. It is also phenomenally expensive.

I've looked at what can be raised from remortgaging the house, talked to a music manager about licensing or selling Morgen's back catalogue, accepted every poxy speaking engagement going, and even then can't see how to make it work long term, because in all cases but the worst, Morgen will need ongoing care. There's the colonial option, of course, moving to a lower-cost country and hiring local labour. I wonder about life in Lençóis. It is strangely tempting to return to the scene of the crime.

It cannot be put off any longer, this telling. *Infinite diversions are possible, but at some point, patience snaps and there's another reader lost. So, here goes.*

Since dawn, my nightmare has trailed us, though nobody else notices the dust it kicks up in our wake. *Caio sets a fast pace, taking advantage of a comparatively flat stretch of the country to let the horses trot or canter. When we stop around noon, it is not, as on previous days, to rest. There's a cave system to explore, the twist being that the chambers are at least partially submerged and linked by underwater tunnels. A man sits at the mouth of this netherworld with piles of masks, snorkels, fins and torches for rent by the hour. He also sells posters of Pelé, Taffarel and Romario.*

Morgen worries about the wisdom of our enterprise, but I am gung-ho, both because it is my default and to fill every minute with activity. Unstructured time is the agar jelly in which ideas grow, no matter how dangerous these might prove.

Soon we are stripped down and kitted out in yesterday's pants and T-shirts, with masks that give us the aspect of sci-fi monsters, the snorkels a single antenna each. Caio leads the way, encouraging us to admire the prehistoric fish that continue to spawn here, and reassuring a querulous Morgen that they feed off dead matter, decomposing plant and animal life and faeces, not living flesh. We don't yet spot them, distracted by the difficulty of wading in fins through the shallows, tripping over our own feet like a troupe of clowns. The chill of the deeper waters takes our breath away, which is unfortunate, for we are to hold it. To reach the next cave, we must duck-dive to an opening in the cave wall, swim

*through it, and stand up only when Caio signals us to do so. He goes ahead,
using his torch to light the route, and I follow.*

*The channel is no longer than an MRI machine and just as claustro-
phobic. Jagged limestone tugs at one fin, but already I've reached the exit
and Caio motions me to surface. We both breathe in, immediately expelling
some of that air to discuss Morgen, who ought to have appeared hard on
my heels.* Wait, *Caio says, retreating through the tunnel, the light escaping
with him.*

*Darkness presses in, heavier than the water. I glimpsed the fish as I swam
– ugly creatures, the colour of dirty salt, with red eyes. Now I imagine them
swarming around my legs. The air seethes too; things touching my face, whisk-
ing past. To banish the phantoms, all I need do is switch on my own flashlight,
but I'm paralysed, the protagonist in a Gang of Four song* History is the
reason I'm washed up.

Before I make a move, the waters glow and erupt, two heads this time.

'Morgen!' I scold. 'Where were you?'

*'Didn't you feel me pull your fin?' Morgen asks, also a little punchy. 'My
mask strap tangled. I wanted your help, but you just buggered off.'*

'Oh.' My voice loses its edge. 'I'm sorry.'

*Caio intervenes. He urges us to look up while he plays the torch across the
cave roof. Stalactites hang above us like Damoclean swords, and between them
clusters of fungus – except that fungus doesn't shiver and pulse.*

'What the fuck!' exclaims Morgen, meaning this as a question.

'Bats,' says Caio.

'But they're white.'

*Their eyes are red too, like the fish. Afterwards we worry about all the
droppings in the water. Do bats spread contagion, or is that a danger only if
they bite?*

Despite its challenges, we get through this day intact. *It is
the night that undoes us, our last before staring up at ceilings where now there
are stars. We lie side by side, pupae in padded cocoons, and, for a while, all
seems peaceful. Then Morgen extracts an arm from the sleeping bag, rolls to
face me, says, 'We should spend more time together.'*

*This is clearly not a complaint, but an expression of contentment. A few
scratchy moments aside, we've had a lovely vacation, a proper one, the first in*

years, our bodies tired in good ways, spirits replenished. The obvious and only reply ought to be Yes.

What emerges from my mouth instead is a sigh, as if Morgen's observation were stupid or irritating. I follow that with a sentence as crude as a rusty skewer, and just as cruel.

'Actually, Morgen, I've been thinking we should spend less *time together.'*

A subject that arises in any discussion about whether or not to have children is our independence. *We prize it. We are together of choice. This luxury is denied to many couples, who are bound neither by love nor joy.*

The barriers to partners leaving might be literal and physical. A friend of ours endured more than two years locked in a bedroom, sometimes chained, too, any flicker of resistance punished, though he also beat her for imaginary crimes and out of contempt for the submission he himself demanded. Another woman in our circle, a prominent public-relations executive, was allowed to go to work each day, her preschool son under the care of her boyfriend to guarantee her good behaviour. She fled only when he began to direct his rage at the child anyway. For a long time afterwards she would debate returning to him. Perhaps he could get help. Maybe the fault lay with her. She had failed to make him feel secure.

PR execs are not the only professional liars. Abusers and the abused acquire excellent skills at deception. Angela rushed into marriage because a stigma attaches to spinsterhood, then hung on for grim death to avoid the shame of divorce. She also feared being single until she found life to be lonelier in the wrong company than none. Even then, economics kept her rooted to the spot for quite a while. Break-ups are expensive, in their immediacy, and – especially for women – the longer term. You might walk out on bricks and mortar, a future mapped out, perhaps a share of a pension further down the line. Even Mum, for all she gave the impression of a bird on a wire, waited until Dad died to take flight.

Morgen and I not only choose to be with each other, we renew that choice on a daily basis. We can afford to decamp if ever we wish to do so, awash with money by most standards, if not enough for Ignis. We have separate accounts, regular work, enough friends to go round or split between us, identities, private and public-facing. As we lie down to sleep that night in Chapada Diamantina, we still possess the remnants of youth and our health, unless you count Morgen's asthma, which is under control.

The words I speak come from terror and ignorance, the first sparked by my dream of loss, the sudden dawning that to lose Morgen is to lose everything. As for the profundity of my delusion – well, that's harder to explain. As I deliberately mutilate the life I cherish, I somehow imagine I am acting for the best, a conjoined twin hacking at the throat of the person who shares her body.

No wonder Morgen stays silent. I have cut my darling's windpipe. On I go, talking nonsense about feeling stifled and needing space. Finally, I falter, and after a pause, Morgen responds.

'Do you love me, Dory?'

Again, the only answer required is an emphatic Yes. *Once more, that isn't what comes out. The phrases might be benign in other contexts, but in this situation, they are toxic:* respect, admiration, affection. *Pushed to explain, I produce another skewer – or maybe I'm a knife-thrower, except that Morgen, not I, wears the blindfold.*

'Sometimes you seem so... needy. Clingy, even.'

'Is there someone else?'

No, apart from occasional fantasies about other universes, different paths taken or yet to pursue. Simply put, I'm still refusing to accept the limits of the dream house, that options close as you get older. It would have been better for me to try to express this idea, disjointed as it is, but of course I keep slashing and stabbing and slicing, wielding whatever weapon comes to hand.

'There has only really ever been you, Morgen,' I insist, but then I keep going. 'And João, of course, but that relationship wasn't like ours. It would never have sustained – so passionate.'

Morgen recoils and the space between us yawns.

The next years will be difficult. *The reflex to erase painful histories has left me with a bag of scraps from which to stitch together the narrative, but my sense-memory of the period endures intact. I become that space between us, hollow like a cave. The body that moulded itself to me, warmed me, comforted me, is cold and unyielding. The being that trusted me enough to lower every defence now bristles, green eyes narrowed, not the signature*

Morgen photoface, but taut with anguish. My darling – am I still allowed to use this endearment? – listens to 'Seven Nation Army' on a constant loop, as if the White Stripes can fend off thoughts of my betrayal.

In the immediate aftermath, we ride back to Lençóis, take two rooms assailed by the song of the water, the next morning drive to Salvador and then, I think – amnesia creates a gap here – separate, Morgen to São Paulo, me to TIME's New York offices. On my return to London, I move out of our home, sleeping, not that I sleep, on Angela's sofa, not that she answers to Angela. Once shot of her disgusting husband, she embarked on a process she terms 'deinvention', retrieving her birth name, Ayotunde, and stripping back layers of conditioning to determine who she might be.

It isn't, she insists, that she rejects her beloved parents, who fought a legal case before they could take custody of her. (The authorities, happy enough to approve a transracial adoption, had balked at placing a Christian baby with this sweet Jewish pair.) What concerns Ayotunde is the extent to which she was brought up to deny difference. We don't see colour, her father would say, and like a person with achromatopsia, neither did she, merely fifty shades of grey. She can't be sure how her Blackness – a word she now capitalises – has impacted her life, just knows that it will have done so, in manifold and subtle ways as well as more obvious ones. 'I'm not doing this for me, you know,' she insists, glancing at her daughter, who in that instant looks up and smiles.

If I expected sympathy, I'm disappointed. Ayotunde is annoyed at me for cluttering up her small flat, and, I suspect, feels greater loyalty to Morgen. Everyone has always liked Morgen more than me – Mum, my uncle, our friends. Certainly Ayotunde blames me for the split, and who am I to disagree? But something else is going on, too. She keeps picking over our distant past, uncovering ways in which I let her down.

'Do you remember at the Shit?' she asks, our nickname for the Ship, the hotel that employed us in its laundry room. 'You wanted us to organise a strike.'

I do remember, except that our memories are not the same.

'You have no idea,' she continues. 'Even now, you have no idea.'

'What?' I am genuinely bewildered.

'I shouldn't have to tell you that the consequences could have been worse for me.' Innocence is no defence. 'When are you going to do the work, Dory?' she demands, and for a moment I think I've left my dirty mug on the floor.

A month of Ayotunde's hospitality is more than enough for both of us. Morgen agrees to my return. At home, everything has changed, and nothing is different. *Mornings I get up before dawn, creep downstairs, avoiding the creaking treads, bring Morgen tea as and when requested. We maintain the outward appearance of togetherness, dinners and walks with friends, the occasional red carpet or private view. Mostly we avoid serious conversations, less frequently force ourselves to address the future. Divorce has been discussed, and at least for the time being set aside, but we are far from recovered. Our silences, once companionable, suck the air out of the room. I notice that Morgen is wheezing more than usual, asthma aggravated by stress, or so I assume.*

Time heals some of these conditions and worsens others.
It will be another year until Morgen is diagnosed with sarcoidosis, perhaps twice that long until we begin to reckon our relationship as good as new. At some point, Morgen compares us to kintsugi, *stronger and more beautiful for our mending.*

But we are not a reconstituted pot, though the distance between us has narrowed to a series of hairline fractures. We survive, but we are not the same. Once something happens, it repeats to infinity or until memories of the event die with its participants and witnesses. The terrible thing I did will always be lodged in our past, indelible as blockchain, Morgen pierced through the heart, a butterfly on a corkboard.

Except that isn't true either. Because what happens in the future counts too. Though I imagine the remaining space between us to be unbridgeable, Morgen and I are about discover that no gulf, whether physical or temporal, can part us. The thread that binds our souls may stretch dangerously tight, but it never snaps.

Dory found it tough to sit still unless immersed in writing, the only reliable method of telescoping time available to non-scientists. Otherwise she controlled her restlessness by venting energy in the gym, something she had made herself do at least twice a week since the virus nobbled her.

Like fate, the disease had waited to strike until she began to imagine herself invincible. So much exposure to the damn thing she survived, first when Morgen contracted it, then in other settings and circumstances, always without succumbing – until she did.

She really should have twigged that something was wrong. For two nights she slept long and soundly, though without the benefit of waking refreshed. On the third day, even before she opened her eyes, she knew.

'You got me,' she said. Nobody else was there to hear her, Morgen by now consigned to a rented hospital-style bed in their room and Dory on a fold-out sofa in what had been her study. *Fucksticks*. She would have to self-isolate, shutting herself away just as the world made another false start at reopening. The logistics, with Morgen ever more reliant on her care, appeared daunting. She made herself get up, returned the sofa to its daylight form, then lay on it while she rang the care agency and friends.

The magnitude of support the calls unlocked astonished her. Every single day Ayotunde brought containers of home-cooked food. An American writer living in London, though herself clinically vulnerable, delivered idiosyncratic selections of groceries, Gatorade and Hershey's and a plush toy shaped like a lobster. She herself had only just recovered, the writer reasoned, so was probably immune for the time being. Morgen's brother, noting Dory's shallow breathing on a Zoom call, insisted on driving her to hospital, lingering outside until Dory texted confirmation that she'd been admitted.

By then Dory's heart had run down like an analogue watch, its ticking irregular and slow. As she lay on a trolley, she remembered Morgen in a similar position, still in Resus awaiting assessment but already deprived of agency and fettered to machines. There the parallels ended. Morgen fell sick before anybody could have guessed at the cause, much less vaccinated against it. Dory's recovery took little more than a month and, to the untrained eye, appeared complete. Few would guess at the rich legacy the incubus gifted her in joint pains, rashes and a heart that continued to dawdle.

Medicine either lacked solutions for these problems or the instinct to provide them, its practitioners bleary with exhaustion and so acclimated to triage that a woman of Dory's years would never be a priority. The specialists may have worn poker faces, but their constant invocation of the phrase *wear and tear* was an obvious tell. At first Dory pushed back. Her current health problems postdated the infection, her blood levels and inflammatory markers all over the place.

Eventually she stopped chasing answers from clinicians, enrolling instead at her local gym. Endorfit was a place of permanent night, pumping music and burly regulars who trailed talcum clouds or grunted like cavemen as they threw dumbbells to the floor. The fierce exercise programme would either kill her or make her stronger, either outcome fine by Dory.

Watching Doctor Roweena, she reflected how easily people with bodies that obey them take their luck for granted. She had counted among their number until the virus catapulted her to the future, one day young for her age, the next as ancient as the hills. How had she nursed Dad, observed Morgen struggle for air, and not seen reflected in their battles a time when she too would need help?

Not that she had yet reached that moment. The hours at Endorfit paid dividends, and she remained resolved to keep up her regimen no matter the external calls on her time. Even here, in these cramped quarters and at the compound, she started her day with a stretching and strengthening routine, to Elo's derision. In his view, the only exercise worth doing was a high-tech exercise in living longer. Their first exchange on the subject helped explain why the disappearance of the machine had hit him so hard.

They had been on the terrace closest to the creek, Dory on the flagstones, head cupped in hands, mid-crunch, him pacing, his shadow falling across her like a blanket, only to be ripped away. The waters drowned some of his rant, but she got the gist. It wasn't only that they were potentially stuck here for ever, but that they were stuck here at all. The longer the interruption to his life-extension programme, the greater the risk to his progress in turning back the clocks. It was imperative that he depart the future present for the present-day present without further delay.

Since quests for immortality are driven by fear as well as ego, Dory had tried to be kind, focusing on the ambition rather than the person. 'And if science conquers death? The global population already exceeds this planet's ability to sustain life, including its own.'

'I'm working on that,' he said.

'Hmmm.' Again she made an effort to connect rather than challenge. 'But look at what's happening right now. *A Handmaid's Tale* has become a manual for populists. Add eternal life to the mix, and—'

'Your problem is solved.' Elo looked pleased with himself. 'At a stroke. No more pressure to breed.'

'Maybe, but the war on reproductive rights will just shift to new ground,' she said, 'only a privileged few permitted to have the right kinds of babies. Also, do you really expect most of us to be given access to life-extension technologies? The only people who would live for ever…'

As she tailed off, Elo finished her sentence, '…would be people like me,' he said.

'And despots. Death is a terrible thing, but it redistributes money and power in useful ways, if not well enough.'

He was grinning. My, what big teeth he had. 'Such a Holy Joe you are, Dorian. Putting my body at the service of science isn't without risks, you know, and everything we discover, every significant piece of learning, we pass to Johns Hopkins. But never mind that. Riddle me this: what's the difference, ethically speaking, between me putting in the hours to live longer and you busting a gut to keep the sainted Morgen alive?'

'That's completely different!'

Her vehemence had surprised both of them, and for once he let a subject drop. She continued to fume. How could she have been so foolish as to confide in him about Morgen's struggles? It was like pointing out a bird's nest to a passing wolf.

Fortified by a breakfast of Weetabix, Elo submitted to another round of Doctor Roweena's interrogation. Dory struggled to concentrate. They hadn't left the suite for, what, thirty-six hours? He was fielding questions on what his inquisitor called *crustacea* and he termed *focking big lobsters*. As he proceeded to the next part of his story, the Doctor flinched. Her movement, though small, triggered a response from her chair, which raised itself and her, swivelled and then retreated to its original position.

Elo responded by picking up his pace. It was startling, the way he did this, as wordy and discursive as usual, but the content delivered faster – a reflex that helped him dominate media interviews. In the round triggered by the announcement of his memoir, he had talked about his addiction to audiobooks. Knowledge is power and audiobooks meant he could devour non-fiction at triple speed while engaged in physical activity, exercising or, God help us, *bonking*. (The term appeared in a tabloid article, the detail provided by his last-but-one wife.) Elo could speak at triple speed too.

He resumed his narrative where he'd left off, in the time machine with Professor Zachary on the back of a lobster in the middle of a sea. As another of the creatures bore down on them, claws wider than the jaws of a great white, the pod took flight. Elo couldn't be sure, but thought the evasive manoeuvre was probably the machine's own initiative. The Professor, scrabbling with the controls, lurched with the motion, no opportunity to brace, his mouth a perfect O.

After that came colours, sounds, flavours, a pull like a riptide or a giant magnet, then a nothingness more monstrous than any mutant crayfish, and finally a washing to and fro, as if they yet rested on water.

This, too, stilled. Now Elo and the Professor found themselves under attack from above, in the teeth of an almighty hailstorm, chunks of ice large enough to inflict bruises and smaller pieces pirouetting and bouncing on impact. The machine had touched down on a lawn fringed with tall palms and rhododendrons, their blossoms cowed by the onslaught or ripped from their stems. A presence loomed over the treeline, headdress and beard striped with gold. Elo saw that it was a sphinx, rearing like an angry lobster, its wings spread wide, not in welcome but warning.

Though his assessment of the surroundings lasted no more than a second or two, the weather took even less time to effect a transformation. The hand Elo raised to protect his lenses from the downpour stayed aloft to ward off daggers of sunlight. Brightness poured through new wounds in brown clouds, turning ice to diamonds. Butterflies, large but not abnormally so, returned to the blueing skies and a hare bounded across the glistening grass.

The time machine's passengers heard voices before they spotted their source. As three or four figures rounded the statue, the Professor made a sound like a shellfish hitting boiling water, part scream, part hiss, scrambled to his feet and jumped out of the pod. Elo barely had time to register his anguish or the matching terror on the identical face staring back at them before a fireball enveloped almost everything, machine, Professor and companions, statue, trees, rhododendrons and lawn. Only the hare and the butterflies carried on seemingly unaffected, and then the flames disappeared, leaving neither trace nor trail, but for a shimmer where seconds earlier the Professor and his twin had stood.

'Touch nothing,' said Doctor Roweena. 'All that we asked was that you touch nothing.' Elo sat on a corner of the bed, elbows on knees and head bent forward so they couldn't see his face. His voice sounded muffled.

'The machine acted by itself. You know it has a mind of its own.'

'Indeed,' said the Doctor. 'That's why it demands respect.'

Dory had to ask something. 'I think I understand,' she began, then stopped, realising that wasn't true. 'No, sorry, I don't understand anything, but am I right to assume that Elo saw the Professor meet himself?'

When the Doctor nodded in the affirmative, a tear finished its journey to her chin and hung there. She ignored it. 'What happened next?' she prompted Elo.

'How many bleeding times?' he sighed, but kept going, and there really wasn't much left to relate – just a brief account of a second, convulsive launch, the pod again acting without instruction, and the return to Tantalus.

'A plausible tale.'

'Because it's the truth.'

'Mr Ó hAllmhuráin, nobody should be surprised by your mendacity, least of all those of us who still suffer its consequences.' The Doctor paused. 'Your story is threadbare.'

Dory wouldn't have believed Elo capable of blushing if she hadn't witnessed it, or perhaps it was anger rather than guilt that blotched his neck and burned scarlet on his cheeks, a second set of eyes.

'You think I'd invent Giant. Focking. Lobsters? Cop on to yerself.'

'Nobody doubts those details. It is your sin of omission that troubles.' The Doctor sounded, Dory noted, not so much angry as sad. 'Would you describe the following as an accurate summation? Zachary encountered himself, vanished and the ship took flight?'

'Dead on,' said Elo.

'Then why, Mr Ó hAllmhuráin, were you sitting at the controls when I entered the laboratory?'

10:00

*S*oaps represent the world as it could be if no bad deed went unpunished, no betrayal concealed. *To lie in soapland is to create a butterfly effect that plays out across multiple storylines.*

Scene: the modest lounge of a brick-built house in a close of brick-built houses. A woman enters. If viewers do not already suspect that something is afoot, the disparity in styles alerts them. She is vivid, unlike the room and its occupant, an older man in a cardigan. Her hair blazes bright as her lips; her hoop earrings are large enough to serve as perches for hummingbirds. She dusts and tidies – anything to avoid looking the man in the eye. Plumping a cushion, she dislodges a feather which, in landing, sends a sleepy fly careening into the air. There it performs a loop-the-loop and plops into the man's tea.

'Botheration,' he says, or perhaps he uses an earthier vernacular.

This is just the excuse the woman needs. She takes his cup and goes to make a fresh brew, only to witness, from the kitchen window, two further characters locked in intense conversation. She shakes her head, remembering where and when she last saw them. She had been creeping out of a hotel, managed to hide before they spotted her. They too looked furtive.

Many episodes will pass before the significance of these sightings is revealed. In the mean time, the woman has spun an elaborate series of lies to protect her own secret, each falsehood compounding her original sin until her cover-up demands a cover-up. She has realised, too, that her fellow characters are responsible for a crime – arson or murder. Serious stuff, yet if she were to blow the whistle, her tapestry of deceit would unravel.

Because this is soapland, everything is bound to emerge anyway, no matter what she or other people do. The die is cast. Her universe will crumble. The miscreants will go to jail. Lying doesn't pay. Except, of course, that, in the real world, it does.

Mum enjoyed these programmes and, in her later years, we watched them together. *They allowed us to swerve the minefields of conversation. They enabled us to maintain a slough of lies.*

We lied to each other, Mum and I. Both of us pretended to look forward to my visits. I also fooled myself into believing that they represented a clear-cut exercise in filial duty, no love involved. After she died, I understood that this too might be a lie. Apparently you can miss someone whose company you barely tolerated. Who knew?

Not that honesty would have improved our relationship. After a certain age, people don't adapt. You either rub along or you don't. We didn't. Sometimes I considered calling a halt to the charade, but Morgen was right that a breach would have been worse than the alternative. Lying paid off. Lying convincingly might have yielded greater profit, less friction, an illusion of family. Neither Mum nor I possessed that skill.

Perhaps you're tempted to counter my argument with examples of public figures who fell from grace when their lies were exposed. *These stories are catnip to the media,* Grimm's Fairy Tales *for the modern era. Think of my reporting on Curasis, or the fates of Elizabeth Holmes and Anna Sorokin. Yet there are many more examples that reinforce the value of lying. The vast majority cannot be cited here because the liars haven't been rumbled, nor will they ever be. For every Holmes and Sorokin, hundreds of fraudsters in the business world go undetected. Look at politics, and you'd need to add zeroes to that number, then quadruple it, and that's without including populists, who lie in plain sight and without shame, reaping rewards despite – or because – the public knows they are lying.*

Technology has created new ways to lie while complicating the act of lying. *At some point, playing about with Zoom, I activated a filter that makes me look fresher. I've never removed it, lying to myself as well as others. This is a face I can live with. Most of us perform similar deceptions on social media, curating the images we post, selecting our favourites, showing ourselves as we wish to be, rather than as we are.*

141

Tech conceals more than turkey necks. It is the fraudster's friend. Apps make it easy to clone email addresses and phone numbers; voice changers to take on different genders and identities. Right now, sitting at my computer, I could launch a phishing expedition, dispatching a flurry of emails that purport to come from a storied financial institution. Were you to call back on the numbers provided, one of my virtual employees (me, perhaps channelling Leslie Phillips) would deliver a sales pitch, nothing too high pressure, before pretending to transfer your call to another employee (me again, this time Doris Day), all to give you a false sense of the scale of the operation.

Like a novelist, I'd invent not only a cast of characters but the world they inhabit. Unlike a mere writer, I would bring them to life in multiple dimensions beyond the page. Each member of my digital boiler room would get a social-media account, interact with real-life humans, and festoon Fleet, Facebook, TwXtter and Instagram with photographs and film clips fashioned by AI. You no longer need to be a programmer to do any of these things, and with a little knowledge and a VPN, you'll be able to cover your tracks.

Cheating on a partner, by contrast, has never been more difficult, your options and actions circumscribed by technology. *London is the tenth most surveilled city on the planet, with 13.2 cameras per a thousand residents; facial recognition detects you seconds after you walk out of your front door. Mobiles function as tracking devices, so if you're up to no good, it's wise to leave yours at home, and maybe also buy a burner phone to avoid the perennial problem of intercepted messages. Of course, you'll then need a reliable hiding place for it. Even so, your partner might be suspicious about the frequency with which you forget your phone and your serenity when this happens. Many of us are welded to our mobiles and go into meltdown if deprived of them for as little as an hour or two.*

You could minimise these risks by delaying your assignation until your partner is away for the night. That doesn't mean you're safe from being rumbled. Most houses are full of connected devices, all of them potential grasses. 'Listen,' the dishwasher complains. 'I haven't been run today.' 'You think you've got problems,' the alarm system replies. 'She left me on for a full twenty-four hours and I'm tired.' In the corner, Alexa listens, records and for once keeps quiet.

'Do you love me, Dory?' Morgen asks me that night in Brazil. *As you know, I give a cruel answer. You probably assume that my cruelty is a symptom and function of truth-telling, brutal honesty, but you'd be wrong. Guilty people are cruel. Popular culture might depict cuckolds as avenging furies, but it's their unfaithful partners who behave as if they've been wronged. In pushing the injured party to retaliate, the adulterer establishes pretextual reasons for any derelictions.* Look how unreasonable they are.

So it is with me. Both my reply to Morgen and my confession to you in the previous chapter of this book are defined by evasion and half-truths – and half a truth is no truth at all.

I do love Morgen. It is a sudden vision of life without Morgen that prompts me to precipitate a severing, the thing I fear most. That doesn't mean I am loving towards Morgen in the moment of giving my answer. Relationships are complicated beasts. As I say, the more you hurt someone, the greater your desire to hurt them. Heaven has no rage like love to hatred turned, but the fury of a woman scorned is as nothing to the white-hot fury of guilt. I itch to punish Morgen for my sins.

'Is there someone else?' Morgen wants to know. No, I insist. *A game-show buzzer sounds.* Wack-wack-oops. *Incorrect!*

My mistake isn't to lie, but to lie badly, viciously, stupidly.

A week before this conversation, I did meet up with João, for one evening. Out of curiosity, nothing more. A terrible idea. I imagined reconnecting with him would exorcise demons. Instead, it raised more. They plague me still.

'**M** r Ó hAllmhuráin? We're waiting.' Elo had frozen, his desire for flight overwhelming his usual urge to fight.

Dory broke the silence with another question. She needed clarity. At the outset of this strange journey, she had assumed Elo to be criminally reckless in the way of many tycoons, their products and services faulty, their data-gathering dangerous, their contributions to climate change oversized, their wealth obscene. If pushed, she would have guessed Elo responsible for industrial quantities of global misery and, indirectly, more than a few deaths. Hatred is a virus that leaps from one host to another, and on his watch Fleet had become the preferred platform for extremists, a gateway to radicalisation for many, including its new owner.

Her assessments hadn't changed, but people are easier to dislike in the abstract (another reason Fleet so effectively incubates hostility). Proximity had forced her to see him as a person – flawed but human. Now this.

'Doctor Roweena.'

'Yes, Ms Szary?'

Briefly Dory let herself be diverted. Szary had been her dad's name before he came to England.

'Silver. Dory Silver. Anyway, when I travelled in the pod—'

'The pod?'

'Your time machine.'

'The ship.'

'The ship,' Dory confirmed. 'There was turbulence. Is it theoretically possible that on take-off—'

'Launch.'

'…on launch, the turbulence might propel one person from the ship and another into the – I'm sorry, I don't know what you call the big chair.'

'The cockpit seat.'

'…into the cockpit seat? Could that have happened?'

'Let us hear from Mr Ó hAllmhuráin,' said the Doctor. 'If he isn't ready to tell us today, we have tomorrow and tomorrow and tomorrow.'

In the end, it took Elo another twenty-four hours to revise his story to the Doctor's satisfaction. When he finished, it turned out that Roweena was aware of the outlines already. After all, the ship kept detailed logs. It could even replay the scene, and unfortunately for her, had done so, the imagery searing into her memory. The footage had a habit of spooling across her inner eyelids several times a day, its edges ragged like an old home movie.

The assault it showed and to which Elo had finally admitted matched the other data from the ship, but that didn't mean the Doctor could close her file on the case. Elo confirmed what had happened, not why. Whilst quite a few of the science-fiction books, films and TV series of the twenty-first century featured brain scanners, the devices, like many other tropes of the genre, could never exist in the form such primitive societies imagined them. Human minds resist being read, even by their owners. The only text to anticipate the real science of brain-scanning was a play called *Danton's Death* written almost two hundred years before the Doctor and the Professor arrived at Tantalus. 'Know one another?' its titular hero says to his plaintive lover. 'We'd have to smash open our skulls and extract our thoughts by their tails.' The Doctor had helped to develop a clinical method very much along those lines, but it was messy.

For now, she and the authorities she represented would make do with a telling of events stripped of key insights and therefore of some of their meaning. Naturally this rankled, since any death is a tragedy, but a meaningless one all the more so.

In the version of the story synthesised from Roweena's own experiences, data from the ship, including the film, and Elo's mutable confession, the Professor had not left the machine of his own accord, nor was the force that ejected him the buffeting of spacetime. Indeed, the machine remained stationary throughout the incident.

As the weather calmed, the Professor had become agitated. 'Mr Ó hAllmhuráin,' he said, detaching the control panel, 'I remember this storm and fear that the ship has returned us to a time just ahead of the point of departure, rather than after it. We must leave immediately.'

Elo either failed to understand him or pretended not to. It was he, not the Professor, who clambered over the edge of the pod to stand on the lawn, declaiming 'Take me to your leader!' and laughing at his own wit.

'No,' the Professor replied, and within seconds Elo's humour drained, and they were tussling – verbally at first. This was a time zone that interested Elo, its civilisation capable of producing the miraculous machine and who knew which other transformative technologies. He was eager to discover everything he could, carry that monetisable knowledge back to his own era. The Professor ignored his explanation, feverishly programming a new flight path as he spoke.

'Take your seat. The machine is ready to depart.'

Instead of complying, Elo leant in to give the Professor what appeared to be a bear hug, then lifted him from his perch and slung him over his shoulder. The control, dislodged from the Professor's grasp, landed next to the pod and Elo, back straight despite his burden (all those hours of exercise), bent his knees to retrieve it, stowing it in a trouser pocket.

It was at this point that the Professor began struggling in earnest, kicking and flailing until he wrestled himself from Elo's grip. As he plummeted headfirst to the ground, a trio, two humans and a Mekon, emerged from behind the statue, not sauntering as described in Elo's earlier iterations of the story, but running. Elo moved fast too, leaping into the pod. He recognised the first of the humans to reach the Professor, and in her wake another familiar figure. Even before the world turned to flaming, sodium orange, Elo had jammed the control into its socket exactly as he'd seen the Professor do, hitting and haranguing it – *eejit* – as the Professor had not. No matter. The machine sprang into tumultuous life and next thing he knew, Elo sat in his laboratory fielding questions from his staff and the woman he'd only just left behind, at a date some half a millennium into the future.

That night Dory didn't speak to Elo. This wasn't a deliberate policy. She hadn't sent him to Coventry, or any other English city. She simply didn't know what to say. Words, her support and staple, deserted her. Nor did he try to initiate conversation. They ate dinner silently, approaching breakfast the next morning with the same Trappist concentration, but for a sudden pained observation from Elo: he'd forgotten that Pop-Tarts attain temperatures *hotter than the earth's core*.

Though the Doctor had wrapped up the previous day early, visibly exhausted from reliving the Professor's death, she began the new session by worrying at the same events, her line of interrogation focused on Elo's decision to hoist the Professor from the machine. His answer – that he couldn't think how else to override the Professor's objections – seemed credible. After all, Elo responded aggressively to anyone who stood in his way. Professor Zachary had refused to act as his tour guide. Elo insisted that he meant to set the Professor free once far enough from the machine to thwart an immediate retreat. This too struck Dory as plausible until Doctor Roweena raised a fresh concern. If Elo acted without premeditation, how had he managed to produce such a carefully constructed pack of lies on his return to Tantalus?

Time travel is disorienting, and Elo by this stage had endured four temporal leaps in rapid succession, from the laboratory to the empty banks of San Francisco Bay, thence to the sea of lobsters and onwards, if backwards, to the lawn, only to make a final journey to arrive at the beginning, albeit plus the few rontoseconds necessary to avoid the Professor's fate. Elo's synapses should have been fried. Yet when HOG, the WEEN team and the Doctor crowded around the machine, firing questions at him, he gave them, without hesitation and in much detail, the false story that he had maintained until yesterday.

'What can I say?' he replied to the Doctor now. 'I've kissed the Blarney Stone.' (This, at least was true. Dory remembered the news footage, part of the circus that always accompanied one of his occasional trips to his homeland.)

'We do not believe you, Mr Ó hAllmhuráin.' The Doctor's voice was flat.

'Who's *we*, Roweena?' he demanded, but she ignored him.

'You planned to take control of the ship one way or another,' she said. 'Your intentions were malevolent.'

'No,' he replied, oddly serene.

'You planned to abandon Zachary rather than killing him, though to abandon a passenger in another time is to inflict a kind of death.'

'No,' he repeated.

'You planned to plunder not only the ship but whatever else of value you could find.'

'No,' he said, 'not plunder. Find. Develop. Share. Make the world a better place.'

'Your world, Mr Ó hAllmhuráin.'

'My world,' he agreed. 'And I make no apology for that. Why would anybody worry about a notional race or civilisation of the distant future when so much needs fixing right now?'

'We are not notional, Mr Ó hAllmhuráin.'

'You are to me.'

Something shifted in Dory as she listened. Until this moment, she had read the Doctor as a truth-teller to Elo's dissembler. Suddenly she wondered if each might be as self-interested as the other. Did the Doctor really care about the well-being of long-dead races and civilisations except inasmuch as their actions rippled through timespace? Dory couldn't recall any mention of responsibility to the past in the Doctor's explanation of her work of a bioethical historicist.

That thought prompted Dory to wonder at her own behaviour. Docile, she had been these past days, trusting even, utterly unlike herself. How could she have failed to challenge her own imprisonment, demanded to know how long and to what ultimate purpose she was being held? These people had no argument with her. Why had she not insisted they take her home to Morgen?

Elo was speaking, but she cut across him.

'I can't do this any more,' she said. 'I need a walk, I need to be on my own, I need to be in my own time. I need,' she finished, 'to know what the hell is going on and why you're holding us captive.'

'This is not,' the Doctor replied, 'captivity. Rather, like the first part of your stay, it is quarantine. I appreciate that the difference might appear semantic.'

'Quarantine?' Surprise inflected Dory's final syllable. 'If we're contagious, aren't you in danger?'

'All known incubation periods have elapsed. The contagion we must continue to contain carries a different set of risks,' said the Doctor. Noting Dory's puzzlement, she added a clarification. 'Ideas spread. The price of social cohesion is control. This is the work of the Chancellery.'

'You must be joking!' Dory exclaimed.

Elo, in a departure from his usual style, responded with a single syllable: 'Twats.'

'What possible threat could we pose to your social order?' Dory demanded.

'That is a complicated question. I shall be happy to explain at length over time.'

'Time is what I don't have. Somebody at home needs me urgently.'

'I'm sorry, Ms Szary. You can't go home.'

Before the Doctor finished speaking, Dory and Elo were on their feet, shouting at her and each other, whilst a wall dissolved to admit a half-dozen squaddies.

11:00

*I*t takes me half an hour to work out the ways in which João has changed. *Most are obvious. He has become a grey man – grey at the temples, grey suited, probably expensively. He's still handsome, stockier than I remember but jawline firm and forehead smooth as if few thoughts trouble him. He wears glasses, wire-framed, the kind that survive being sat on. The most significant difference eludes me until he grins. His teeth, younger than he is, are blindingly bright.*

He has remained in Minas Gerais, but for an interlude in Brasilia, where he advised the President on improving the mental health of the nation's physicians. After her impeachment, he returned to Belo Horizonte and an academic job. He hasn't worked as a doctor for years. I smile when he says this. 'Do you remember,' I ask, 'how it bothered you, the English phrase to practise medicine? *A trained doctor has no need of practice, you said.'*

This is when he flashes those teeth. 'Six years I studied, more than 7,200 hours on placements, and your colegas *made it sound like a bar job.'*

He wasn't wrong. They enjoyed teasing him, my friends, and there had been an edge to their antics. 'Such a pretty boy,' one commented later, 'but so earnest.' The misunderstanding was less of language than culture, though my Portuguese was better than his English. Our gang put a lot of effort into appearing effortless, plus we mistrusted the adult world and felt no compulsion to join it. He never got our humour either. That was why my comment about the cheese sandwich riled him so badly.

If João and I hadn't split, who knows whether I'd have fallen into journalism, and I certainly wouldn't have found Morgen. In the early days of aftermath, ignorant of these blessings to come, I of course dreamt up parallel universes with João. My imagination never filled in the blanks about how I'd have spent my time while he doctored beyond vague ideas of writing novels (an undertaking that surely demands filling in blanks).

It has taken until this moment, decades into separate lives, for reality to bite, veneers whiter than João's. His arm rests next to mine on the counter, close enough to sense its warmth. We order drinks, a second caipirinha for me, mineral water for him. Around us, the other customers laugh and gossip, most too young to worry about options closing or even to suspect that they might. The din forces João and me to lean in to hear each other.

Not that we say anything of consequence. Our conversation is polite. I pose none of the questions that suddenly assail me, do not ask if he thinks we might have survived marriage and children, or still believes that, in severing our bonds with surgical precision, he spared us a worse breach at a later date. Another vision is bleaker still: the two of us locked into the long, slow, living death of making do.

Once I met Morgen I rarely thought about João. If a key interviewee weren't based in João's hometown, and if social media – in João's case, LinkedIn – didn't make it ridiculously easy to dig up the past, I wouldn't be here at all. Morgen is my love. What harm can come from looking up an ex?

Weirdly, it's that sort of thinking that causes the problem. Another cocktail and I'm comparing Morgen to João as if this were a livestock competition. Since you ask, Morgen triumphs in every particular. João has a decent brain, the kind that retains technical knowledge, but he is often obtuse and always literal. Morgen, by contrast, is perceptive, intuitive, wildly imaginative. Add to that a fundamental sweetness of character and you have in Morgen one of the best people on the planet. Also one of the funniest. Morgen could have done stand-up.

They are both head-turners – or were, though Morgen doesn't just draw the eye but hold it. Despite the terrible things I will soon blurt out in Chapada Diamantina, it is Morgen, not João, who is my lodestone for passion. Yes, João and I used to have chemistry, our energies untrammelled by age. Perhaps an inkling that we wouldn't last the distance added to the intensity. But a greater physical connection? Absolutely not. Of this I am certain. So why do I test the proposition?

In case you wonder, it is nothing more than a kiss; nothing less than one either. What happens seems inevitable, though this is choice, not fate. While the fourth caipirinha blurs my vision, erasing the few lines time has incised into João's face, this just makes our encounter messier.

I mean, for god's sake, I stumble when I stand, my skin is slick with heat and alcohol sweat, my tongue furred.

Nor are his moves graceful. Perhaps he is stilted by a lack of drink rather than its excess. In his eagerness to avoid being seen, he makes himself conspicuous, scanning the street like a cartoon villain ensuring that the coast is clear. Satisfied, he pushes me against the nearest wall, thrusts his groin against mine. It occurs to me that he has done this before, maybe at this exact spot. He chose the bar, which is neither convenient for my hotel nor his place of work, but I'm guessing that the youth of its clientele offer some protection from accidental discovery. His children have already left Belo Horizonte for the lights of Rio and São Paulo, and this isn't the sort of establishment his students are likely to frequent.

When we kiss, I feel nothing. No, let me rephrase that. His kiss sparks no excitement. Rather it reminds me of a teenaged effort, a slimy exploration of my oral cavity. I do feel quite a lot, none of it pleasant. His erection presses against my lower abdomen, reminding me that I should have used the loo before we ventured outside. His belt buckle adds to the pressure. There's something pushing into me from the other side, a sharp-edged stone embedded in the concrete, though it could be a finger, jabbing me in the back to demand what in hell I think I'm doing.

Whatever it is brings me to my senses. I wriggle out of his hold, say, 'This is mistake, but it was nice to see you,' start looking around for escape routes. Maybe I can find a cab.

Except that isn't what I do. I return the dental kiss, otherwise remaining passive. He has already unzipped himself and painfully works his whole hand past various barriers before I call a halt. Not that he responds other than to do something with his fingers he presumably deludes himself will change my mind. Soon I'm struggling, and more of those fingers are around my neck. For a second or two, I think he will win because he has three hands, except that the third is his penis, slapping me with as much effect as a truncheon wielded by a toddler. I stop trying to detach his hands and grab the truncheon.

'Just stop,' I say, adding idiotically, 'or I'll hurt you.'

'Você é uma puta,' he replies, but lets go, rearranges his clothing and walks off without a backwards glance.

T heir captors rehoused them in separate quarters of the Chancellery, and if Elo faced further questioning, Dory wasn't summoned to witness the proceedings. Her new accommodation at least gave her a glimpse of the world outside, though the building's height and soundproofing rendered the scenes dreamlike. She watched vehicles move silently over the cobbles, three-wheelers and articulated conveyances that rippled like caterpillars. Horses clopped noiselessly past; wagons made no sound as they jolted across the rutted surface. People walked and ran, talked and called across the street to each other in mute animation. A crocodile of children chattered away inaudibly until a wordless command from their teacher brought them to a respectful halt.

This last phenomenon might be more than a function of a window fashioned from the same material that doused the decibels of the creek back at the compound. During a testy visit on the first day of Dory's solitary confinement, Doctor Roweena revealed that the Trochilians, *Persona trochilianis*, the subspecies Elo called Mekons and Dory dubbed Apostles, generally communicated by telepathy, although also able to speak. Indeed, they were natural linguists because their non-verbal exchanges consisted of shapes and feelings constant from one language to the next. This, and an immunity to many of the diseases afflicting other branches of humanity, made them natural guardians, instantly alive to the basic needs of anyone under their watch.

The *Persona sapiens* line, though it had also evolved since Dory's time, depended on cortical implants to interact with visitors. The translations these devices produced, the Doctor admitted, were far from perfect. She preferred to rely on the English she had learnt ahead of her arrival in Nevada and augmented during her incarceration at Tantalus. The problem with most assistive technologies, she said, was a dearth of datasets, any inputs limited to information extracted from surviving artefacts and the academic research of scholars like her.

'What do you think of the food we provide?' she asked suddenly.

'Not terrible,' said Dory, reworking her dad's phrase, 'and not too little of it.'

'But is it an accurate representation of the meals you might expect in your own time?'

'Not really.'

The Doctor sighed. 'So much knowledge lost for ever.' Then she reached for Dory's hand. 'I understand that you don't want to be here, but really you are fortunate in ways you cannot yet imagine.'

'Try me,' said Dory.

'You will learn in due course. Assimilation is a process that cannot be hurried without significant psychic risks.'

'Oh for fuck's sake!' Dory erupted with rage, then found herself silenced by the same emotion. She detached herself from the Doctor's grip, breathed deep, tried again. 'Time is what I don't have. Nothing you say alters the basic facts. You're holding me here against my will, however much you try to dress up your actions as concern, and...' She interrupted herself. 'What is this country called, by the way?'

'The concept of countries did not endure, Ms Szary. History showed it to be a root cause of many conflicts. We are the Guerglas.'

'Whatever. And my name is Silver.' Dory waved as if batting away a mosquito. In another life, she'd have pushed for for more information. Right now, though, she was consumed with the urgency of her mission. 'Please understand,' she continued. 'I pose not the slightest danger to you and yours. I will sign anything, do anything to prove it. Cut out my tongue, wipe my memory. I have to get home. Do you understand? I. Have. To. Get. Home.'

'Ms Silver – as you prefer,' the Doctor replied, 'without memories there is no home.'

She left Dory to stew on the observation. This Dory refused to do. The Doctor seemed to think Dory's sanity would be threatened if she ingested too much information too quickly, but it was the slow drip-drip that was driving Dory mad. Also, she had already confronted the cruellest reality of all. No matter how advanced the science or brilliant the clinicians she found or funded, the old

Morgen would never return. That home was for ever barred. She had known this since the day she and Elo searched for the pod.

Yet love conquers all. Those of you lucky enough to love and be loved will understand the meaning of Virgil's dictum. He wasn't suggesting that love protects its subjects from harm or death, however hard it tries – and believe me, love explores every avenue, even those signposted *HOPELESS*, *SILLY* and *DELUDED*. Whatever steps you take, the worst you can imagine will happen, and that is when love discovers its superpower: to endure the worst and keep going. Dory loved Morgen, now and always, in every incarnation, whether near or far, vibrant or fading or a little more than a shape under a sheet, there and not there.

So yes, the Doctor hadn't been wrong. Love – or to call it by its other name, home – consists of memories, including those in process or still to be made, yet it is also more than that. Dory remembered a film clip of a patient with advanced Alzheimer's, a former prima ballerina tiny as a hummingbird, listening to the finale from *Swan Lake*. As the music swelled, her arms lifted and extended, then folded together like wings, the choreography stored not in her brain but her body. Love is exactly like that. It changes us at cellular level, becomes as much a part of who we are as any genetic coding.

So despair be damned. Dory refused to give in. She would keep busy – not easy under current circumstances, but not impossible either. To begin with, she paced her new quarters establishing and memorising the number of steps needed, toe to heel, to traverse the bedroom and bathroom in every direction gravity permitted. Then she performed the same exercise backwards, Ginger Rogers to an invisible Fred Astaire.

She was crossing the diagonal from shower to bidet in this way (five steps) when Doctor Roweena called out. Returning to the bedroom, she found her gaoler accompanied by a Trochilian.

'We have secured permission for you to take exercise as you requested,' the Doctor said, ignoring Dory's immediate and repeated query: *Permission from whom*? 'Bifron will guide you.'

Dory switched approach. 'What's to stop me from overpowering Bifron?'

The Doctor looked perplexed. 'Where would you go?'

Unlike the Trochilians at the compound, Bifron spoke to her, if only to determine their route. *You wish? Yes, no, better here.* Dory might have attempted a conversation were she not in the grips of sensory overload.

In this respect, the outing mirrored her first few hours in this future. Once again, the profusion of sights, sounds and smells overwhelmed her; so too the fact and presence of many living, moving things. As if this were not enough for her brain to sift, the experience resurfaced memories, a night to forget, the jagged pieces bobbing up like spars from a shipwreck.

Picture this: Dory primping for a party after months of lockdown. She half-heartedly styles her hair, changes out of her tracksuit bottoms. Now she arrives at the venue, the function room of a hotel bedecked with birthday banners, already crowded, the only familiar figures distant acquaintances or stars of stage, screen and the dispatch box. Good. 'Ignorance and incuriosity are the comfort of strangers,' as somebody once observed. She can't recall the source of the quote, but the evening confirms its accuracy. Nobody thinks to ask her about Morgen, nor does she volunteer information, responding to every *How are you?* with a cheery *Good, thanks* until a former *TIME* colleague turns up, embraces her – she rigid at the strangeness of human contact – and loudly declares, 'You must be in bits.' *Please,* she begs him, *don't talk about it. We're trying to keep this out of the papers.* She does not add: *and I'm hanging on by my fingernails.*

More spars. As the news ripples through the room – nothing spreads faster than a secret – guests recoil. The stink of mortality cannot be disguised, but Dory does make an effort. She puts on one of the funny wigs the organisers are distributing. *Ha ha! Be merry for tomorrow we will be merry!* Revellers contort with joy beneath their new multicoloured afros, braying and shrieking, grins like snarls. But then, a shushing – Birthday Boy is in the building, and everyone must hide, sardining into tiny spaces, all except Dory, frozen in the middle of the room.

In the nick of time, with the door squeaking open to admit him, she dives under the buffet table, right into a spillage of egg mayonnaise. No matter. She'd curl here for the rest of the night if allowed, but no such luck. They have reached the set-piece of such occasions, the grand reveal. She emerges from her lair as Birthday Boy clutches his heart, in surprise or pain, while fellow guests serenade him at the tops of unscarred lungs.

Happy birthday to you
Squashed tomatoes and stew
Your life's disappearing
And soon so will you.

Challenging as isolation was, Dory found the opening of prison gates tougher. While nobody was allowed to leave home except to work, shop or exercise (one period per day), Morgen's confinement within the bars of a hospital bed felt part of a shared normality. Everyone was in this together – the loss, the sacrifice. Who knew that politicians were already breaking the rules they themselves had set, carousing and splattering the richly wallpapered corridors of power with indigestible lies or hawking public-health contracts at bargain-basement prices.

These were days of innocence, a new Eden, the air sweet, bird-song in city centres. Time performed magic tricks, blurring and merging the days, conjuring nights that lasted for weeks. In the empty streets, foxes lost their fear, approaching humans for food or company. An entire family, russet-furred, took up residence in the strip of scrubby gardens behind Dory and Morgen's terraced house. The adults often patrolled the roadway out front too. Once Dory watched them successfully defend a discarded takeaway from marauding rats, dragging the box across the pavement, its cargo of jewelled rice leaving the sort of trail that in a fairytale leads to a happy ending.

There were, of course, precedents for the restrictions on public movement, good and bad, both in intent and execution. Opponents drew wild comparisons with some of the worst, the Warsaw ghetto, Léopoldville. Dory, if she had considered the historical parallels (which she did not), might have spotted similarities with Ancient Rome, whose senate sought to stem the burgeoning cult of Bacchus by banning gatherings of six or more. Where's the harm in a bit of fun? critics howled, but worship of the god had taken a dark turn, involving not only revelry but ritual slaughter.

So it was in the age of the plague, when to exhale irresponsibly might be to commit murder. Where the parallel faltered was in the outcome. Modern lockdowns, far from stamping out Bacchanalia, fostered their practice. The instant strictures lifted, people surged from their hiding places as if at a surprise party, drank for England, fought and frolicked. At dusk, silent in the shadowed house, Dory listened to the noises of the world leaving her and Morgen behind.

Now, as then, she shrank from the thing others embraced with such fervour. Bifron had steered her to a busy square. Curiosity helped to quell her nerves, but even so she found the clamour and press of crowds difficult to take, and gratefully acquiesced when Bifron gestured her to a seat at a café. A Trochilian server brought drinks without them ordering, an iridescent liquid, hot and sharp.

Humans as she knew them mingled with unfamiliar beings. She stole a glance at the next table, a group of four, chairs adjusted to accommodate their smaller stature, footrests extended and seats raised. Though heavy-set, their skin hung loose, faces folded like shar peis'. They laughed frequently, their eyes disappearing completely and wattles swinging.

Open-air restaurants and cafés clustered against the long wall of what might be a church. Arcaded buildings formed the remaining three sides of the plaza, walkways shaded and cool. Upper storeys, clad in reflective materials, angled sunlight away from each other and the people below.

'What's that?' Dory pointed at a black monolith dead centre of the space, the crowds, despite their numbers, giving it a reverent berth.

'Pancasila,' said Bifron, or that's what Dory heard.

The next day, Doctor Roweena attempted to canvass Dory's impressions of the city, but her captive dug in her heels. 'Why should I answer your questions if you won't return the courtesy?'

The Doctor smiled without warmth, recalling a counsellor Dory saw a few times before deciding therapy wasn't for her. 'You mistake caution for reticence, Ms Silver. But please do ask what you wish, and I will reply to the best of my ability.'

Dory longed to quiz the Doctor about the barriers to her departure, who ran this place, what future they planned for her. However, a skilled journalist never goes straight for the money shot, the revelation with the power to generate headlines or raise a profile piece to a work of literature. The trick is to lull your subject into confessional mode by starting with easy topics and edging crabwise towards your prize.

Though the technique worked for the majority of interviewees – a category Dory labelled Arthur Dents – certain personality types resisted this approach. Bond Villains, for example, liked to prove themselves cleverer than reporters by thwarting every line of inquiry. Their fatal flaw was a compulsion to show off. The interviewer simply had to bide her time, pretending to flounder until, swelled with self-regard, her targets began to boast. Tougher nuts to crack were the Jay Gatsbys, introverts except that the word means inward-lookers, and this sort of person prefers to avoid psychological probing, whether by others or themselves.

Dory was beginning to think the Doctor might be an amalgam of a Jay Gatsby and a Bond Villain. Originally she had found her sympathetic, assumed her honest, but recent events suggested the opposite qualities. In either case, Dory couldn't figure out what made her tick. This was hardly surprising. Dory had learnt to adjust her interview techniques and expectations from one country and culture to another. If she struggled to empathise with members of Moms for America or Brazilian gangsters, how should she connect with this woman from a remote spacetime? In the circumstances, Dory decided to approach the Doctor as an Arthur Dent, softballing and meandering, her initial questions about the Trochilians. She assumed this to be uncontroversial, but even here the Doctor proved tricksy.

'Can Bifron read my mind?'

'Reading and understanding are wholly distinct.'

'Does Bifron understand my thoughts?'

'Somewhat.'

'Say I did plan to escape: would Bifron alert you?'

'You seem to be working from the premise that Trochilians share their insights.'

'Don't they?'

'Everybody has secrets, Ms Silver, from themselves as well as others.'

'Is Bifron male or female?'

'No.'

Dory resisted diverting into a discussion of gender – such conversations tended to be blind alleys full of drunks – instead inquiring about the furrow-faced quartet in the square. When Dory referred to them as a race, the Doctor corrected her. *Persona fremens* was a subspecies of humankind, significantly different in biology to other branches.

'Are there many such subspecies?'

'A number.'

'Do subspecies intermarry?'

'Marriage is not a concept that endured.'

'Do subspecies interbreed?'

'Breeding does not take place as once it did.'

'Don't people have sex?'

'Naturally.'

'Naturally they do?'

'Naturally.'

'So how does breeding take place?' *And what would happen if I punched you on the nose?*

This last question, never vocalised, prompted a flicker at the corner of Dory's vision. All at once, Bifron stood between the two women.

'You look fatigued,' the Doctor said. 'We shall resume this conversation when you have rested.'

It would be more than a week until she saw Doctor Roweena again. In the meanwhile, Dory paced, stared across the cityscape or at the ceiling. Insomnia was reclaiming her nights. Only her expeditions with Bifron offered a distraction, but today she had waited in vain. Now she sat at the window, watching time leak away.

Sunset put on a show in this place, ripening like a nectarine until dusk consumed it in wolfish bites and the city subsided into darkness. Streetlamps targeted only roadways and pavements, nor did the buildings bleed light, no matter what took place inside them.

Tonight they surprised her. As the last traces of red disappeared from the sky, every structure came alive, pulsing like the pod or transformed by moving images, dancers and armies, Anansi and abstract shapes. This, at least, resolved a mystery for Dory, who had wondered about the glow that first alerted her to the city. Like many explanations it raised fresh questions, but she would gnaw at those tomorrow. The carnival of light provided the diversion she sorely needed, and here came another, the wall shimmering into air and behind it not a hostess trolley but a second shimmer: Bifron.

They descended in one of the crazy lifts – the sideways lurch startling her even though she had learnt to expect it – and exited into festive crowds. Behind them, the Chancellery showed its true colours, military camouflage travelling from dappled forest shades to marine blues, and onwards to the white and grey of ice, only to land in a desert of dirty beige, brown and olive. For a few blocks they went with the flow of merrymakers, then turned off the main drag, down cobbled passageways, some stepped. Their destination proved to be a restaurant occupying its own miniature square – or rather, triangle, the city wall forming its hypotenuse. This evening the wall functioned as a giant kinetic screen, sparking and flaming. Beams of gold illuminated a quartet of musicians playing an unfamiliar syncopation to diners in glad rags and glitter. It looked as if every outdoor table were occupied, but no, here was a prime spot, a reserved card positioned in the centre of crisp linen. The server – why were they always Trochilians? – brought drinks, perry, by the taste of it, and handed Dory a card emblazoned with the legend 'Tourist Menu'. *Entrées*, she read, *Main Courses*, *Side Dishes*, *Desserts*. Beneath each category, handwritten, were the same three words: 'Seasonal Greens. Vegan.'

'I guess I'll have the seasonal greens,' she said, raising her voice against swells of conversation and music and, in the distance, fireworks.

'Good choice, madam,' she, he or they replied.

161

The first two courses, though not unlike the food at the compound, bore hallmarks of fine dining, prettily arranged on plates. Portions were small, but only in keeping with the elegance of presentation. While their starter, a warm salad of stem broccoli or *cime di rape*, the dressing sweet and spicy, matched the menu's description, a main of fondant root vegetable with morels in a rich sauce with a swirl of almond paste strayed further from its billing. The dessert, *îles flottantes*, neither counted as green nor vegan, Dory thought.

'The meringue is made with aquafaba, coconut cream and agar,' said Bifron, then, correctly reading Dory's unspoken reaction, added, 'As my mind learns to mingle with yours, my ability to speak your language improves. I'm sorry you're sad.'

Dory stirred her crème anglaise into waves, rocking the little island of egg white. 'You're kind, Bifron.'

'Not really,' Bifron said. 'I'm sorry because I experience your sadness.' A tear fell into his custard. Was it still vegan?

12:00

We are lucky, Morgen and I – always have been. *If my love must fall ill, at least our personal catastrophe unfurls in prelapsarian times. Nobody blocks me from travelling in the ambulance to St Thomas's, or waiting in Resus until they assign Morgen a bed for the night. I promise to return first thing in the morning, and we kiss. Though the diagnosis is pneumonia and sepsis, we aren't too worried, and neither are the medics. How can they be when their patient, bright-eyed and sharp, keeps making them laugh? One of them asks Morgen for an autograph.*

My mobile sounds at 2 a.m. Morgen is being transferred from the general ward to ICU. I arrive to find that Morgen has scored an annex designed for two patients but, for now, ours alone. Hospitals are running at normal capacity, and this one is particularly well resourced. Staff allow me to turn up whenever I wish and stay into the early hours, enforcing the rules just once, when they find me sipping a beer. No Corona permitted on the premises.

Over the next twelve weeks, I more or less live in ICU but for brief trips home to pretend to sleep. In the early days, I pick up kit Morgen requests for work – external hard drives, messy sheafs of lyrics. ('The album still won't finish itself, Dory.') The only exercise I get is walking to and from home, a route I know well. By coincidence, I've been a St Thomas's regular for over a month already, with Mum installed in a different wing of the same building. The end is nigh. Seventy-two hours after Morgen's admission, they halt medical interventions for Mum. To make sure she is undisturbed in her final hours, they hang the sign of a swan above her bed – a bird she happens to resemble: long necked and majestic until roused to squawking rage. Just one more night and that anger stills, moulding her face into its last expression of disapproval. This is not the grand exit she would want.

Even then, she doesn't get my full attention. I rifle through her handbag for her house keys, dash through the corridors of St Thomas's as if on a treasure hunt, collect the medical certificate, catch a cab to her place to pick up her passport and other papers, and somehow make it to the register office in time for my appointment. Nobody should be considered truly dead until bureaucracy records the news.

The next afternoon, I seek out a funeral director – a jolly little man who pronounces 'deceased' as if it rhymes with 'diseased'. I give him Mum's death certificate plus a green slip permitting the disposal of her body and order a no-frills package, despite his valiant attempts at upselling. Mum will get the cheapest coffin (the cost of these things!) and a cremation without ceremony – the woman literally has no friends and broke with remaining relatives when she moved to London. The funeral director consults his computer, exclaiming that we're in luck: the smaller East Chapel at Golders Green Crematorium has a slot available in less than a week due to a cancellation. I agree the date, wondering under what circumstances a person cancels a funeral. Resurrection? You hear stories of people declared dead only to wake as the coffin lid is nailed shut.

Back in the hospital, Morgen, always considerate, asks me how I am coping. 'It can't be easy, Dory. I wish I could support you instead of adding to your stress.'

'Don't worry,' I say. 'I'm all the better for seeing you.'

And so I am. Apart from the IV line and a nasal cannula delivering oxygen, Morgen seems fine, eager to go home and focused on the more distant future, mixing, mastering, promoting, touring, and maybe, further down the line still, a move. A warmer climate could suit us both.

We are lucky, but the timing that enables me to keep Morgen company in hospital also works against us. *Nobody suspects that the virus drawing pretty patterns on Morgen's lungs – like hoar frost, the consultant remarks, holding up the latest X-ray – might be the same that plagues a city in central China. Health authorities theorise that the original infection resulted from zoonotic transmission, for example from pangolin or horseshoe bat to human, and insist that the leap between species took place no earlier than the dying days of the old year. Morgen's gigs in China predated the outbreak.*

More recently, cases of the Wuhan virus have begun popping up outside the country, isolated and easily traced to international travel. As we watch the news on a screen suspended over the bed, Morgen remarks that life seems to be imitating art, the ancient TV series Survivors. *Decades into our relationship Morgen and I are still discovering fresh commonalities and convergences. This drama, set in a world ravaged by pandemic, made such an impression on teenaged me that I asked a hairdresser to copy a cut inflicted on one of the lead characters with shears in a post-apocalyptic commune. 'Ohhhhh kayyyy,' he said. 'Coming right up.'*

Morgen, suddenly animated, opens the laptop, searches YouTube, swears at the hospital Wi-Fi, and eventually coaxes the Survivors *title sequence to play. A masked Chinese researcher in his laboratory drops a vial. Later we see him board a flight for Moscow, only to collapse on the tarmac. Here the story might end before it has really begun, except that the fury science has unleashed continues its journey, hitching rides across the world, each destination illustrated by a stamp in a passport: Singapore, New York, Montreal, Rome, Madrid, Paris, London and, oddly, Corfu. We presume that somebody on the production team had recently holidayed on the island. Little did the programme-makers know that, near half a century after the first broadcast, a pair of lovers would decipher the lettering and make fun of their editorial shortcut. The last laugh is on us, though. Corfu aside, this version of events comes closer to reality than any of the news reports beaming into the ward.*

If science fiction gets to truths journalism misses, that's because it tracks political and social trends to their inevitably dystopian conclusions. Utopias aren't impossible. It's just that the conditions that currently prevail couldn't possibly lead to one.

For this reason, please jettison any thoughts of a world perfected and consider instead the huge differences small tweaks to the past could make to the present. Say, for example, there had been prompt alerts about the contagion, transparency from the Chinese authorities, sound political leadership in more than a handful of countries, sharper reporting. Imagine that the factors that were spreading a different disease, populism, had not also combined to transmit health misinformation and mistrust of mitigations. Think how many deaths, how much suffering, could have been avoided.

As it is, the scale of loss blurs understanding. People find it easy to empathise with individual pain, but as the numbers ticked upwards, we tuned out. One reason I am compelled to tell Morgen's story is because if I can show you how the global convulsion impacted two of the most fortunate people on the planet, you might inch from our experience towards a sense of the brutality visited on others.

Morgen is still with us, however diminished. Millions died and those they left are damaged. The widow of Morgen's friend Andy Gill tells me he achieved a singularity of sorts, a melding with machines that might have enabled him to live indefinitely, but that she gave her agreement for doctors to switch them off. She doesn't know how much longer she can carry that responsibility. I too struggle with survivor's guilt. If Morgen didn't need me, I might, like Andy's widow, consider death the easier option. I worry that Morgen and I may have been inadvertent carriers, given Mum's cancer a helping hand, infected her carers and their patients, our friends, strangers.

Hindsight replays the past from new angles. See when you spread that picnic blanket? You crushed a butterfly, an endangered plant. In following best practice for treating the range of symptoms the first iteration of the virus produces, medical teams take decisions that turn out not to cure but kill, lying sufferers flat, in Morgen's case stopping the steroids that keep sarcoidosis contained.

Two weeks into Morgen's hospital stay, a senior consultant draws me to one side to discuss my love's worsening condition. The team is stumped, frankly. Microbiology has identified an opportunistic infection – as opposed to what, a careful plotter? – called Pneumocystis jiroveci. The targeted antibiotics should be taking effect. Instead, Morgen needs more and more help to perform that most fundamental of tasks: breathing. The nasal cannula has been replaced by a Venturi mask, and even that is not enough. They don't want to intubate, however. The hoar frost has done what hoar frosts do. Lung cells are ruptured, the alveoli delicate as lace.

The consultant and I briefly touch on the Chinese epidemic. Its genome has been uploaded to the GenBank database, but he doesn't think it worth testing Morgen; the timelines can't be reconciled. Try not to worry, *the consultant says.* We still have a few tricks up our sleeves.

The sign on the door of the East Chapel reads 'Reserved for Service to the Late Gloria Mundy Silver'. *Mum hasn't used the family surname for years, but officialdom always insists on having the last word. As for late, she's bang on time, six black-clothed men shouldering* *her in that overpriced coffin from hearse to bier. This is choreography she might appreciate, though it cries out for a show tune.*

Before her arrival, I argued with an attendant, who warns I'll regret the lack of music. Think what you like, *I tell him,* but please switch off the digital display. *A computer screen, high on the wall, is flicking through a carousel of images, sunsets, fields of yellow flowers and a hummingbird on the wing. After he does my bidding and retreats, I realise that he has been right for the wrong reasons. It's not Mum I've let down but myself, stranded in this moment, feeling its weight, no plan, no eulogy, no ceremony. Awkwardly I hug the coffin, speak to the woman inside it, tell her where she is. 'You know this place,' I say. 'Red brick. Romanesque revival. Pretty gardens. Also,' I add, 'the ashes of Freud – Sigmund, not Lucien – Bram Stoker and Anna Pavlova are all interred in the Columbarium here. Not that I know what a Columbarium is.'*

A voice from the coffin. 'Just like you to use big words you don't understand.'

Dry eyed and distracted – I must get back to Morgen – I bid Mum a clumsy goodbye and head towards the front gates. The Columbarium is signposted, but access is by prior arrangement only. Which resident still draws so many fans that restrictions are necessary? Probably Freud, the least admirable. In Dracula, *Stoker created a character that successive generations reinterpret in their own image. That the undead of this era are defanged teen heartthrobs, poster children for the anti-ageing industry, is hardly Stoker's fault. About Pavlova I know little except that she gave her name to one of Morgen's favourite desserts. On the Tube back to the hospital, I read her Wikipedia page, discover that she redrew the aesthetics of ballet with her* Dying Swan. *I click on a link and land on the* New York Times' *report of her death:*

> *The end came despite every effort of two Dutch physicians and her own Russian doctor, Professor Valerski, to save her. Yesterday an operation was performed to withdraw water from one of her lungs. At 10 o'clock last night her condition was extremely serious and as a last resort it was decided to administer Pasteur vaccine. It came too late, however, for she was already sinking, and she died soon after midnight.*

Horror seizes me. Suddenly I realise how it might feel to read obituaries for my love, strangers invading life's most intimate act, the leaving of it, or drawing portraits at best incomplete and often plain wrong. At Waterloo station I take the stairs two, three at a time, run all the way to St Thomas's, barrel into ICU, heart thudding, almost forget to stop at the hand-cleanser or to put on the PPE that is in such rich supply.

Thank god. The tableau that greets me is not a pietà but a nativity, Morgen reborn and surrounded by visitors, musician friends, Ayotunde, Morgen's brother. Even in oxygen mask and hospital gown, my dearest darling is beautiful. I exhale.

Everything will be all right. It has to be.

Morgen understood Dory well enough to read her thoughts. Bifron scanned Dory's mind on a daily basis yet struggled to make sense of her. The confusion was mutual. Dory neither comprehended Bifron nor, at this stage, herself.

Each dawn brought feelings that couldn't be reconciled: anguish, yearning for Morgen, a heaviness of heart and soul, yet excitement too. Her excursions with Bifron reminded her of the thing she most loved about journalism, the immersion in unfamiliar worlds, her fierce pleasure as the silt settled and new landscapes came into focus.

The outlines of Guerglas were still occluded, but she learnt more every day. Bifron, unlike the Doctor, made serious efforts to give direct answers. He – for at this time of the year Bifron was male – wouldn't know how to prevaricate even if so inclined. His kind never lied because they assumed themselves to be open books, their pages on view to fellow Trochilians, if not to other humans. The idea fascinated Dory, and she immediately peppered Bifron with follow-up questions. Did Trochilians commit no crimes? Were they eternally faithful, endlessly sincere, or merely more likely to be caught out in their betrayals?

Bifron had been about to lead her on another stroll through the city, but he paused to answer. Some of his responses revealed temporal gulfs between them. The sincerity of his efforts to grasp the concept of sincerity stirred a memory, of a German with tombstone teeth. Another of Bifron's remarks revealed less about Trochilian telepathy than the wider organisation of Guerglas society. Criminality had long been eradicated, he said. It requires a mulch of secrecy to root.

'But I thought only you Trochilians read minds.'

'We sense intentions, feelings, beliefs. Pancasila sees what you do.'

That word again. She hadn't misheard the first time. But what could it mean in this context?

A few years before Dory and João landed in Indonesia, its regime had passed a decree requiring citizens to study the country's founding philosophy: faith in god (any god) and in Indonesia, a just and human approach to each other, adherence to democracy and to social justice. This philosophy took its name from the Sanskrit *pañca*, five, and *śīla*, principles. Quite a few of the people they met on their travels expressed pride in the ideology and its enforcement. This was an archipelago of more than eighteen thousand islands and at least as many belief systems, cultures and ways of living. Only through the active practice of Pancasila could such diverse strains peacefully cohabit.

Dory could imagine how a similar philosophy might evolve in a place that accommodated not only different influences but distinct subspecies. Bifron seemed to refer to a different Pancasila, however. Perhaps the issue lay in the gap between intention and practice. Dory remembered a conversation at a bar in Mataram about the irony of Indonesia's dictator promoting live-and-let-live ideas by decree and with force. But does it work? João had asked. The speaker, who like Bifron had lowered his voice, put down his glass and left the bar.

A few weeks later, adrift in Labuan Bajo after her split from João, Dory brushed off a warning from the young owner of her guest house to steer clear of a local restaurant, the haunt of a group called Pancasila Youth. She felt too listless to ask him why. Nothing mattered but her personal distress. Perverse logic – she might as well add danger to misery – soon found her staring at a congealing plate of *Nasi goreng*. Even with her diminished appetite, she saw that nobody would come to this place for the food. It was still early, just one other table occupied, all boys, seventeen, eighteen years old tops, their styling, crew cuts and camouflage, making them look younger. They paid little attention to the sad girl in the corner. It would be a decade or more until she learnt of the killing sprees carried out by members of their organisation. She recalled the sweet faces, felt no surprise. By then she had become wise to the ways in which benign creeds might be twisted into nooses.

'What is Pancasila, Bifron? You called that sculpture Pancasila too.' She waited. While most of us dissemble easily, persuading ourselves that so-called white lies are kinder than honesty, Bifron had never before attempted to edit his words. Dory watched him wrestle with this unfamiliar process, huge eyes closed, veins throbbing beneath the silvery skin. Otherwise, for the first and only time in their acquaintance, he remained static. Then he skimmed across the floor to tap the wall, gesturing her to the waiting lift and, still wordless, guiding her to the street, where he set a faster pace than usual.

Their route led down the hill, took a left on to another artery. She had no memory of passing this way before, but suddenly they were at the town gates and through the thick city walls.

'Are we allowed to leave?' she asked, surprised.

'I don't know,' he replied, but kept going, across the drawbridge and on to the scrubby field beyond. Only after they reached the long grass did he slow, mainly because Dory lacked his ability to navigate the tangled undergrowth as if it were a manicured lawn.

'Everywhere,' he said, 'is under their eye.'

'Whose eye?'

'Pancasila. Whom you might call gods, except that Pancasila is more than that, the fabric of the world. We Guerglas are custodians and beneficiaries of Pancasila; we look after Pancasila and Pancasila looks after us.'

'That sounds like an equitable arrangement, Bifron.' When she tried to hold his gaze, he looked away. 'So why are you scared?'

Once more she observed him struggle with his answer. 'The price of social cohesion is control.'

This was the sentence the Doctor uttered seconds before squaddies burst in to restrain Elo, flipping him face down and hefting him away by his arms and legs. Dory felt a prickle of guilt. How little thought she had paid to him since.

'What forms does control take, Bifron?'

'For severe infractions, there is an apparatus that inscribes your misdeed into your skin. But we must hurry. Pancasila is in everything, yet there is a possibility to speak in the grasslands.'

'And in the city?'

He maintained eye contact now. Every cobblestone, he told her, logged the impact of her feet, gauged where she had been, calculated her destination, assessed her mood. Every building observed her. Every room, every piece of furniture learnt her patterns, absorbed and analysed what she did and how she felt.

'How I feel,' said Dory, 'is dizzy.' She sat down, right there, in the long grass. 'Dizzy and disgusted.'

171

Bifron didn't ask her to lie on his behalf. Quite possibly he couldn't do so. Nevertheless, when finally Dory spoke to the Doctor again, she avoided confronting her with any fact that risked revealing the Trochilian as its source. Journalism had trained her in such balancing acts. Intelligence provided on a background basis, though not quotable, was often invaluable, clearing the silt from those underwater landscapes until vague shapes resolved into crags and troughs, corals and creatures.

During this visit, Doctor Roweena anyway seemed more expansive, almost playful at times, resuming their conversation at the point she herself had interrupted it, and rattling off a few details about the Guerglas approach to reproduction. This varied across different biologies and combinations thereof. The Lebre, whose life cycle was shorter than other humans', produced offspring in batches of up to six. By contrast, Poikilos, long-lived and usually conjoined – as many as three individuals inhabiting each body – spawned infrequently and sparingly. The birthrate of fewer than one child per head of Trochilian population could be explained by their short windows of fertility, at most three or four months a year when primary sex characteristics, chromosomal and endocrinal systems aligned. No matter the differences between Guerglas subspecies, thirteen in total, a single principle prevailed for all: sex and reproduction had been permanently delinked, the former permitted in all consensual circumstances, the latter tightly regulated by the authorities.

'Which authorities?' Dory interjected. The Doctor ignored her.

'Your time spoke of reproductive rights,' Doctor Roweena said. 'We speak of reproductive responsibilities.'

'Oh, that phrase exists in my time too,' Dory told her. 'It slides easily between meanings, at one moment deployed to urge women to breed like weasels, at the next used to tell them they can only do so if they're moneyed and married.'

'Marriage and the nuclear family,' the Doctor replied, flatly, 'are not concepts that have survived.' These forms of social organisation had lasted but the blink of an eye, *a mere four or five centuries*, confined even in their heyday to industrialised countries. At no point, she added, did the system function smoothly, forcing parents into breadwinner or homemaker roles, babies born without guarantees of adequate care. Guerglas young came into the world assured a sufficiency of the economic and emotional resources required for their successful raising.

Dory nodded, remembering her wintry childhood, but just as she might have expressed agreement, the Doctor pivoted. 'Children are the future of society. That means society must take primary responsibility for nurturing and shaping each child, from conception to adulthood.'

'Conception?'

'Of course. Breeding without controls propagates defects in the population.'

'That sounds like eugenics,' Dory said.

'No,' the Doctor replied. 'Eugenics was grounded in confirmation bias, not science. Qualities such as personality, intelligence and behaviours are not heritable but socially determined and, as such, a matter for society. We long ago came to a better understanding of which characteristics are the gift of genes, whether those genes are active or unexpressed. No child should be denied the genetic, pedagogical and environmental benefits of multiple parenting. The measures we take are not intended to promote one genotype over another, but to eliminate disorders.'

'Such as what? Thinking the wrong things? Being different? Or...' Dory gestured towards the Doctor's three-wheeler.

'I did not enter this world with impaired mobility,' said Doctor Roweena. 'Mr Ó hAllmhuráin must answer for my injuries. To which point, our investigations have concluded. Sentencing takes place tomorrow. You are of course invited to attend.'

The judges assembled in the hall Dory had mistaken for a cathedral. It stood atop the city, perfectly positioned for the panoramic views its opaque walls repudiated. Four roses of stained glass smeared the floor with colour. More light streamed from the spire, a translucent pyramid above the far end of the nave. Bifron stopped halfway along the central aisle, at a row marked *CONSERVED FOR GUESTS*. Her dad used to scramble his words in a similar fashion. *Cheers, ears,* he'd say, or call out to Mum when the postman brought one of her endless mail-order purchases for signature: *Give me a sign, sweetpie, give me a sign!*

Nobody joined Dory and Bifron in the pew-like seating. Late arrivals squeezed on to benches already full to capacity, then craned their heads to inspect the stranger. At first she experimented, locking eyes with members of the congregation, even waving, but they stared right back, no human connection, just a blank curiosity. She glanced at Bifron. He seemed to be communing with his own kind. The conversation didn't look easy.

She shifted her weight. Already the lip of the bench dug into her hamstrings. It puzzled her, the archaic traditions and technologies this world chose to retain alongside cutting-edge science. As if to underscore the thought, three notes sounded, the trio Morgen's IV feed emitted whenever it kinked. Simultaneously a shadow fell, lengthened, draping the congregation in darkness. The monolith that cast it, blacker than a collapsed star, descended without obvious assistance to hover above the brightly lit platform. Three more bleeps, and the judges made their entrance, twenty-six in addition to the Doctor, including subspecies new to Dory but with *Personae sapiens* in the majority.

Roweena remained in her own transport. The rest slid into a semi-circular quire to face the audience. Elo came next, the force propelling him all too evident. His cage was on castors. Two squaddies manoeuvred it into position, tipping the structure. The action threw the prisoner against the rear bars. As they righted it, Elo crashed forward, and Dory saw that his wrists were manacled. Worse, his glasses had been removed. He squinted against the brightness, unable to use his hands as a shield.

A Sapiens, bullet headed and bull necked, strode to the larger of two lecterns, gripped its edges with big, pink hands, and shouted something incomprehensible before switching to plosive English. 'I'm Chief Prosecutor Hassard. This is my court and there will be no funny business. Right?' It wasn't a question. 'We're using cortical interpreters because the Cro-Magnons are too thick to understand us. Got a problem with that? Speak now or for ever hold your bloody tongues.'

He glared, swivelling that chunk of a head like the barrel of a mortar, and coming to rest on the quire. 'You lot ready to serve?'

The judges answered in unison, variations in their timbre and pronunciation weaving a strange music: 'We swear before Pancasila that to the best of our abilities we shall fulfil as justly as possible our duties, that we shall uphold faithfully the precepts and principles of Guerglas, conscientiously implement all statutes and regulations, and shall devote ourselves to the service of the greater good.'

Hassard pointed to a Fremens. 'Defence Attorney Tarkin, read the buggering verdict.'

The attorney walked to the second lectern, pulling a scroll from the heavy furls around her neck. A New England accent and gruff voice did interesting things to both versions of the defendant's name and the list of charges.

'Elo Ó hAllmhuráin né Robert O'Halloran, you have been convicted of fraud, larcency, false imprisonment, manslaughter through the negligent misuse of restricted technology, and murder. Do you understand?' Without waiting for a response, she cleared her throat and addressed the assembly.

'Chief Prosecutor, judges, Guerglas, this has been a most difficult case. Ordinarily we might summon witnesses to prove the defendant's innocence. But the crimes of Mr Ó hAllmhuráin are, by their nature, visible.' She coughed, swirled the product in her mouth and hawked into her hand.

'The ship recorded the vilest of his deeds. We could only hope that Mr Ó hAllmhuráin would accuse himself. Instead, he at first denied his actions and, when confronted with irrefutable evidence, attempted to obscure his motives. Therefore, we relied upon the plaintiff, his surviving victim. She certainly did testify.' Tarkin bowed to the quire and returned to her seat.

Hassard gestured at Doctor Roweena. 'Go on, then.'

'Thank you, Chief Prosecutor,' said the Doctor. 'The court evaluates the evidence. I live and relive it. For that reason, I nominate 'Oumuamua to present my impact statement.'

A Poikilo uncoiled, flowed to the stand, opening a fresh scroll, and reading tonelessly from one of their mouths. 'My name is

Roweena Falou. I trained as a bioethical historicist. It was my ambition and destiny to draw lessons from the past to protect the future. Since returning gravely impaired from the field trip on which this case centres, I have devoted myself to research in the field of psychoencephopathology, contributing to advances in the understanding of thought and memory. It seemed that if I could not pursue my vocation, and must live in unremitting agony, physical and psychic, that I could at least find ways to mitigate such experiences for others.

'I do this work to honour Pancasila and in celebration of Professor Zachary Pandai. His life was my past, present and future. His death exiled me from hope as surely as if I were stranded in the undiscovered bourne from which colleagues by the beneficence of Pancasila rescued me.'

Dory sat transfixed. 'Oumuamua's delivery, in stripping the statement of sentiment, added to its power. Years ago, Dory had quoted *Dr Faustus* on a postcard to João, a line from Mephistopheles' complaint. At the time, she imagined herself banished from happiness, little realising that their split had opened a path towards it. Now the devil's words drummed in her chest, a broken heartbeat, the lament of the Fall. Like Roweena, she had lived in Eden, and like her, must live with its loss.

> *Think'st thou that I, who saw the face of God*
> *And tasted the eternal joys of heaven*
> *Am not tormented with ten thousand hells*
> *In being deprived of everlasting bliss?*

Pain coursed through her, a creek over rocks. She watched the Poikilo refurl the scroll and themselves, while Hassard machine-gunned the room with details extracted during the investigation. The congregation remained motionless, intent, but more than that, controlled, Bifron rigid but for the slightest of vibrations. He was shivering.

As Hassard embarked on an account of Elo's original journey through time, the monolith transformed into screen and projector, footage of the events described playing across its surface and in

four dimensions along the aisles. These must be the recordings
from the ship. Though Dory had heard multiple versions of the
climactic sequence and the other landings, the images startled her.
How beautiful the Bay looked without its crust of human activity.
Here it was again, but now the coastline had vanished. When
the giant lobster reared in quintuplicate, terror overwhelmed the
quieter fears enforcing order. All around her, people screamed,
scrambled to their feet to evade the beasts, flapped useless hands.
Amid the hubbub, the Doctor raised her little voice.

Hassard banged his gavel, once, twice, and the film stalled,
paralysing the crustacea upright, bellies exposed, Venuses in half
shells. 'Do you know what nemesis means, mateys?' He paced
the platform, glowering at those audience members unfortunate
enough to be caught in the light of the tableau. 'Well, do you?'

The Doctor ended the stand-off. 'Chief Justice Hassard, with
your permission, I will take a moment to expand on my statement.'

'Make it snappy. And you...' He pointed into the gloom. 'Keep
your traps shut, you absolute tits.'

Doctor Roweena rolled herself to the centre of the platform.
'Behold,' she said, pointing at the monsters, 'our future, unless we
change it. Your fear is rational, even if your loss of discipline is
regrettable. These creatures carry the clearest of messages. We
humans have no automatic rights to this earth. This was a tenet
Mr Ó hAllmhuráin and his contemporaries ignored at their peril
– and ours. The Anthropocene epoch could not hold. Things fell
apart. The process of rebuilding has been long and hard, and still
we risk doing too little.'

She glanced at the quire. 'It is the sacred purpose of this court
to hold not only criminals to account, but we Guerglas ourselves.
Ignorance is no defence under our laws, nor should turpitude
be. We must take equal responsibility for our actions and our
inactions.

'I will return momentarily to what that means for these proceedings, but first let us consider the defendant. True justice seeks not
merely to punish, but to punish appropriately. True justice lays
bare the past to protect the future from recidivism. True justice
aims not only to offer redress, but where possible to restore.

'Mr Ó hAllmhuráin's crimes are heinous. What can be made of this series of decisions and acts? They cannot be attributed to incompetence alone.

'Moreover, he neither can give assurances that he will mend his ways, nor offer any options for restoration. The damage he has caused to me personally is irreparable. To suggest otherwise is an insult that minimises the nature of his transgressions.

'You will shortly witness Mr Ó hAllmhuráin's assault on Professor Zachary. This was not the defendant's worst sin. There is one crime that outweighs all others, a crime so unspeakable that we Guerglas prefer not to name it. I shall, with your permission, use a synonym: *erasure*.

'It is a weapon used in every period we have visited, from the most primitive to those that flattered themselves with labels such as *civilisation*. The conquering armies of Hittites and Assyrians razed towns and cities, salting the earth so that nothing of those settlements should remain, no shoot push through the soil to indicate that once life flourished here. Governments of the defendant's era industrialised such processes.

'Whether he meant to or not, Mr Ó hAllmhuráin destroyed Zachary and salted the earth on which he walked. Were it not for the quirks of human memory, and of the ship's, no trace of that precious soul would survive. But we remember.' She wheeled herself to the foot of the cage, stared at its occupant. 'It is the cruellest irony that my beloved lives on in the minds of those most closely bonded with him, me and the ship, and of the man who cut those bonds, his murderer.'

The Doctor lowered her head. 'I have watched so many times, and each time I lose him afresh. Steel yourselves, for this is an indelible sight.' At her signal the film restarted, replacing lobsters with the final landing. Though better prepared, some spectators ducked under the onslaught of virtual hailstones or stirred as if to intervene when Elo and the Professor tussled before them. Now the innocents approached, running across the glistening lawn, a second Zachary in the lead, and then the horror. The horror.

The fireball engulfed the cathedral, nothing left but light and, at its core, the absence of light, the monolith. As Dory's vision cleared, she looked around, marvelled at the way different physiognomies displayed identical emotions, fear, revulsion, anger, the Doctor alone calm, though grief streaked her face.

Again, Roweena spoke. 'It is terrible, is it not, this obliteration? The sight evokes primal responses in us. It tempts us to unwisdom. That is not the way of Pancasila.

'Pancasila is the fount of justice, as Pancasila is the basis of everything. In passing judgement, we also judge ourselves. In the enforcement of justice we demonstrate our values, our commitment to the future, our humanity. You scarcely need reminding that the second principle of Pancasila is humanity. We do unto others as we would have them do unto us.'

Relief flooded Dory, much as pain had flowed through her minutes earlier. Her body was a riverbed, barren of emotions or overwhelmed by them. *Do unto others.* The doctrine of reciprocity, more often honoured in the breach than in the observance, especially by Christians – well, evidently the Guerglas took the idea seriously. Dory wasn't sure why Elo's fate mattered so keenly to her; she owed him nothing. Perhaps it was her own version of do-unto-othersism, or the opposite, self-interest, an intimation that his treatment prefigured her own. The Doctor's magnanimity moved her, as the impact statement had. Love breeds love. Throughout this process, she'd avoided looking at Elo. Now she tried to gauge his reaction, but not a muscle moved in the white face, tiger-striped by the bars.

Hassard was strutting the stage again. 'And what about this See You Next Tuesday?' he demanded, cocking his forefinger at Elo. 'If any Guerglas moron breaks the law, the law breaks him. Can't see why it would be different for a Cro-Magnon.'

The Doctor gave one of her glacial smiles. 'Exactly,' she replied, and Dory suddenly grasped the real meaning of the words she had construed as forgiveness. 'Mr Ó hAllmhuráin embodies every impulse in ourselves we must excise if Guerglas are to survive. If we show him leniency, we show ourselves leniency. We must show no leniency.'

It started tentatively at first, a clap here, an emphatic *yes* there, then more affirmations, and suddenly every spectator was applauding, some on their feet, and the chants began. 'Do unto him! Do unto him! Do him!'

When, after a short recess, the court resumed, its functionaries speeded through the last – if substantial – segment of evidence to their foregone conclusion. Where accounts from Elo and the Doctor conflicted, Hassard employed the simple expedient of discounting the former. To be fair, which the Chief Prosecutor was not, Doctor Roweena's testimony about her imprisonment at Tantalus was the more believable.

The court accepted a narrative that saw her, after the loss of the Professor, gain importance to Elo as the only remaining keeper of the secrets of the time machine. He wasn't to know that she could barely programme a ship, much less unpack the science. Luckily, she was Sapiens, not Trochilian, and as such an accomplished liar. Her best chance of escape lay in pretending to cooperate. So strong was her survival instinct that she avoided challenging Elo, even in the moments after she entered the laboratory to discover Zachary missing from the ship. Not a single element of the original story Elo had concocted did she believe, whether the giant lobsters, the ship's evasive lurch or that its action tipped Zachary into the maw of a passing whale.

Her consternation was real enough, though – no play-acting required. Whatever the real explanation, Elo's determination to cover it up boded ill. She wanted to scream at him until he stopped prevaricating. Instead, she forced herself to say that such things had been known to happen, humans ending up in the bellies of cetaceans. Historical texts bore this out. Then, as if struck by inspiration, she began citing the story of a man who survived for months in the digestive tract of a sea creature, only to be vomited up. Perhaps if she trained Elo to use the time machine, he could retrieve a regurgitated Zachary. Elo looked her in the eye and lied right back. Of course. Finding the Professor would be his top priority. *What professor?* asked HOG. The rest of the team seemed to be suffering from collective amnesia too. Roweena feared she knew the reason, but then again, she and Elo had not succumbed to the outbreak of forgetfulness. Surely that meant Zachary still lived.

Soon Roweena was demonstrating to Elo how to set destinations, simultaneously exploiting her access to the ship to input a series of hidden instructions. If she got it right, he would be able to make journeys into the near future and back, but anything more than a short hop would prompt the machine to head for the concealed coordinates.

She had conceived both an escape plan and a fallback. The former would see her so thoroughly gain Elo's confidence that he let her accompany him on his next voyage. Her second line of defence, a nuclear option, would maroon anyone who flew long distance without her. In either case, at any distance above a calendar year, the concealed overrides would automatically deploy, directing the machine to a future date, then depowering it. She havered over the ideal timing, didn't want to risk an encounter with her pre-departure self, so decided to add a buffer of a decade.

Neither option would be ideal, stranding her as well as her enemies – and they were enemies, this much was clear – but she had faith that even if she were not aboard, the ship carried enough data to lead rescuers to her and, *please, oh please*, to Zachary. Fear clutched at her heart, yet she refused to abandon hope. If her love had suffered an ordinary form of death, clever navigation to the moment before his slaughter might permit an intervention swifter than an assassin's knife. It could be done.

In the mean time, she became that knife, her lethal edges concealed. Did he know about *Granulomae temporalis*, she asked Elo the day after his return. His doctors should be monitoring him for symptoms, shortness of breath, confusion. Travellers who undertook too many sequential temporal shifts put themselves at high risk of contracting the disease, and Elo's travels could easily have breached the advisable upper limit. It was like scuba diving – you had to wait between dives, let the nitrogen leave your body. Elo should pause for at least a month before venturing back into the further reaches of the future. Time travellers absorb subatomic neurotoxins.

Again, pure invention, but the Doctor needed time to win his trust. This ruse worked too, and might have borne fruit were it not for HOG. He didn't exactly see through Roweena, indeed continued to underestimate her, but paranoia served him quite as well as perception. One day, he took her for questioning, conducted the session a little roughly, and inflicted the first of her serious injuries. He hadn't meant to let her fall from the window, just to frighten her. Even then, she probably could have regained most motor functions, given appropriate medical care. But that was not on offer at the makeshift sick bay inside the Tantalus laboratory.

And then it came, the contagion, and of course she succumbed – no natural immunity to the diseases of this timeline, not that the virus was natural. Already she was fighting pneumonia triggered by impact trauma and partial paralysis.

If Guerglas rescuers hadn't found her, she would have died. That they retrieved her at all was close to a miracle. Without the original machine, they had no way of knowing its current coordinates, but they were able to follow its original flight path. A garage owner called Wilson provided the detail that led them to Tantalus. From there it was a question of landing their ship inside the perimeter, evading capture, finding her and bundling her aboard. Like the vessel she arrived in, this was a two-seater. As her saviours arranged her as best they could across their laps, a shard of broken vertebra pierced her spinal cord.

Nor were the consequences of their daring restricted to the Doctor. One rescuer developed a dry cough the morning after reaching Guerglas city. The other sickened a few days later. Belatedly the authorities installed them in a sealed wing of the infirmary, closing off a neighbouring ward to accommodate anyone who might have come into their ambit. The first rescuer died from the disease, as did seven more Guerglas; three sufferers, including Roweena, survived, but after-effects lingered, multiplied and shapeshifted.

Once released from the infirmary she began to piece together the news she dreaded. She quickly realised that nobody else recalled Zachary. The rescue mission had been launched for Roweena alone, and her anguished pleas to find him had been written off as the product of hallucinations caused by her sepsis.

Years passed, and the questions faded for everyone but the Doctor. It wasn't until Dory and Elo arrived in the original ship that its logs yielded to researchers the recording of the extinguishing of a person unknown to them.

Now the footage could not be gainsaid. The professor had existed, should exist in the flesh, across time and in official records.

He did not. There could be no retrieval, no reprieve, no turning back of clocks.

The first thing the Guerglas authorities did was to issue an interdict against further time travelling. For all that the technology had yielded many useful lessons, its deployment would henceforth be barred. It was too easy to abuse, and the consequences of mishaps and misconduct too dreadful to contemplate.

The judges produced black rectangles of material, monoliths in miniature, placing them on their heads as Tarkin husked and expectorated through a final, redundant piece of ceremonial.

'Whereas Elo Ó hAllmhuráin stands attainted and condemned of high crimes, the sentence pronounced against him by this court is that he shall be put to death by fitting means, which execution yet remains to be done. By the grace of Pancasila.'

Then it was over, or should have been, except that the squaddies loaded Elo's cage on to a tumbrel. For hours they paraded him through the bright streets, one circuit of the city after another. Dory, once more confined to her soundproofed room, was unable to hear the jeers and catcalls, the wheels on cobbles, but felt them in her bones. Eventually she noticed another noise too – a strange keening. Only then did she realise she was sobbing.

She could never go home.

She could never go home.

There's no place like home.

13:00

*W*hen Elo stands onstage at TechCon, claiming to be the world's first time traveller, his lie happens to be – almost – true. *According to conventional chronology, the Guerglas won't conquer the fourth dimension until centuries after Elo appropriates their achievement. He is also and by any standards a king not of truth but truthiness. The reason he sweeps people along with him like a river is that he believes whatever he says in the instant of saying it. More than that: he feels that he* should be *the world's first time traveller, and in Elo's universe,* should be *and* am *elide.*

Of course, I don't know any of this yet. Until we meet in Las Vegas, the man is little more to me than a background presence, a voice on the radio I'm inclined to mute. We haven't met, nor would I expect our paths to cross except that he's exactly the sort of overpromoted public figure who keynotes at conferences and bestrides those abnegations of journalism, power rankings. TIME *magazine, which built its brand on fêting the rich and famous, often includes Elo in its annual list of the world's most influential. Soon he will notch up the publication's highest designation,* Person of the Year, *a title previously bestowed on Hitler, Trump and Rudy Giuliani. (You think I'm joking? Look it up. Stalin got the nod too.)*

So right now, on the worst day of my life, Elo couldn't be further from my thoughts. Nor, until this terrible, wrenching morning, have I yearned to travel through spacetime except in the distracted way that comes with age and loss. Who wouldn't wish themselves younger, the people they love healthier, the dead to rise? I ache for Dad, even Mum, and a clutch of beloved ghosts incidental to this memoir, if not to me.

Dreams revive them. By day the past feels more remote. Still, at least you can pick and choose the moments to revisit. Memories of a Morgen unscathed glint with promise, but their edges are razor sharp. It's safer to explore a time before love, take respite from the present, rather than reproaching it.

Even then, the mind plays tricks. Often I have touched down at a golden evening atop white cliffs, my friends and I glowing in the light and with optimism. So many of us jammed around the table, yet our souls, they soar like seabirds. Today of all days, the memory glitches, forcing me to wheel and swoop too, watch from on high as we fade and fall until those benches empty.

Everyone is travelling through time, and not one of us will survive the journey. This much I have long accepted for myself, yea though I fear the landing. Let it be quick – a gunshot to the temple. Go ahead. Make my night. It is Morgen's life that I refuse to relinquish, and not ten minutes ago doctors informed me that it hangs in the balance.

The bare minimum you should do for the people you love is defend them in their hour of need. Morgen will have looked for me, called for me with breath more urgently required for living. It has been, without doubt, my worst betrayal, to listen to the nurses who urged me to go home. Morgen is stable, *they said.* You need your rest. This is a marathon, not a sprint. *Reluctantly I agreed, gave Morgen a Judas kiss, promised to return at dawn. As sure as dusk follows day, the tea delivered at breakfast would be undrinkable, so every morning I have brought my love a cappuccino from the café at the main entrance.*

'With cocoa. You always forget the cocoa,' chides Morgen.

'I don't.'

'I door you, though you forget the cocoa.'

'I window you. Sleep well, sweetheart.'

The call comes at sunrise – one of the doctors. Already I'm back at the hospital, phone wedged under my chin while I pay for the coffee. The doctor informs me that Morgen experienced significant distress, had to be intubated. There's a phrase she repeats – the patient has been placed in a coma *– as if monstrous claws plucked Morgen from the bed, deposited an empty shell in Morgen's stead.*

The cup drops from my hand, contents drawing a map on the floor, but directions are unnecessary. After weeks of navigating these corridors, I could find my way blindfolded. A turn here, a dogleg there. Fast I run, faster, fate at my heels, its breath sour. The lifts seldom work, but it's only two flights to ICU and my feet barely touch the ground. Fear gives me moth's wings, a gossamer as delicate as Morgen's lungs.

185

Even so, I am too slow. There lies my love, an effigy except for a metronomic beat of air, more sound than movement, another texture to the plangent music of the ward. Morgen, who joked about sampling the breedle and feep of the machines, has become part of the soundtrack.

Impossible to be certain, but it seems likely that Elo will have embarked on his ill-starred expedition with the Professor at around the same date Morgen breaches the rules of time. *For Morgen is a time traveller too, one minute subject like the rest of us to time's dictates, the next pausing its flow to hover in suspended animation.*

If the bed were a capsule, the mattress dry ice, the scene that confronts me as I tear into the ward could be lifted straight from a movie, Morgen aboard the Nostromo *or* Discovery One, *insensible to the danger ahead. Staff lead me away, usher me to a family room, lay out risks and probabilities as best they can. Morgen's body and mind are under siege. The coma could give the team the time they need to address the physical onslaught. The downside is that patients awakened after protracted periods of induced oblivion do not simply open their eyes and welcome a new day. Most suffer post-traumatic amnesia; many will never fully recover.*

A nurse asks if he can give me a hug – nope, sorry – then starts listing ways I might improve Morgen's odds. Most of these offer empty reassurances, whistles on airline lifejackets. Sleepers are astronauts adrift from their mothership, yet he encourages me to talk to Morgen as if my words might weave a tether. Should I remind him that sound is the vibration of particles, space a vacuum where nobody can hear you scream?

There's also a Goldilocks quality to this advice: too little stimulation bad, too much worse – the last thing comatose patients need is to be roused to reality – and no more than a one-in-three chance of getting it just right. Caution must be exercised around the equipment, nor is the danger of infection to be underestimated. Touch nothing, *the nurse warns. What, not even those elegant hands, bruised and porcupine-spiked with cannulae? This privilege is to be denied all visitors but me.*

He has one more rabbit in his hat – an exercise book. 'Take it,' he says, thrusting it towards me. This will be a letter in bottle for the future Morgen, a way to understand the currents that washed us to whichever place and time Morgen's consciousness returns.

I stare at the title without comprehension: Critical Care Patient Diary. *The phrase is printed in large type above a form – Patient's Name, Patient's Medical Record Number, Date of Admission. A slogan occupies the bottom right corner of the cover:* SHOWING WE CARE. *The font casts pretend shadows.*

Somebody has written a sample entry on the first page – another nurse. 'Hey Morgen, it's Chris. Early this morning when we met you had been struggling with your breathing, so you agreed for the doctors to put you to sleep and help you with your oxygenation and carbon dioxide. Also, you have had lines inserted into your neck and groin to allow us to give you important medications.' Might Nurse Chris prove the last person to talk to my darling in realistic expectation of a reply?

It will be over a week until I write anything. 'Dory here, with apologies for the delay. I've been crazy-busy organising your social life. You've always been a wonder of the world. Now you're a site of pilgrimage.' After that, the friends and family clamouring to see Morgen complete the diary on my behalf, their contributions quickly filling all but a few pages. 'You're gonna need a bigger book,' I tell Morgen, mimicking Martin Brodie in Jaws. *The joke falls flat. During this period, my love isn't the most receptive of audiences.*

Also, the image is unfortunate, because there's a fin circling the bed, blood in the water, a gathering menace of bass notes, just the two, dunnn dunnnn, dunnn dunnnn. *Once or twice I glimpse the disturbance out of the corner of reddened eyes, convince myself it's an illusion, clouds reflected in water.*

Of course the monster breaks surface, as monsters always do. Restrictions will be imposed, unprecedented precautions, to stem the spread of the virus that is dominating news headlines. From tomorrow, only Morgen's brother and I will be allowed to visit.

Soon that dispensation too is denied. Morgen continues to orbit while we observe from a distance. When the nurses hold up their mobiles, I see my beloved as through the wrong end of a telescope, dwindling to a point of light. Otherwise nothing about Morgen changes, no deterioration, no improvement. The clinicians profess themselves flummoxed. They also look ragged. ICU is overflowing with non-contagious critical patients transferred from other units in a vain effort to contain the virus. Plague carriers are consigned to a single floor of the hospital dubbed the Red Zone.

Then another call – a senior consultant. It must be serious, and it is. Morgen has tested positive, is being transferred to the Zone.

The news comes as an axe at the end of a slow-motion arc. You'll recall those days, all of us frozen like deer, eyes turned to rubies by oncoming beams. How could we stand there, passive in the face of avoidable tragedy?

Before I loose a barrage of questions – Will the light of my life survive? What does this mean for a body already so ravaged? *– the consultant delivers a second blow, one I didn't see coming. The team has revisited Morgen's original diagnosis of a sarcoid flare complicated by sepsis and pneumonia. Had this been correct, Morgen's lungs would be striated like sedimentary rock. Instead, ground-glass opacities are disappearing into the whiteout of a cytokine storm. Radiologists see such patterns often nowadays. Though the date of Morgen's admission theoretically rules out the virus, doctors have retested bloods taken that day and there it is, squatting amid Morgen's genetic material, the alien RNA.*

The results are astonishing but irrefutable, unmasking my love as a serial offender against temporal laws, who manages to contract the virus before it officially exists, only to opt out of the initial lockdown it unleashes.

Morgen's greatest trick of all is to survive. When months later those beautiful eyes finally reopen, they find me in my usual spot by the bedside, as if I had never not been there. Later the same day, Morgen asks, haltingly, for a cappuccino. Oh, if this is not the sweetest music ever heard. I rush to the café, collect the order, apply cocoa in the shape of a heart.

Dory wasn't on hunger strike. Sorrow sat in her throat like an infected tonsil. Yearning pressed bony knuckles into her solar plexus. For so long she had feared Morgen's death, never imagining there could be a form of separation more agonising. If she had taken a lesson from Elo's show trial, it was that mercy found no quarter in this future. This, combined with the Guerglas ban on time travel, stripped away any reason to do so much as lift her head. It wasn't a conscious decision – more of a shutting down. When Doctor Roweena entered, she barely stirred.

'You must eat.' The three-wheeler halted by the head of the bed.

Dory curled around her silence, knees pressed into hollow body, the Doctor's lap at eye level.

'I have given orders that you be transferred to the infirmary.'

'Leave me alone.' A sigh, but the Doctor heard her.

'Pancasila holds life sacred.'

A residual prickle of anger gave definition to Dory's words. 'The same Pancasila that demands the death penalty.'

Doctor Roweena inclined her head.

'Mr Ó hAllmhuráin obliterated life. His punishment asserts and upholds the sanctity of life. The voice, a tinkle of canned music, seemed to pipe from the far corner of the room. Dory looked for a wall-mounted speaker, but spots obscured her vision, bobbing like signets chasing their mother.

'All lives matter,' she mumbled. 'But some more than others.'

'I understand your feelings,' said the Doctor.

'Bollocks you do.'

'Ms Silver, believe me.' The Doctor turned from the bed towards a newly formed exit. 'I know what it is to lose hope.'

'Hope makes things worse,' said Dory, but she was speaking to the wall.

After that, Dory misplaced a chunk of days, whether to the combined effects of malnutrition and dehydration, or the remedies prescribed. When she regained clarity, the physician in charge, a Poikilo, explained that they aimed to address not only the headline issues, but a series of underlying problems detected on Dory's arrival at the infirmary. Some of these appeared to be the legacy of her encounter with the virus. Guerglas doctors were alert to its mischievous ways and long tail. Though the contagion would never again land in their midst, they continued to develop responses to it. A civilised society cares for its vulnerable and prepares against public-health emergencies, whether unforeseen or foreshadowed by the work of bioethical historicists.

Dory already knew about her sinus bradycardia, had tried to ignore it and other hangovers from the disease, determined to stay strong for Morgen. Without this incentive, the prospect of replenished strength taunted rather than tempted. As the physician's trio of heads conferred with her and each other about her heart, she wondered if their narrow chest housed multiples of the treacherous organ. Medicine in this diverse age must be beset by complexities. Drugs developed for one biology rarely work well in another, as the women of her era could testify. Decades of exclusion from clinical trials had condemned this global majority to inaccurate dosages and aggravated side effects. Guerglas physicians had to accommodate many more differences than their earlier counterparts.

Even so, there seemed to be continuities in heath care. Dory's first excursion beyond the single occupancy ward recalled St Thomas's, disinfectant contending with organic smells, a corridor so long that the distant swing doors must conceal a vanishing point. She didn't get the opportunity to test the proposition. An orderly steered her into a curtained bay where technicians applied gel and ran a probe over her chest. Scan completed, she was bundled back into the chair and at a fast lick along another hallway, passing blank doors to either side until they reached a sign marked *Radiology*. Beyond it, all sense of the familiar fell away.

A lake kissed misty shorelines and flattered a rosy sunset, both planes untroubled by breeze. A wooden jetty extended towards mountains whose only purpose seemed to be separate water from sky. The orderly pushed the chair to the lakeside, grasses yielding like goose down beneath its wheels.

She supposed she might have questions, but before she formulated a single one, the orderly set the brakes and retreated. An answer of sorts came from somewhere behind her.

'Goot mornink. We goink to look your insides.' Eyes closed, she'd have thought the speaker one of Dad's cousins.

'Please to remain calm and not to movink.'

The Trochilian wore robes of scarlet and flamingo. A second, in Lincoln green, held out a beaker, beaded bubbles winking at its brim.

'Drink, please.'

A week ago, less, Dory would have flung the contents to the ground. Now she accepted the beaker, took a swallow – nothing to lose but her life. In any event, this must be a barium meal or advanced equivalent. The liquid, though thick and oily, fizzed. She gagged, persevered, waited to be trundled to a scanner of some kind. Instead, the first radiologist repeated the instruction – *remain calm and not to movink* – and Dory found herself alone.

Most of us will never hear a silence so pure nor gaze on a landscape too flawless for beauty. Briefly, Dory contemplated messing it up, heaving her chair into the water, kicking divots out of the perfect lawn. Then again, she doubted she could so much as stand.

After an hour or six, the Trochilians rematerialised at her elbow with the largest syringe Dory had ever seen.

'Is not goink to hurt.'

'Data collection,' said the second, hands a blur of motion. The needle, as fine as its housing was large, lodged in Dory's forearm before she could protest. As her blood filled the barrel, not red, but frost and pearl, another colour overwhelmed her, black, binding her tight.

When the darkness finally receded, she sensed a transformation. Back in her own time, she had woken to the virus, addressed it. 'You got me,' she'd said. Now she adapted the message. 'They got you,' she murmured, speaking as to a ghost, because that's what it was, undeniably and reliably dead, every lingering trace excised from her system.

From ancient times, humans have predicted the future, a triumph of hope over experience given that the predictions business rarely makes the right calls. The antichrist, like Godot, never arrives. Armageddon – well, that's another story. Fortune-tellers read tea leaves, palms, cards and entrails, charging handsomely for their flummery. Psychosis passes itself off as connection to divinity or spirits. Astrologers have adapted their trade to the advent of mass media, scripting horoscopes with a generality that gives them the hit rate and utility of a stopped clock.

Algorithms and computer modelling more often drive than avert disasters; so too the financial analysts and management consultants who depend on them. Technology attracts the most gobsmackingly off-beam forecasts of all.

'The Internet,' said a BBC interviewer, 'is just a tool'.

'No,' his interviewee, David Bowie, replied, 'it's an alien life form.'

'Remote shopping... will certainly flop. It has no chance of success.' That was Dory's former employer, *TIME* magazine.

'The automobile is a fad, a novelty. Horses are here to stay,' a banker told one of Henry Ford's potential investors.

'Television will never hold on to an audience,' opined a movie mogul.

The last three examples demonstrate another principle, too: stick to an opinion for long enough and it might come good after all. By the advent of the Guerglas era, these industries had disappeared.

Science-fiction writers alone prophesied their flowering and decline, the only profession to do a half-decent job of anticipating what might lie beyond the visible horizon. H.G. Wells wrote about atomic bombs a quarter of century before the discovery of nuclear fission, and described airplanes and tanks when these machines did not yet exist. He even imagined a time machine of sorts, though wide of the mark on the science. A year before Hitler stormed to power, Wells urged universities to appoint professors of foresight. 'There is not a single person anywhere who makes a whole-time special job of estimating the future consequences of new inventions and new devices,' he said in a radio broadcast. Every such invention arrives 'fraught with consequences, and yet it is only after something has hit us hard that we set about dealing with it.'

Elo, the proud owner of a shoehorn that once belonged to Wells, never engaged with this warning or referred to the author. The one person Elo quoted almost as often as himself was the futurist Ray Kurzweil, particularly Kurzweil's aperçu about progress: 'Fire kept us warm, but also burned down our villages.'

Of the two men, just Elo thought both halves of the sentence a good thing, giving a TED Talk called *Let's Burn Down the Village*, in which he mocked legacy companies for respecting tradition over innovation. A similar spirit underpinned the high purpose he proclaimed for himself at TechCon. Until chance delivered up the time machine and with it the means to plunder the future, he was planning to direct scores of untested technologies at the climate crisis, burn as many metaphorical villages as it took to position himself as saviour of the world.

Even if the cure for the impending apocalypse really did rest in more of the technology that sired it, Elo's first solo experiments in time travel quite literally harnessed the science to casino capitalism. Had he managed to exploit its potential at scale, his wealth and power, already gargantuan, would surely have blotted out the sun. Once chance is eliminated, every bet becomes a certainty. Where there's no luck, there's brass. To know the future is to hold a golden ticket – unless others are privy to the information too.

The Guerglas understood these dangers, neutralising them by publishing every finding by bioethical historicists. Guerglas policymakers extrapolated from that data; they never conjured predictions from thin air. It remained to be seen whether the suspension of time travel would erode this approach. Meanwhile few aspects of their epoch had been foretold by Dory's contemporaries and then generally within the bounds of fiction.

The infirmary served up a rare exception. After Dory awoke, the physician in charge came to discuss her treatment, declaring her well enough to leave. The strange cocktail given to her in the radiology department had contained nanobots, programmed not only to scan but to repair, the tiny machines swarming through her system to replace endothelial cells damaged by the virus, nuke microclots in her bloodstream and boost her neutrophils. While they were at it, they repopulated her biome too, mended a labral tear and removed inflammation from joints and organs, returning via the syringe to log their activities.

'There's a limit to what can be done,' said one of the Poikilo's heads.

'You won't be as good as new, but you should definitely notice improvements,' said another.

A third chimed in. 'Certain conditions are more susceptible to our techniques than others.'

It was too much to process, so Dory's mind performed its usual trick, staving off messier reactions by assessing the information as an editor might. The headline here would be that nanorobotics had lived up to the hype. Ray Kurzweil foresaw this, a moment of singularity, man and machine combining to augment human capabilities and extend human lives.

When Dory first encountered this theory, Kurzweil's optimism had seemed misplaced. The scenario assumed artificial intelligences would outstrip the human variety only to submit to the will of their makers. What if they simply seized control? After noodling about on ChatGPT a decade or so later, Dory stopped worrying about the rise of intelligent machines, fearing instead the rule of stupid ones. Yes, large language models synthesised reams of data in an instant. They did so indiscriminately. They reasoned, but with plodding logic, *this* because *this*, that nevertheless failed to stop them from jumping to wild conclusions. Where was the critical judgement, the intuition embodied by thinkers such as Kurzweil?

He was that rarest of beings, a futurist with a track record of useful predictions, also an inventor, his technical expertise allied to social and psychological insight. Like H.G. Wells, he imagined things that didn't yet exist; unlike Wells, he imagined quite a few of them into existence.

Dory knew of him long before she begged him for an interview. Her friend Richard suffered from cerebellar ataxia, a disease that killed in stages, targeting coordination, sight and speech. As the first of these failed Richard, he used Kurzweil's voice-to-text software to send Dory flurries of emails begging help with the older technologies on which his life depended. His glasses broke or fogged; his motorised wheelchair malfunctioned as often as most futurists.

She often thought about that wheelchair during Elo's interrogation. The Doctor's three-wheeler, life-sustaining and life-enabling, reminded her that not all innovations came wreathed in dangers and downsides. This was a point Morgen made whenever Dory went off on one of the *end-is-nigh* diatribes that marked her pivot from technophile to doom-monger. Technology was eviscerating journalism and, indeed, the music business, she would say. Music, like other content on the Internet, supposedly yearned to be free, or distributed for fractions of pennies on streaming services. Record companies sustained themselves by commandeering ever bigger slices of musicians' waning income. Yes, Morgen replied. But there are upsides too. In their basement studio, a hulking Atari ceded to a series of Apples; Cubase and Pro Tools gave way to Logic; Kurzweil-branded pedals, interfaces and midis proliferated. Yet alongside this march of progress sat racks of battered Gibsons and Fenders and boxes of vintage microphones, while an analogue Neve mixing desk dominated the control room. Old and new are not inevitably in opposition, said Morgen. The trick is to recognise what retains value and what adds it.

Dory described the studio to Kurzweil the day they met, intending this glimpse of the personal as an icebreaker. Counterfeiting intimacy, a technique she originally learnt to disguise her otherness, had morphed into her way of persuading interviewees to open up. Kurzweil needed little coaxing. The subject of her research – amortality – lay close to his (potentially defective) heart. His living room drifted with papers. He explained that he was bringing back to digital life his father, lost to heart disease at fifty-eight, the same age cancer destroyed Dory's dad. Kurzweil planned to upload his father's writings and records to computer to recreate a facsimile of his mind, then connect it to an avatar.

In the mean time, fearing cardiac problems of his own, Kurzweil was aiming to extend his lifespan, to survive until the singularity in order to live for ever. Should this scheme fail, he had a back-up plan: his head would be cryonically frozen. During the interview with Dory, he broke off to swallow supplements, his regimen recently streamlined to 150 capsules daily thanks to improvements in their bioavailability, each capsule, whether or not it delayed death, also a reminder of its fact and inevitability.

Their encounter lent colour to her book on age and ageing. Were she a novelist and her fictional protagonist modelled on Kurzweil, she'd give the character a name without such thudding symbolism – *Kurz* is German for brief, *Weile* a period of time.

All life ends but humans, unlike other animals, live with fore-knowledge of our fate. Some of us worship at the altar of wellness, seek comfort in fairy tales of an afterlife or trust to technology as our ancestors leant on gods. Others keep too busy to think. This is another reason that artificial intelligences will never match our output. We magic up distractions from thin air, products, businesses, pieces of art or personal dramas, anything to avoid staring down the barrel of our own mortality.

Dory believed herself to be an exception, not merely a realist but ready to die. Why, then, did the Poikilo doctor's next words prompt a violent reaction? 'You've gained a good few decades,' said the first head, and her detachment crumbled into relief. Then came desolation. Without Morgen, she might be physically whole, but in the manner of a Henry Moore sculpture, a solid thing enfolding emptiness.

Squaddies collected her, escorting her not to the Chancellery but a café where Bifron waited. He looked different, though she couldn't immediately identify the nature of the change. Finally, as he pushed aside a purple drink, she spotted it, his movements slowed from quicksilver to merely fleet, as if invisible weights dragged him down.

He was talking about a new life, hers. Like any other resident of Guerglas, she would be given lodgings and the means to sustain and clothe herself, encouraged to work but not forced to do so. The authorities did have something in mind for her: an academic job. Now that the cessation of time travel had cut off historians' richest resource, she held significant value as a living artefact. They hoped she would assist researchers in building a detailed picture of her society, perhaps also tour Guerglas schools and universities. There was a curatorial position on offer too, at the Pyramid Museum. She barely listened.

'Bifron,' she said, 'what's happening with Elo?'

A pause.

'He appealed his sentence.'

'And?'

Bifron shook his head.

'How long…?'

'Soon.'

'Might I see him?'

Bifron hesitated again, a sign she now recognised.

'So I can't see him. Bifron, what do you think about any of this? I accept that Elo has done terrible things, but… executing him?'

'Pancasila,' he murmured.

'All of you use that word to shut down conversations.'

Bifron looked away and she continued. 'A long time ago I read a book called *The Moon Is a Harsh Mistress*, which posed the following conundrum: are there circumstances in which it is right for a group to commit an act that would be immoral if carried out by an individual? Why don't you solve it for me now?'

'That's a trick question.'

'No, Bifron. Yours is a trick answer. What's happened to your famous Trochilian honesty? You do know that evasion is a form of lying, don't you?'

'Yes,' he said. 'I apologise.' Then he dodged the question again. 'Let me show you to your new quarters.'

Dory had been allocated rooms in a residential block on one of the narrow lanes tracing the city's perimeter. The small balcony looked over ramparts to a stretch of sky, speckled like an egg. If she craned over the balustrade, she could see the city gates.

Someone had taken the trouble to recreate the clothes she had worn every day since her arrival, identical copies apart from the tops. She looked down. Hers, once white, had yellowed. These boasted stripes and scrolls and plaids in coral and apple green and lavender and faint orange. Such beautiful shirts, and not her thing at all. She remembered that distant morning in Las Vegas, dressing at speed, glimpsing herself in the suit that made her look like a flight attendant. Her old jacket hung in the closet alongside facsimiles, cleaned, pressed and mended.

The apartment contained a shower, toilet, bed and chaise longue, no kitchen. It took her a few days to learn how to mould the space, dissolving some partitions by day and reconstituting them at night to keep out noise, though this precaution owed more to habit than necessity. Guerglas architects put as high a premium on sound insulation as other aspects of construction. She heard almost nothing through walls or floors, though families lived either side of her apartment and directly below it.

Her downstairs neighbours introduced themselves in the refectory. They were a mixed household, Fremens and Sapiens, too numerous to permit an easy decoding of familial relationships. She studied the children. Pure Sapiens, she thought – or perhaps not; something puppyish about a few of them.

The adults immediately engaged her in conversation, other residents joining in, peppering the meal with odd questions. The clothing of her era: what had been the point of fake pockets? Why, they wondered, had somebody inscribed a sentence about recreating life out of life into the DNA of a bacterium still found in Guerglas cisterns? How had she endured a social order that rewarded luck and aggression?

She attempted to answer the last of these with another inter-rogative: 'Do you like everything about the way your society is organised?' A silence fell. 'Let me rephrase that,' she said. 'If you disagree with something and want to change it, how do you go about that process? Are there elections? Protests? Strikes?'

Around the long table, implanted sigils delivered translations of Dory's words, but not their meanings. She attempted to explain, and just as quickly faltered when the phrase *industrial action* raised fresh queries. The withdrawal of labour might not provide much leverage in a culture without paid employment or, as far as Dory could tell, markets or money of any kind.

Her descriptions of demonstrations, millions of people marching, against nuclear weapons, despots, environmental disasters,
killer police, for women, drew a blank too, though a Fremens,
cheeks flapping, attempted his own interpretation. He'd been
told that old-world humans were wedded to the step counters in
devices they carried or wore. Yes indeed, Dory agreed, but protest
predated such devices by centuries, an essential tool of progress
throughout the ages and into her present day.

'So you walked from one point to another and things changed?'

'Um, not exactly.'

And elections? 'Ah,' said a Poikilo. They had learnt in school
about the fraud practised so successfully for so long by so few on
so many, fostering an illusion of participation while denying the
majority any meaningful agency.

Dory countered. Democracies were imperfect, yet far better
than the alternatives.

The same Fremens shook his head, a stream of drool dropping
from one corner of his baggy mouth. Guerglas had found a
solution to the democratic deficit: *constant engagement*.

'If I may?' A Sapiens held up her hand as if at a lecture.
A psychocultural anthropologist, she could shed light on the roots
of the Guerglas system, which, though grounded in Pancasila, took
elements from other regions of the past and a geography people
once called China – in reality two countries: a hefty landmass
and a small island. Both parts, despite being locked in conflict,
had drawn similar conclusions about the importance of knowing
what their citizens thought, pioneering the use of technologies to
achieve this goal. Big China understood the importance of data
and metadata, compiling detailed profiles of every national and
visitor, tracking their interactions and movements. Little China
invited its peoples to shape public policy via a platform engineered
against the grain of social media of the time, to sow consensus
rather than outrage.

While sigils had rendered such external interventions unnecessary, the Guerglas authorities could not be better informed about
the dreams and wishes of their citizenry; any information missed
by sigils would be captured by other means. This was a democracy

more profound than any Dory could have experienced, said the anthropologist.

'Do you know the expression "the tables have ears"? Most do.'

Dory looked down. The furniture appeared normal enough, not that she cared. What was she even doing, acting as if there were a point to getting to know these people, their world?

'I'm sorry,' she said. 'I must go. I'm tired.' This wasn't just an excuse. The earth's gravitational pull seemed to have intensified. She thought of Bifron and his strange transformation. Mostly, though, she thought about Morgen, ached for Morgen.

Bifron slowed further, as if waterlogged. His unexpected torpor suited Dory. They no longer strolled, heading instead to the nearest city square, slumping in the same spot until evening. There was only one way to animate her.

'Tell me about Morgen,' Bifron would say.

She responded with stories, fragments of memory and melody. Talking hurt, but so did her chest. Anguish left to gather in the pericardium will either burst the thin membranes or seep through them to spread around the body.

How different it would be to sit in a sunny corner of Guerglas if this were merely an assignment, her return home just a matter of days away. Once upon a time Dory had enjoyed getting under the skin of cities and cultures. Now she upbraided herself for past stupidity. Imagine seeking new interests when life with Morgen offered pretty much everything she needed.

She had been smug, telling friends that their relationship worked not because of the time they spent together but their periods apart. It was good for them, she would say – and mean it – that Morgen toured and she jetted off on research trips. When Morgen lay in a coma, she'd committed a greater idiocy still, wishing the hours away. They had been precious, every one, no matter the discomforts, the stink and groan of the hospital, the relentless bleeping. Her love lay right there, within reach in relative terms, even after lockdown.

Occasionally she would free herself from these looping thoughts just long enough to ask Bifron about his own life. His answers might have been scripted to dampen interest. She remembered the spies she met after British security services approved her to receive direct briefings. These men – and a woman, yes, there was one woman – had no need of disguises. It was enough to be dull. Most people were caught up in their own lives. Show them a business card proclaiming consultancy work in an obscure, technical field, and they swiftly moved on.

Bifron appeared to be adopting a similar playbook, robes dreary, hair scraped back, replies a colourless gruel of yeses and nos and statistics, two siblings, no partner. Nor did Dory ever witness signs of him mind-melding with other Trochilians. This morning, however, he volunteered an unsolicited piece of information. In a week, maybe less, he would begin transitioning to a female state. Dory wondered then if Bifron's mood might be hormonal. Though she had never experienced premenstrual tension, menopausal madness or related joys, many of her friends were tormented by them. Only a fool would tease Ayotunde in the days before her period or presume on her patience in recent years (and Dory had been that fool). Perhaps what ailed Bifron was a version of PMT or perimenopause, only worse.

Then again, he radiated despair, not rage. As he dissembled once more, sidestepping a question about his parents, she put a hand on his arm.

'Bifron, why are you behaving so strangely? Is this part of your transition? What's wrong with you?'

'You are,' he said. 'I told you. I feel your sadness.'

This sounded true. She knew that he couldn't shut out the feelings of others, had witnessed a Trochilian server touch a hotplate and seen every Trochilian in her line of vision flinch. Yet something rang false. Might an unaccustomed freight of lies be weighing Bifron down?

An alternative explanation presented itself soon enough. Bifron came to her in the pre-dawn, a shadow at the end of her bed.

'Jesus! You scared me!' she exclaimed, pushing herself into a sitting position. 'What on earth are you doing here?'

He said nothing, dematerialising a wall to admit a second strand of moonlight, then holding a finger to his lips. When she signalled understanding, he began to mime: she should get up, come with him.

She shrugged. *Where? Why?*

He extended both hands, palms down. *Patience.*

She wrapped herself in a sheet, trailed to the wardrobe, waited until he left. Once dressed, she took the stairs to the street, almost missing him, first in his stillness, then his renewed speed. He skimmed ahead, through the city gate and across the open plain, a ship with the wind in its sails, pausing only beyond the scrublands, where long grass grew.

'Listen carefully,' he said then. 'My transition has started. As soon as they realise this, they will replace me as your guide. I will help you to return to your present, but we must act right away.'

Joy exploded like a fireball, leaving Dory and Bifron unscathed and the world around them transfigured. How beautiful this place was, its scented night, its sparkling skies. She struggled to respond, and finally managed a single word: 'Why?'

'It is unbearable, what you feel.'

'Thank you, Bifron. But how… Isn't it dangerous?'

'Do not thank me. I have no choice. And yes, it is. We have already tripped alarms by leaving the city. To reduce the risk of detection, I am doing my utmost to block channels to my own people, but this too will be noticed. It is now or ever.'

'Where?' she asked, skipping over his mistake. She mustn't let herself dwell on the possibility of homecoming either. Too much to do. So much to play for.

'First,' he said, 'you should return to your lodgings and collect the panel.'

'The what?'

'The panel. You removed it from the museum.'

She understood. He meant the object that looked like a TV remote.

'How did you…?'

'Your thoughts. You will need it to operate the ship. As soon as you have it, go to the Chancellery.'

'Is it there, the ship? And won't it see us? The building, I meant, but the ship too? And the squaddies? Won't they be on guard?'

'It will be hard,' he said. 'We may fail.'

'Will they kill you if we're caught?'

'This is not living.'

Dory retrieved her old suit jacket, the panel and dead mobile next to each other in the inner breast pocket, and headed back out. Should she walk as though she had nothing to hide or cling to the shadows? In the end, she managed neither, adrenalin forcing her into a staccato rhythm. Near the top of the hill, Bifron beckoned to her from an alleyway.

His route seemed to circle the Chancellery rather than approaching it. On one of their descents, he swerved without warning or backwards glance through a doorway and into darkness. She followed, barking her shin on something hard, a little table of white metal, laid with the remains of a meal. The light, when it flickered and caught, was faint. By the time Dory understood its source, the glow had receded.

She chased after Bifron as a child pursues a firefly. Down staircases and tunnels he went, deeper into the earth. Somewhere nearby she heard a whump of heavy machinery, caught the glint of animal eyes, tasted blood or rust on the lifeless air. Finally he turned that lantern face, and she saw that they had reached another door. He waited until she stood next to him before opening it.

The atrium rose above them like a Falcon Heavy, its scale grandiose rather than grand. These impressions were fleeting. Something far more compelling caught her eye: the machine, sitting in the middle of the polished floor, and there, in the passenger seat, paler than ever and still without his glasses, Elo.

14:00

*T**he thing about happy endings – in films, not massage – is that they're really beginnings.** Those red skies aren't sunsets. Our heroes ride off into the metaphorical dawn to live ever after in a place like home or their loved ones' arms (for me, the same thing). The movie* Blade Runner, *with melancholic genius, inverts the trope. As Deckard escapes with his replicant lover, he remembers his colleague's warning. She'll die, of course. Everybody does.*

When Ignis brings his roadshow to London I book an appointment. There's not a single reason to believe in him and many that should send me screaming from his hotel suite – not least the nurse. She cannot be real, straight from central casting, a vision just this side of pornographic, breasts pushing against starched bib above a waist cinched to anatomical impossibility. Of course, she sounds Nordic. The Doctor is looking forward to meeting you, *she sing-songs.*

I doubt this is true, but I have been counting the hours to meeting him. This is what desperate people do: cling to figments as the grief-stricken clutch at ghosts.

It was a famous actor who told us about Ignis, in the innocent past when Morgen's sarcoidosis caused little trouble and the virus had yet to be born or created. That the subject came up was a matter of luck – the bad sort. Our hosts one evening owned a cat, a calico called River Song. We did warn them; Morgen's allergy meant we couldn't come to dinner unless they kept her at bay. No problem, they said, then showed Morgen to the sofa that River Song favoured for her grooming rituals.

It is never enough merely to banish the original source of contamination. Cats, like viruses and populist politicians, leave inflammatory trails. As River Song glared through the bay windows, Morgen started to wheeze, took a drag of a Ventolin inhaler, then another. I noticed but said nothing. Morgen dislikes fuss. Anyway, a debate had already kicked off, about the line-up for the opening ceremony of the London Olympics, the actor slighted at his omission. We almost missed a small voice from the corner: 'I think I might be in trouble.'

Thus the evening ended almost before it had begun. Paramedics helped Morgen to the ambulance, while River Song, in a final act of revenge, rubbed herself against our departing legs.

An injection later, Morgen was back to normal, though they held us in A&E for several hours in case the Aminophylline triggered side effects. Apparently it belonged to a class of drugs called bronchodilators. 'Not a dinosaur I've ever heard of,' said Morgen.

The next day brought an email from the actor, littered with mistakes and half sentences, as if grammar were for little people, or to gloss over his Etonian education. Some years earlier, his husband had been diagnosed with a life-limiting chronic condition. Harley Street specialists told him they could manage, not fix it. Then a Hollywood connection directed them to II, the Ignis Institute. Magicians, those II people, enthused the actor. And Ignis himself, what a character. His husband returned to the UK as good as new.

My lip may have curled as I read this testimonial. Miracle cures belong to a class of medicine called snake oil, and the email, brief though it was, contained a checklist of phrases associated with its promotion. II supposedly offered treatments traditional clinicians didn't want you to know about; *they had been developed outside of and in opposition to* the pharmaceutical-industrial complex. *A core component involved a new form of blood-cleaning,* as yet unvalidated by clinical trials.

The website confirmed my scepticism. 'Anyone who claims they have a one-step solution to your health problems is selling you something,' read the slogan above an image of a white-coated doctor whose lower lids looked capable of sliding upwards to mask his eyes. 'Life is complicated, so we treat the whole person to bring mind, body and spirit into optimal harmony.' The institute combined bleeding-edge technology with natural therapies developed — and forgotten — over centuries.

In person, Ignis turns out to be even more reptilian than his portrait. Had I already encountered Poikilos and were the species not a number of evolutionary cycles away from drawing breath, I might wonder about his parentage. He cups my hand between both of his, his skin dry and scaling.

'How is the patient?'

205

The nurse will have informed him that Morgen is too sick to leave the house. I pull away to retrieve the medical records I've offered to send over in advance of this consultation. He takes the folder from me, drops it unopened on to the coffee table.

'No,' he says. 'How is the whole *patient? Traditional medicine' – he waves at the folder contemptuously – 'too often reduces people to lists and numbers, percentages, prescriptions, tests, physiological monitoring data. These are the trees that stop us seeing the woods.'*

'They're quite important trees,' I counter, instantly regretting extending the metaphor, but ploughing on anyway. 'These trees are *the woods. Morgen's lungs might as well be made of paper. Liver and kidney function are badly impaired. Mad and inexplicable things are going on with the bloods. At this stage it's hard to unpick the effects of sarcoidosis, the virus and the impacts and interactions of the treatments prescribed to address the primary causes. Also, what kind of life is it, bedridden, medicated and denied daylight by severe photosensitivity? In summary, the whole patient is, to use the technical term, wholly fucked. I think that about covers it.'*

'You're angry.' Ignis is unruffled. 'Which is only natural.'

'I'm angry because I'm in a fancy hotel talking to a stranger who is holding out hope. And I don't believe you can make good on your promises.'

'Again, understandable.' Ignis turns that unblinking gaze on me. 'What would it take to convince you? Would you like to speak to former patients? Visit the institute?'

'I won't believe your methods unless and until they are supported by double-blind clinical trials and those results peer reviewed.'

The bastard actually laughs, a parched sound like that Bostonian accent. 'As they will be, in ten years, twenty.' He picks up one of his own leaflets, reads from it. '"The evidence cannot tell us when it is best to ignore the evidence." This line is quoted in a paper on the limits of evidence-based medicine published by no less than the American Medical Association. Would you listen to the AMA?'

I try to incline my head but I'm rigid with fury, at myself more than Ignis. What am I doing here?

'Evidence-gathering is vital,' Ignis declares, getting into his stride, 'but speed matters just as much. Every second a patient is left without effective interventions is a second wasted, an opportunity for disease to do its work. In the USA, it takes seventeen years for research evidence to translate to clinical practice. Tell me: how much time can your Morgen spare?'

Hope makes things worse. *It is insidious. I see Ignis for what he is — a charlatan, a leech — and yet I sign up. After all, what is there to lose, except our house?*

In describing the Ignis Institute to Morgen, I am complimentary, optimistic, parcelling out the hope I mistrust. We'll get you there, *I say. Just a few formalities to complete.*

And funds to organise. This issue I don't mention. My love's public profile rules out a crowdfunder. We'd become a story. Anyway, wealthy people like us shouldn't exploit the soft hearts of fans and good Samaritans. I've started to remortgage our home, liquidated a straggle of half-hearted investments and am exploring the possibility of selling Morgen's back catalogue when the email arrives from my speaking agent. TechCon has offered a humungous fee for me to conduct an interview live onstage in Las Vegas. My interviewee will be Elo Ó hAllmhuráin.

How could she ever repay him? Bifron brushed the question aside. Dory's greatest service would be to leave, fast, and take the condemned man with her. Should they aim for the TechCon stage? Again Bifron swatted away her words. The ship would deliver them to the place they needed to be.

He pushed the panel into its slot, setting the machine vibrating and dancing with colour. Like her soul, she thought.

'Listen carefully,' Bifron said. 'The first destination is programmed. You will be able to set coordinates for one additional journey, short haul only. After that, or if you attempt to input coordinates beyond a month either side of your original landing date, the ship will automatically return to Guerglas.'

She understood, said Dory, though she wasn't sure she did. Elo squinted at her, pointed at Bifron.

'Yer wan here. Is he sound?'

'Yes,' said Dory. 'Bifron's a mensch. Bifron, you're a mensch.'

'It's time,' Bifron replied, leaning forward to activate the panel. As the machine took flight, he seemed to disappear in a puff of smoke.

This was the roughest trip yet, a rollercoaster that felt as if it were coming off the rails amid a hail of distressing images. If some history is tough to live through, how much worse to experience it in reverse, the dead reanimated only to lapse into nothingness; a flaming tower block shaking off its cladding to reveal its skeleton before collapsing into a hole wider than a mass grave. It was hindsight all the way, the fury of a tornado dwindling to a breath of air, the flap of a butterfly's wing.

The machine came to a halt in room Dory had never seen before but recognised from the Doctor's descriptions, vast and circular, its central core partitioning the space, and floor-to-ceiling windows forming the exterior wall. Next to her, Elo drooped, head too weighty for his neck. Maybe she should feed him water, revive him like a plant. A cooler bubbled away next to a double set of lift doors.

She stood, shakily, looked around. Immediately below them she could see a promontory laden with lower buildings, each deferring to this high-rise and bearing the Tantulus apricot. She had no idea if the sun were rising or setting. Certainly it was doing one of those things, its angry red spilling across the white carpet.

Her untrustworthy legs folded, returning her to the captain's chair. In front of her, the panel flashed through three sets of numbers, 2025, 37.50992 and 122.18469. Suddenly her pocket pinged. Her mobile. Dory pulled it out, studied the screen with disbelief. A message from Morgen.

'Enjoying Vegas, oh queen of the space aliens?'

An idea gripped her. Willing her hands to stop shaking, she opened Maps, searched for the location marked *home*, retrieved the latitude and longitude, and began to input those numbers into the panel. The phone sounded again.

'Miss u.'

'Back before you've noticed I'm gone,' she typed.

Then she had another thought, put the mobile down, detached the panel, altered the third coordinate by one numeral. She didn't want to risk landing in the house. Now to figure out a safe date.

'What's the craic?' A growl beside her. 'Are you trying to fock around with my machine?'

In her exhilaration, Dory had forgotten Elo. In seconds and though debilitated from captivity, he had pinned her to the seat, grabbing for the panel, a struggle he would easily have won had a noise not distracted them. Both turned towards the source: a crescent above the lift like a half moon or bisected clock, its single hand whirring from left to right. At once Elo's face began to describe its own arc, from startled to fearful and then, as a figure exited the lift, relieved.

The newcomer reminded her of Chief Prosecutor Hassard, thickset and choleric.

'HOG!' Elo exclaimed, with what sounded close to affection. Then his face altered again. A second person ambled into the room, wrap-around sunglasses reflecting the Bluetooth buds that winked in his ears while he issued a stream of words at an unseen caller.

'Yes,' he repeated. Yes, yes. Top billing, natch. I'm a bazillion miles more interesting than anybody else they'll be having on their poxy programme. I mean, it's radio. What technology do they need? Tin cans and string? We'll take the Gulfstream to Vegas later today. Yep, yes. Right. Yep, I do the interview down the line from TechCon or not at all. Their choice. And we know what their choice will be. When all is said and done, I'm the world's only time traveller.'

Finally he noticed the interlopers in his living room, stepped back in surprise, but the fireball caught him all the same. For a second Dory imagined she saw his glasses melt, the flaming eyes flame. Next to her, another human torch crackled and sputtered. Then it was over.

The machine thudded down at an angle, teetering on the edge of the Bay, no Tantalus buildings in sight, just a gorilla of a man, floundering in the waves and bellowing at her.

Dory seized the panel – no time to make further adjustments – pressed buttons until concentric rings expanded and burst like bubbles in the sky. Within no time at all she was back in her house, except that it was airborne, falling, spiralling. She glimpsed Morgen, hale again, Dad with a net, Mum. How she missed them all.

'There's no place like home,' she said, and passed out.

III

Postscript

*A*lways we have been lucky, Morgen and I, and again our luck held. *The machine landed in our tiny, overgrown garden, burying itself in a corner where the nettles and the dock leaf grow. True, there were limits to the luck. As I write, nettle rash burns along my arms. So much for the power of dock leaves.*

I was desperate to rush inside, hug my dearest love, never let go again, but first I covered the machine with a tarpaulin. Our neighbours are sociable – or nosy, depending on your viewpoint. It wouldn't do for them to mistake the coloured lights for a party and turn up with a bottle. A shame to leave Morgen's beloved SL to the mercy of London's acid rains, but we only have the one tarp. Also nothing endures, however fiercely you protect it, not even structures like the Mercedes, forged from steel and built to last.

As for humans, our little lives would barely make a mark on the ungrand scheme of things were it not for our collective powers of destruction. Morgen is an exception, a rare spirit who gives the earth beauty and meaning, rather than merely extracting resources from it.

Now that life is guttering. Though I've been away for no more than a day in Morgen's terms, I see a deterioration. Obviously the round trip to Vegas couldn't have been completed within that time frame, but my love doesn't notice the inconsistency. The carers are scarcely more curious, immediately satisfied with my story of an air traffic control meltdown and delighted to receive an unexpected paid holiday. Take the rest of the week off, *I tell them, deciding to cancel the district nurses too. Over the coming days, I intend to manage Morgen's care by myself. There's enough food, solid and otherwise, to keep us*

211

going; the curtains, always shut in our bedroom, are drawn downstairs too, the front and back doors bolted from inside. Who knows when or whether I – the other Dory – might return. I wonder what she thinks she's doing in Nevada.

One task remains: to write.

Dear readers, whosoever you are, I am under no illusion that you will believe my account. *In erasing Elo Ó hAllmhuráin, the Guerglas authorities also wiped everything he has ever built or destroyed. What does that mean? At a basic level, no more* Morlock *or* Tantalus, *I suppose; perhaps increased sales for* Minecraft *and iPhones. What of his former employees and wives and families? Might they sense a gap in their lives, find themselves suddenly, inexplicably adrift? Have his many children vanished? As for time travel, it will once more be relegated to the realms of science fiction, dismissed as a nice idea, but fanciful.*

Of course, I've considered upending this narrative. All I would have to do is reveal the machine rather than use it, securing, in the process, a journalistic coup of planetary proportions. The Guerglas correctly anticipate that I will not do this, just as they have played me perfectly throughout my time under their eye. It helps that they benefit from foresight – they know my choices because in their universe I have already made them. Even so, I incline to a different theory. I believe the Guerglas understand my susceptibilities because of our common humanity. Most people, of whatever era, cling to comforting stories over hard realities; we let our guard down if others appear empathetic; we are led astray, again and again, by false hope.

Was Bifron lying from day one? I intend to ask him, or her, if the chance arises.

The main reason I have chosen to document the past weeks, future years and my plans for a final rescue mission is that I am able to do so. Others are not so fortunate. Andy Gill's widow published a grief memoir. I'm not ready to follow in her footsteps. I can't imagine that I ever will be.

There's another motive too. Although this manuscript may be misinterpreted as a suicide note – Morgen and I will, after all, vanish without trace – perhaps at least a few of you might accept my words in the spirit I intend them. They are my parting gift, the lessons of experience.

So much I have learnt on my travels through time – and how poor our choices look from a distance. We reject the limitations of medicine, even death itself, while accepting global reductions in the human life span after a century of increases. We normalise health and mortality gaps that see elites lead better lives and longer ones. Their power will eventually be checked, but only by the environmental catastrophes and violent conflicts they sow.

Anyone in a position to agitate for change, for equality, for a course correction, should do so. It might be too late, yet the future turns out to be surprisingly malleable. As for the visions we pursue, gods and utopias are distractions. Societies are built on trade-offs, and in my opinion, the Guerglas, like us, have made some terrible decisions. We should trim our ambitions to aim for a better world, not a perfect one, unless that bleak place of giant lobsters represents your notion of perfection.

For as long as humans survive, there will be man-made problems, glitches, stupidities, messiness; also art, invention, kindness, friendship, joy and love. The greatest of these is love.

Will the Guerglas kill Morgen and me on arrival or agree to help us? Their infirmary has the capacity to work the miracles Ignis offers to perform but could never deliver. I veer between visions of extinction and salvation, both scenarios, in their own ways, credible. Here's what I do know. It is worth the risk. Morgen is worth any and every risk.

And if our journey should end in pain and fear, as all journeys must, we might yet snatch a blissful moment, Morgen and I, together in the sunshine, breathing the scented air and watching the butterflies dance. I would give anything for that. I would give anything for just a few more minutes with my love.

The end/The beginning

TIME/LIFE

↓

↓

↓

A Note from Catherine Mayer

Her email arrived without a covering message, just an attachment, so I moved it straight to trash, assuming she had been hacked. Dory Silver and I barely knew each other and had corresponded only once before, when she sent me condolences on the death of my husband, Andy Gill.

This would have been an end of my involvement had I not sat down to supper that evening with Radio 4 for company. The headlines at the top of the hour spanned the usual range of man-made catastrophes, but then three words seized my attention: 'mystery', 'disappearance' and 'Morgen' and – well, you know the rest. I retrieved the email, read the document in one sitting and the next morning called the police, who took a statement along with copies of the email and Dory's condolence message.

Press speculation spiked and waned. Weeks ticked by and apart from two calls from different units asking me to go through the meagre contents of my original statement, I heard no more. During another solitary meal, the radio news informed me that the investigation had been shelved.

What to do next? To be honest: nothing. I gave up. This wasn't my story, and I anyway wasn't sure what to make of it. It was my friend Bee Rowlatt who persuaded me to show it to her publisher, Will Dady.

Having launched Renard Press in lockdown, Will applies the same fearlessness to his editorial choices. He immediately contacted my agent Eleanor Birne – who during the course of this project time-travelled from PEW Literary to RCW Literary Agency – to sketch out a plan for publishing Dory's manuscript.

215

When I mentioned *TIME/LIFE* to my own long-term publisher, Lisa Milton at HarperCollins, she asked to see it and soon Harper-Collins's audio division proposed putting it out as an audiobook. Her colleague Rebecca Fortuin took charge of the recording.

A final piece of the puzzle dropped into place during a conversation with Andy's close friends and collaborators, former Gang of Four singer John Sterry and musician-mixer-producer Santi Arribas, at the time launching their new band, Rear Window. Phrases and ideas from *TIME/LIFE* continued to haunt me and I suggested these fragments might make a good basis for a song. They agreed. 'Rocket Men', a kind of theme tune to *TIME/LIFE* co-written by us, appears on the audiobook and the band's debut album with Dharma Records, *Happiness by Design*. (To listen, scan the QR code below.)

Dory is not in a position to give thanks to anyone mentioned above or to the publishing teams who contributed to bringing her story to a wider audience. I am and do so in my own right. Thanks also to my wonderfully supportive friends and family.

Getting to know Dory through her writing, I felt a kinship, not least in our shared flaws. Morgen and Andy were twin spirits and towering talents. For these reasons – and because everything I do is for Andy – I hope *TIME/LIFE* moves you to hold those you love a little tighter.

London, 2025

A NOTE ON SUSTAINABILITY

RENARD PRESS feels strongly that there is no denying the climate crisis, and we all have a part to play in fixing the problem.

We are proud to be one of the UK's first climate-positive publishers, taking more carbon out of the air than we put in. How? We reduce our emissions as much as possible, using green energy, printing locally and choosing the materials we use carefully; we calculate our carbon footprint and doubly offset it through gold-standard schemes; we replant the trees used to make our books and we plant a tree for every order we receive via our website.

Find out more at:

RENARDPRESS.COM/ECO

ABOUT THE AUTHOR

CATHERINE MAYER is a bestselling author and award-winning journalist, the former Europe editor of *TIME* magazine and the co-founder of the Women's Equality Party and Primadonna Festival. Widowed at the start of the pandemic, she also runs the music estate of her late husband, guitarist, producer and Gang of Four founder, Andy Gill. She finished and executive-produced a double album, *The Problem of Leisure*, that he was working on at the time of his death. Her books include *Amortality: The Pleasures and Perils of Living Agelessly* about the changing attitudes to age and ageing, *Attack of the 50ft Women*, described as 'a compelling feminist call to arms', and a memoir, *Good Grief*. Her biography *Charles: The Heart of a King* generated worldwide headlines with its claims of dysfunction in the royal courts and was a *Sunday Times* top-ten bestseller.

WWW.CATHERINEMAYER.CO.UK